SHERLOCK HOLMES

The Red Tower

ALSO AVAILABLE FROM TITAN BOOKS

Sherlock Holmes: Cry of the Innocents
Cavan Scott

Sherlock Holmes: The Patchwork Devil
Cavan Scott

Sherlock Holmes: The Labyrinth of Death
James Lovegrove

Sherlock Holmes: The Thinking Engine
James Lovegrove

Sherlock Holmes: Gods of War
James Lovegrove

Sherlock Holmes: The Stuff of Nightmares
James Lovegrove

Sherlock Holmes: The Spirit Box
George Mann

Sherlock Holmes: The Will of the Dead
George Mann

Sherlock Holmes: The Breath of God
Guy Adams

Sherlock Holmes: The Army of Dr Moreau
Guy Adams

Sherlock Holmes: A Betrayal in Blood
Mark A. Latham

Sherlock Holmes: The Legacy of Deeds
Nick Kyme

COMING SOON FROM TITAN BOOKS

Sherlock Holmes: The Devil's Dust
James Lovegrove

SHERLOCK HOLMES
The Red Tower

MARK A. LATHAM

TITAN BOOKS

Sherlock Holmes: The Red Tower
Print edition ISBN: 9781783298686
Electronic edition ISBN: 9781783298693

Published by Titan Books
A division of Titan Publishing Group Ltd
144 Southwark St, London SE1 0UP

First edition: March 2018
2 4 6 8 10 9 7 5 3

Visit our website: www.titanbooks.com

A CIP catalogue record for this title is available from the British Library.

Printed and bound in the United States.

SHERLOCK HOLMES

The Red Tower

"For who can wonder that man should feel a vague belief in tales of disembodied spirits wandering through those places which they once dearly affected, when he himself, scarcely less separated from his old world than they, is forever lingering upon past emotions and bygone times, and hovering, the ghost of his former self, about the places and people that warmed his heart of old?"

Charles Dickens, *Master Humphrey's Clock*

FOREWORD

FROM THE NOTES OF DR. J. H. WATSON

The affair of the Red Tower is a story that I have long overlooked. Not because it offers insufficient intrigue or incident when compared to the vaunted annals of Sherlock Holmes's casebooks, but because it is of such personal concern to me that it has long pained me even to review my notes. Now, with my friend and I both retired, and the subjects of this tragic tale all departed this mortal coil, the time is right to add this case to those stories of the great detective within the public domain.

It was the April of 1894. Sherlock Holmes had not long been back in London after his sensational return from what many had supposed was his death, and this had barely faded from the news. I was mulling over an invitation from Holmes to return to my old room at Baker Street, an offer made more tempting by the interest I had received from one Dr Verner in the purchase of my medical practice. I had hesitated, perhaps longer than I ought to have. In truth, I had never really suited living alone, but nor could I face simply turning back the clock. To resume my professional partnership with Holmes was one thing—I had certainly been reminded of how much I had missed our adventures during his hiatus—but I still could not bear to leave the home that I had shared with my late wife, Mary.

Yet an unexpected invitation from an old acquaintance changed all that. So it was that I found myself travelling to rural Berkshire, against the advice of Sherlock Holmes, in much need of a change of scenery and some friendly company. What I found there instead was a case singular in its strangeness, cruelty and ingenuity.

CHAPTER ONE

AN UNEXPECTED INVITATION

The train rattled noisily through Berkshire—a not at all unpleasant part of the world through which to travel, save for the cold nip in the air that sliced in through the window casements. I looked again at the letter of invitation and, not for the first time since boarding, hoped that my host would not be meeting me at the station in person, for I had managed to secure a seat only in third. As I was to spend the weekend in the company of a Marquess and his friends and family, it hardly seemed a propitious start.

Not that he would care. The host in question was James Crain of Easthampstead, son of Theobald Crain, the Marquess of Berkeley. Through Holmes, I had met many storied noblemen, yet there were none I could ever truly call friends. James Crain, on the other hand, had become close both to me and to my late wife, Mary; so much so that I was among a close circle who called him simply "Crain", at his insistence, rather than using his courtesy title of Lord Beving. Crain had always striven to be seen as a common sort of man, which I suspect not only led to his pursuit of friendships with the likes of me, but was also born of some antagonistic relationship with his father. Certainly, despite our years of acquaintance, I had never before been invited to his family home.

Mary and I had been there for James when his mother, Lady Agnes Crain, had passed away—an event that rocked him in such a profound way that it seemed as though he'd expected her to live for ever. He had never quite recovered, and became somewhat dependent upon us, spending most of his time in our company whenever he was in London. Crain had always been a man of varied and addictive appetites, and the tragedy pushed him towards the misuse of various medications. I had tried to help him once or twice, but he always gave me short shrift. "I came to you as a friend, not a physician," he would say, as if one precluded the other. In those moments, he rather reminded me of Holmes, though otherwise they were as chalk and cheese.

After Mary's death, our acquaintanceship dwindled to the occasional exchange of letters, a situation which Crain often put down to the increasing pressure of his duties at the family estate, but which I had often suspected had more to do with the spectre of Mary's passing. Our meetings had become awkward, full of those moments that gentlemen often cannot bear with the required decorum, and it became easier simply to avoid the circumstances—and each other—altogether. That he had not been there for me as I had been there for him could have been considered rather selfish, but so all-consuming was Crain's grief for his mother, that I felt sure he could not stand to grieve for Mary also. I had written to him only recently, as it happened, telling him of the offer I had received for my practice, and of how torn I was at the prospect of moving away from my marital home at long last and returning to the life of a bachelor. He had been sympathetic in his response, but no more or less than that.

That is, until he sent his latest letter, and the invitation.

All these recollections would have been little more than maudlin emotion stirred in a breast long recovered from the most difficult trials, were it not for the contents of that letter. For although the invitation promised wine, music and song, there was something in it that bothered me. It could have been nothing, or, as Holmes would have had it, it could have been everything. For the guest of honour at the weekend party was a certain "Madame Farr", a spiritualist medium.

The last time I had seen Crain, many months prior, he had at least belatedly begun the healing process, or so I had thought. As it transpired, he had become increasingly interested in spiritualism. He had always given the practice more credence than I, ever since his mother's passing, but the enthusiasm with which he pursued messages from beyond the grave had worried me. The truth was, I had reached out but briefly to a spiritualist "mission" in Blackheath in my darkest moments after Mary's death, but had found it curiously lacking in both comfort and candour, and had resolved never to return.

"In my experience they offer some small comfort to those whose grief is near," I had told Crain, aiming to be circumspect should I inadvertently cause offence, "and they seem harmless enough." I had wanted to add "if misguided", but refrained. I had said instead, "I would always advise caution when dealing in such matters. In my experience, when we mourn a loved one, we begin to see her likeness in every reflection; to hear her voice in every echo. When we are presented with notions of an afterlife, we strive to believe, even if the evidence of our senses denies it."

"But what if the evidence of our senses does not deny the truth of an afterlife?" Crain's hands trembled. "What if it were real, Watson, and it could be proved?"

"Then greater men than I would be forced to eat their

words," I said, thinking briefly of the rationalists at the Royal Society, but more so of Holmes. "The world as we understand it would be changed."

"Aye, for the better," Crain said. "There is no greater pain than the loss of those we love. Imagine if that pain could be diminished. Imagine if we could be absolutely certain that the departed stand with us, as though they had never left at all; that we could speak to them as plainly as I speak to you now; that they could see into the past, present and future, and use their great knowledge for the advancement of us all."

"I think the world functions adequately as it is," I had said. "I have seen grief consume men, Crain. I have seen death in all its forms, natural and unnatural." I always struggled at the reminiscence of past battlefields. I rarely allowed myself to dwell on the things I had seen in my army days. "Throughout it all, I have always known one thing to be true: that those who move on from tragic loss—who look to the future—thrive. Those incapable of relinquishing painful memories are forever imprisoned by their own grief."

Crain had seemed somewhat wounded by my lack of belief, and had promised in jest that, should he ever find definite proof of his convictions, he would present it to me and expect me to eat my words. I assured him that if he could find true evidence, then I would be only too pleased to do so, but I expected that day to be a long time coming.

Some few days later, I heard that Crain had started visiting a medium who had set up her little enterprise in some village near the Marquess's estate, and that news presaged a dwindling of my contact with him. Indeed, he seemed to have retired himself, young as he was, from London life almost entirely, much to the befuddlement of his friends.

In what few brief exchanges we did share, no more was said

about the matter, and that had remained the case until one week ago, when a letter arrived from Crain, along with the invitation. The note was full of the boyish warmth that had so endeared him to me when first we'd met, and contained such familiarities as though we had never become estranged. But it was the way he wrote of the local spiritualists that worried me. "Worried" may seem too strong a word, but if anyone was in a vulnerable state of mind, it was James Crain; and as heir to both title and fortune, he would make a fine prize for a more unscrupulous trickster. After so long in Holmes's company, I was ever suspicious.

Crain had written:

> Watson, as I think you may have heard, about a year-and-a-half ago, a small spiritualist group formed in the village of Swinley. Over the past year I have rather become convinced of their faith, and of their genuine ability to converse with spirits. They have passed on to me messages which I believe cannot have come from any other source than dear Mama. So convinced am I, that I think even you would be unable to deny the truth of your own eyes and ears were you to see her work in person. Her name is Madame Farr, and I would very much like you to meet her.
>
> I am sure that she can help you as she has helped me. Because Mary was my friend, as you are. Because—and this is deuced selfish of me, I know—I need an ally. Someone of sound mind and strong character who can attest to Madame Farr's talents, and support me against naysayers. My family are less convinced than I am of Madame Farr's teachings. My sister, Esther, is a sceptic. I'm rather afraid that her mind is closed, although it has more to do with her fiancé, I'd wager. A chap named Melville—a London barrister. A stand-up fellow in most respects, but stern, as

their lot so often are. A little old for Esther, in my opinion, but keep that to yourself. He was widowed some years ago, but when he first met Madame Farr he didn't take kindly to her words of comfort. He went into a black mood, truth be told. I rather fear his influence has turned Esther against spiritualism altogether. But if anyone can bring her round, it is you, my old friend.

Esther is rather taken with your stories—you must be used to that by now. Even young ladies in the provinces have heard of Sherlock Holmes. Indeed, she fancies herself a bit of a sleuth as a result of reading them. She has even tried to "expose" Madame Farr's séances before, but with no success—how could she succeed, when they are quite authentic. Just give me the chance to prove it to you. Next weekend we are having a small gathering at the house—I hesitate to call it a party, because it's only a chosen few. You can meet Madame Farr and see what you make of her. Even if you don't become a believer, there'll be plenty of stimulating conversation, good food and wine. Sir Thomas Golspie will be there—he's an old friend of Father's. I'm sure you can swap stories of your many adventures.

I knew James had thrown Sir Thomas Golspie's name into the conversation to entice me. I had read about the man's adventures in Africa as a youth, and they had in no small part influenced me to join the army, so that perhaps I might see more of the world, as he had. It was an obvious ploy, but one that I gladly fell for. If nothing else, the chance to meet one of England's most intrepid explorers would make the trip worthwhile. But more than that, I hoped that I could rekindle my old friendship with Crain—so long as he was not entirely lost to Madame Farr's strange beliefs.

The arrangements had been made via telegram. I was to

go to Berkshire by train the following Saturday, arriving at the manor in the afternoon in order to reminisce with Crain before the other guests arrived. There would be an informal dinner on Saturday evening, and then on Sunday afternoon the party proper would begin. I would be home in time for afternoon surgery on Monday, refreshed from a small holiday. What could be more pleasant?

The train's whistle sounded. I had barely noticed our brief stop at Bracknell, and we pulled away, the station fading from view in a cloud of steam. The majority of the passengers had alighted, and I was left to shoulder the draught alone. There was one more stop. I folded up the letter and put it in my pocket.

I arrived at a tiny wayside station south of Bracknell, the only passenger to alight. The sky was the colour of tired linen, and threatened rain. Once the train had pulled away from the platform, a deathly silence fell, and it became a desolate thing to endure. I wondered more than once if I had done the right thing in coming; I had spoken with Holmes just two days ago, and he had sown seeds of doubt in my mind, as he so often did.

"You really intend to go?" Holmes had looked at me down his aquiline nose, incredulity writ large upon his sharp features.

"Why ever wouldn't I?" I'd shifted in my seat as a waiter had cleared away the plates from the excellent fish course. It was rarely that we dined at the Criterion, and usually when Holmes wished to place himself on my good side. The place had long been a favourite of mine, and Holmes had twice reminded me that it was here at the Criterion where I'd first heard of him, and determined to approach him on the matter of shared rooms at Baker Street.

"Because, my dear Watson, to go willingly into the company

of practising spiritists is normally to forfeit either one's reason or one's wallet."

"It is not the spiritualists with whom I wish to engage," I'd said. "Crain is a dear old friend—to me and to Mary. It would be remiss not to accept his invitation."

"Nevertheless, Watson—this medium. Madame…?"

"Farr," I'd sighed. "Madame Farr."

"Quite. I shall make a few discreet inquiries on your behalf. Never fear; if there is anything untoward about Madame Farr, I shall uncover it."

I'd groaned. "Holmes, there's really—"

"Don't mention it! Now, Watson, I know I said I would not press you for an answer, but I really do need to know if I should advertise your old room. Baker Street's not the same since you left. I have some fascinating cases to review, and it would be helpful to me if my chronicler would return. Even if he possesses a penchant for the dramatic."

"Making fun of me will not hasten my decision."

"Then what will?"

"I must consider carefully Dr Verner's offer," I said. "He will take good care of the practice, I'm sure, and the remuneration is perfectly fair. But there is the matter of the house… and the memories it holds." Holmes, to his credit, had said nothing. "Some time away will do me good. I shall go to Crain's weekend party, and afterwards you shall have my answer."

With that, it had seemed we were both satisfied. And yet the bleakness of the day brought with it regrets at accepting the invitation, for reasons that I could not rationally fathom. I was just cursing Holmes's naysaying when at last a dog-cart arrived by the station gate, and my name was called.

CHAPTER TWO

CRAIN MANOR

We took the winding lanes around the fringes of a great forest, some still virgin and black as night, through whose tangles I glimpsed occasionally with some small thrill the odd barrow, or Iron Age earthwork. On paper, Crain Manor was favourably located, being almost equidistant between Windsor Castle and the royal hunting grounds of Easthampstead Park. In reality, however, it was tucked away between hills and forests, and modern roads had apparently not yet extended to Lord Berkeley's estates.

My coachman, Benson, was an earthy man, prone to chatter, mostly about horses. I learned in detail the names of the best hunters and racers he'd stabled at Crain Manor, the ones that had been sold on to the royal stables, the winners he'd groomed at race tracks across the country, and so on. Indeed, once he had fixed on the topic, it was difficult to snatch a moment's peace.

We passed through Swinley, which Crain had mentioned to be the nearest village, some five miles from the manor. It was the sleepiest little place one could imagine, a huddle of low stone cottages with nary a sign of industry. The local church was old, and in dire need of care. It was telling that the village pub, the Green Man, was both larger and better kept than the historic place of worship that faced it across the street.

When at last we came to Crain Manor, it was not at all as I had imagined. A weekend party at a country house conjures images of lazing in the sun, or playing a round of croquet upon manicured lawns. I could envisage little of that as the carriage ascended the sloping drive, flanked by gnarled, ancient trees which formed the approach to an imposing, rambling house of dark grey stone and black mullioned windows. I had rather expected an austere, classical building, as one often found these old families living in. But Crain Manor was an awkward conglomeration of architectural styles, speaking of a long and tumultuous history. Eroded gargoyles peered from shadowed cornices, more in keeping with an abbey than a country residence. The great entranceway was more modern in style, but the eastern wing was dominated by a tall, round tower, draped generously in blood-red ivy and looking oddly out of place—as though it had been plucked from a castle and reconstructed on the side of the house stone by stone.

There was no good reason for a rational fellow to feel apprehensive, but that is exactly what I felt. The sky was overcast, grey as the ancient stonework, and there was a chill in the air, and these things conspired to make me shudder. I chided myself for my foolishness, and thankfully, as the carriage came to a halt, so too did my strange fancies.

A footman opened the door of the carriage, and James Crain himself descended the steps of the manor to greet me, arms outstretched, a boyish grin on his face.

"Watson, my dear fellow." He beamed.

I greeted him in kind, shaking his hand warmly. Then

I noticed someone standing a little way behind him; a young woman, whom I had at first mistaken for a servant.

Crain must have noticed my distraction, for at once he introduced us. "This is Judith. Don't mind her! Judith, this is Dr Watson."

"Pleased to make your acquaintance," I said.

The woman nodded, her expression unchanging as stone. She could perhaps have been described as pretty, were she not so sullen. I could not fathom the familiarity with which she was treated—she was dressed plainly, almost like a governess, and I did not take her for a lady. I looked quizzically to Crain.

"I see you have inherited some of the detective's eye from your famous friend," he said. "Judith is my companion; she's tasked with following me about, in case Mama wishes to communicate with me. These things can happen at any time, you know, and we need someone on hand to interpret the signs."

"Ah," I said. "A spiritualist."

"Ho! Don't sound so incredulous. We must keep an open mind. Come along now, I'll show you to your room and then we can take tea. You must be hungry after your journey."

As I followed Crain into the cool shadow of the house, I cast a furtive glance behind me. Sure enough, Judith followed at a respectful distance.

I was thankful to be inside the house at last, for it was considerably more traditional in its style than the forbidding exterior suggested—reassuringly so. We crossed a great hall, brightly lit by stained glass and a domed lantern window above. Many doors led off left and right to various rooms and broad passages; glimpses of a dining room, a large drawing room, a comfortable lounge, and a parlour bedecked with leafy plants all passed by before we ascended an elegant staircase. A three-sided gallery swept around the upper floor of the hall, and carpeted passages trailed off in all directions.

"Most of what you see here was rebuilt after a dreadful fire in 1775," Crain said. "It's been like this for over a century now, but Father still calls it the 'new' part of the house, as his father did before him. Now, I'll warn you, the manor can be a bit of a labyrinth. The other guests will be staying in the west wing, and the servants will be back and forth there for the rest of the day, getting things ready. We've put you in the east wing with the family so you are not disturbed."

"Most kind. What's through there, might I ask?" I nodded along the gallery, to a medieval-looking door which was open upon a stone staircase. It looked like something out of a fortress.

"That's the oldest part of the house still standing. The Red Tower."

"Because of the ivy, I suppose?"

"One might say so… We don't use it—only three of us in the house, you see, since… Well, it's not like the old days. We could put you up in there if you'd prefer, although it's a bit gloomy, and cold to boot."

"No, no, that's quite all right," I said, perhaps a little too readily. I saw at once that Crain was making a jest, and I was glad of it, for the entrance to the tower induced a strange, prickling sensation at the back of my neck. "I am sure the accommodation you've arranged will be more than adequate."

"I think this one has the *sense*."

I turned, surprised to hear Judith speak. She looked past me, first to the tower stair, and then to Crain. Although her features never changed, her blue eyes shone with inner strength and passion.

"You feel something?" Crain asked her.

"The departed have left their mark on that tower, sir, as well you know," she said. "Your friend feels it, too: he must have the sense. What a blessing."

Crain beamed at this.

I smiled politely. "Let me guess… the tower is haunted," I ventured.

"I wasn't going to say it, but yes, actually. It's said that the ghost of Lady Sybille Crain roams the tower sometimes. I've never seen her, but then, I don't have the sense, unlike the two of you."

Crain continued on his way, and I followed him to my room with an inexplicable feeling of apprehension.

After refreshing myself I joined Crain for tea, which was served in a grand conservatory at the rear of the manor; an impressive, modern construction of wrought iron and glass. The room was filled with large exotic plants ("Most of them gifts from Sir Thomas," Crain explained). On a bright day, I imagined, this glasshouse would be pretty indeed, but unfortunately the heavens had opened, and the pattering of April rain reverberated through iron casements, rippling like applause in a theatre.

"Lord Berkeley—will he be joining us later?" I asked, in a bid to break the latest uncomfortable silence.

"He's out with the estate manager," Crain said, looking almost relieved. "I offered to go for him, with the weather taking a turn, but he wouldn't hear of it. Won't be much longer. Even when he's home he tends to keep to his books these days, but he'll join us for dinner."

I had hoped for lighter conversation with Crain, to catch up on old times, and yet that was made difficult by the persistent presence of Judith. She sat apart from us, never engaging, but always within earshot. Whenever Crain began to talk of Mary, I felt uncomfortable, as though the young woman in the corner was eavesdropping. Perhaps I did her a disservice, for she always appeared engrossed in her sewing or reading if I glanced in her direction. And yet still, the private thoughts of Mary, which I would have been more than willing to share with a mutual friend, were not for the ears of the spiritualists. I confess it: I mistrusted them. I could not be sure if all their ilk were as bad as the ones I had encountered in Blackheath, but I did not want to take the chance.

"It would do you well to talk about her more," Crain said at last. I do not think he realised just why I was being so guarded. "Mary, I mean. One thing I've learned is that talking about those we have lost is healthy."

"Crain, please do not think me unfeeling on the matter," I replied. "It is far from the case, I assure you. But time has passed. I have grieved for Mary, and now look to the future, as all must."

Crain looked downwards, and sipped at his tea. Judith turned the page of her book.

"Ah, this must be Dr Watson!"

I had heard no one enter, and now I turned at the sound of a woman's voice, expecting to find James's sister. Instead, I was confronted by a striking woman of perhaps fifty years, a vision in a high-collared dress of black crepe, which along with her dark, tightly curled hair set off her pale complexion most starkly. Behind the woman, standing near the door, was a rangy man of similar age. He was possessed of an unruly beard, and was altogether too scruffy to be a servant in the Crain household.

I rose at once, and the woman held out a slender hand closeted, rather unusually, in a black lace glove.

"Watson, this is Madame Farr," Crain said, rising also.

"I have heard so much about you," the woman said. Her voice was strange, with an accent that squirmed away from any attempt to identify it. Her thin lips curled into a smile that would have seemed warm and genuine, were it not for the coolness in her dark eyes.

"Nothing bad, I hope," I jested.

Madame Farr inclined her head as though she did not understand. "You mourn." It was not a question.

I glanced to Crain before replying. "I *have* mourned, but no longer. I find time to be a great healer."

"Ah. Physician, heal thyself. But trust me as one who knows, Doctor: to set aside one's grief is to deny it. To deny it is to forget. You do not want to forget your wife, do you?"

I took a breath. It seemed to me that Crain had brought me here specifically for a little show from his new friends, and now it felt rather like an ambush.

"Madam, nothing could be further from the truth. I honour Mary by living a life, as she would wish." Was there a flicker of a smile on Madame Farr's narrow lips when I said Mary's name? It was information she doubtless already had from Crain, if not from my own published work, but suddenly I felt as though the slip had betrayed some weakness on my part, that it might represent the first in a line of such errors, unwittingly giving the spiritualists some intelligence they could use against me.

"We do not dishonour the dead," she said. "Far from it. But they are with us always, Dr Watson; we might choose to deny our hearts, and ignore the messages of the dear departed. Or we can choose to open our minds, and listen."

"Even if that were so, it is my belief that we must all look to our own futures, rather than dwell upon the past."

Madame Farr stepped forward, her dark eyes fixed on mine, and before I knew it she had taken both my hands in hers. "And what of that future, Dr Watson? I sense you have an important decision facing you."

"Important?" said I. I could only think that she referred to my practice, and whether or not I should sell it. "I would not call it so."

"Ah, but the other party might?"

Had I slipped? Had I implied with my words that another party was involved? Or was it simply that Crain had mentioned all this in passing before my arrival?

"He might indeed, madam," I said, "though I should doubt it."

"A friend. A famous and formidable friend," she said.

"This is common knowledge," I replied, tiring somewhat of the game. She spoke now of Holmes, of course, and yet I had seen more impressive feats of deduction from my friend on many occasions, without the need for spirit-guides and crystal balls.

"I should warn you, Doctor, that your friend has made a request of you for the most selfish of reasons. To fall into an old regime will do you little good; indeed, it may even put you in danger. Sometimes, the hardest path is the one we must tread alone, but it is also the most rewarding. This is a sense I have, and I am sure it comes from Mary."

"Mary?" I frowned. "Mary is gone, and can counsel me no more."

"Is she? Like all men, you believe the dead are gone, but not forgotten. And yet once you accept that they are beyond reach, you will forget, no matter how hard you try otherwise. Day by day, you find it harder to picture her face. Yes, I see her clearly, Doctor. It is my gift. My belief is that the dead are not gone, and need never be forgotten. They can reside here with us, if we let them. We can speak to them. Some—those with 'the sense'—can even reach out and touch them. What would you give, Dr Watson, to touch your wife's pale cheek once more? To hold her dainty hands in yours?"

At that, I withdrew my hands from hers. She had chosen her words very deliberately, for had I not used similar words to describe her in my own story some years ago? But what of Crain? How much had he told Madame Farr about my personal life? Or, at least, how much had Judith overheard? I tried to push aside such thoughts, for I knew Crain would not have intended to cause me hurt.

"Who is this?" I asked, nodding to the man by the door. "We have not been introduced."

"This is Simon," Madame Farr replied. "He is my assistant—my amanuensis. From him, I gather much strength. Forgive Simon—he speaks little, which is why I listen to him when he does. Simon, you may leave us now." She waved her hand at the man, and he sloped away without a word, his long limbs carrying him awkwardly, yet quietly as a church mouse.

"I wonder if I might excuse myself," I said. I felt my colour rise, and did not want to upset my host on the very first afternoon by delivering my soul upon the subject.

"Oh, I have made you uncomfortable!" Madame Farr said. "I must apologise, Doctor. It was not my intention—it is merely the depth of my belief that drives me. I hope you will come to see me as a friend before this gathering is at an end. For now, perhaps I should leave you two alone for a while."

"Not quite alone," I said, and looked to Judith, who at once averted her eyes and pretended she had not been paying attention.

"As good as," Madame Farr smiled.

"Come on, Watson," Crain said. "Finish your tea—we can talk about all this later."

"Oh, I do hope not!" Another voice joined the throng, and this time I turned to see a finely dressed young lady enter, a well-attired maid in tow. Her voice was musical in its lilt, her features delicate and paper-white. Her auburn hair shone like polished copper in a crepuscular shaft of light that appeared only at her arrival. She walked slowly, taking only small steps, and passed Madame Farr as if the woman were not there, before greeting me with all the warmth of family. "How do you do, Dr Watson? So sorry I wasn't able to meet you sooner."

"My sister, Esther," Crain said, helpfully.

"Lady Esther," I said. "Finally we meet; your brother has told me all about you."

"I'll bet. I imagine he's made me out to be dull and unimaginative because I don't have time for his silly table-rapping games. Frightful, isn't it? Oh, I'm sorry, Madame Farr, I didn't see you there; I trust you are well."

Madame Farr smiled coolly, bowed her head, and shrank away. She said nothing, but the daggered look she threw at Lady Esther was unmistakable. If Esther noticed, it did not show. Indeed, the warmth of Lady Esther's smile and the lightness of her tone banished all darkness from the room—Madame Farr included. The spiritualist took her leave without another word.

"I must say, James has been simply dreadful for keeping you from us for so long," Esther went on. "He must have told you that I've read all your stories."

"He may have mentioned it, Lady Esther."

"I suppose you find it tiresome, hearing of it all the time, but we must speak of Sherlock Holmes. Will you ever write about his adventures after he dispatched that terrible Moriarty fellow? I for one would love to know what he got up to!"

"It is not tiresome to me at all, my dear lady," I said, fully enchanted by her manner. "Holmes is ever a mine of inspiration, of intrigue and, at times, of annoyance—but he is certainly never tiresome. He is, however, remarkably tight-lipped on the subject of his hiatus. Although I'm sure Holmes would not mind me telling you a few anecdotes from what I know—as long as you promise to keep them to yourself, of course."

"How kind of you, Dr Watson. And rest assured, I shall take your secrets to the grave."

Crain affected a yawn and a stretch, drawing a playful glare from his sister. He winked. “I say, where’s that fiancé of yours, anyway?” he asked.

“He’ll be in presently, I’m sure.”

The lady’s maid dusted off a seat and, oddly, made to assist her mistress.

“Don’t fuss so, Sally,” Lady Esther chided, but still allowed the maid to hold her gently by the arm as she took her seat. Esther was a slight young woman, fine of feature and figure, and it occurred to me that, despite her energetic and sunny conversation, she might be ailing from something. Lady Esther turned to Judith, who was still concentrating on her book. “I say, Judith—your mistress has left. You’d best run along now.”

Judith stopped reading, and looked not at Esther, but at Crain, who hesitated to support his sister.

“Oh for heaven’s sake, James,” Esther said. “I daresay we can have some peace for half an hour. Dear Mama surely won’t be joining us for tea.”

Crain flushed at this glib remark—it was clear that Esther had moved on from the tragedy of their mother’s death even if her brother had not. I sensed she rather shared my opinion on looking to the future rather than the past for comfort.

In the end, Crain relented. He nodded to Judith, who closed her book and stood. At some unspoken signal from Esther, Sally followed Judith, almost escorting her from the room. Judith walked meekly, her eyes so fixed on the floor that she almost bumped into a tall man who was heading towards us. The man exchanged an unmistakably queer look with Esther’s maid, before striding in.

“Melville, there you are,” said Crain. I noted some slight relief in his tone, and wondered how much tension had been caused between him and Esther, perhaps by repeated disagreements over Judith.

I greeted Esther's betrothed, but received rather short shrift. I saw at once what Crain had meant back in London when he'd said Melville was stern. He was tall and fair, with a handsome but rather lined face. He had that look in his keen grey eyes much like Holmes—as though he were scrutinising every facet of one's demeanour, looking for some clue, or some weakness. It was doubtless a consequence of Melville's occupation as a senior barrister, but as we shook hands I rather felt as if I were a witness on the stand.

"Did you journey down from London today also?" I asked, in an attempt to make small talk.

"Thursday," he said, "and it was a tiresome trip."

"I say, Melville," Crain said. "Looking rather glum today. Something the matter?"

"No, no," the man said, distractedly. "Just some business I had to finish. Serious business, but it's done now."

"Good," beamed Esther. "Then you'll take tea with us, Geoffrey, and wipe that frown from your face. Dr Watson must think you're a dour sort of man."

"Anyway, sis," Crain said, before either Melville or I could respond, "you seem in fine form today. I take it you're feeling more yourself."

"Yes, thank you, James. Never better."

"She's been a bit run down lately," Crain said to me. "Look how thin she's become! Perhaps you could take a look at her, Watson. Second opinion, and all that."

"I… that is, I am at your service, Lady Esther." I never liked to tread on the toes of fellow professionals, and Crain's mention of a "second opinion" suggested I would be doing precisely that.

"There's no need," snapped Melville, a little too abrasively. "Esther has seen one of the finest physicians in London, and is well on the mend."

"Really, it was just a chill," Esther said. "I do wish you men would stop fussing. Now, let's find some amusement. If the weather is not going to favour us, we should play cards or something. There's plenty of time before dinner."

We all agreed this was a fine suggestion, and Crain went to find some cards at once.

"It will be a small, family dinner tonight, Dr Watson," Esther said. "I'm sure even Father can be prised from his study for once."

"And… will your brother's *other* friends be joining us?" I ventured.

"Hmm? Oh, them. Judith will dine with us, I'm sure—she's like James's shadow these days. Honestly, he doesn't even notice the doe eyes she throws his way; typical of you men. As for Madame Farr… well, she will be sitting with us tomorrow, and I doubt Father would favour her with two audiences in one week. I imagine she'll dine with that tall fellow, Simon—two peas in a pod."

"I gather you aren't over-fond of the local spiritualists."

"Nor are you, if I'm not mistaken," she said.

I shrugged, not wanting to say any more, lest it place me in a precarious position between Crain and his sister.

Melville fixed me with one of his serious stares and said, "Esther tolerates these 'spiritualists' in her house because she is of a sweet and charitable disposition."

"And I take it you do not share that disposition, sir?" I asked, rather surprised by Geoffrey Melville's brusque manner in the company of strangers.

"Quite right. Thankfully, when Esther and I are married, we shall have no need of the Crain family fortune, because mark my words, that is what Madame Farr is after."

Melville's directness rather took me aback. Lady Esther looked uncomfortable. And yet, I was struck by the possibility that Melville was right. It had crossed my mind already, and

James Crain was in just the frame of mind to allow himself to be manipulated by unscrupulous sorts.

CHAPTER THREE

GHOSTS OF THE PAST

To the evident disappointment of Lady Esther, Madame Farr did indeed join us as we gathered ready for dinner. Her presence was as unwelcome as that of a ghost, to all, at least, but Crain.

She had arrived as Esther pressed me for stories of Sherlock Holmes. Madame Farr was a vision again in black, head held haughtily above a severe high collar, dark eyes peering at us inquisitorially. The conversation of our gathering immediately became stilted, as Crain seemed to desire only Madame Farr's attention.

Last of all to arrive was Lord Berkeley himself. If ever a man could exude the status of stern old patriarch, it was he. Though he was advanced in years, and had a cautious, creaking gait, he was a strong-looking man, stocky, with a shock of dark grey hair crowning his square, craggy features, somewhat like storm clouds over a mountaintop. He nodded to each of us except for Madame Farr, towards whom he did not so much as glance. As the only stranger present, I was introduced, and Lord Berkeley shook my hand with a vice-like grip. With his arrival, the butler announced dinner, and we were shown into the dining room.

Indeed, there was an atmosphere somewhat akin to a séance about the room already; it was dimly lit and gloomy, sparsely furnished and somewhat chilly.

"You are feeling better, Papa?" Lady Esther asked her father, once we were all seated.

"Well enough, m'dear," he replied, his voice a low rumble. "It's me heart, Doctor," he said to me. "On s'many damn pills I'm surprised I don't rattle when I walk."

"I'm sorry to hear that, Lord Berkeley. If there is anything I can do… I am at your disposal."

The formalities over, dinner was served, although it was not a cheery one. If I felt as if I were intruding on a family meal, then Madame Farr and Judith must have felt it doubly so. Lord Berkeley simply refused to speak to either of them, or even acknowledge their existence. If there was any opportunity to make a jibe at his son's expense, he took it. He spoke to Melville of legal affairs surrounding his estate tenants and property portfolio, leaving me behind in the mire of detail, and Lady Esther, presumably, entirely at sea. Indeed, Lord Berkeley's penchant for discussing business and, more particularly, money, was a little vulgar given that there were guests present. I received the strongest impression that this was a man acutely aware that he was in the twilight of life, and somewhat obsessed with his legacy. As a stranger in the house, I could only guess at what difficulties lay between Lord Berkeley and his son, and it did not seem unlikely that Madame Farr had much to do with it. I wondered why Lord Berkeley didn't simply throw them out of his house if he felt so strongly.

It was something of a relief when dinner was over, although that relief was short-lived. Lord Berkeley retired early. Over brandy, I suggested that Melville, Crain and I should perhaps repair to the billiard room. Out of keeping with his character, Melville seemed to warm to this suggestion, but Crain flat-out refused.

"Actually, Watson," he ventured, "I have arranged a private reading for you with Madame Farr—I dare say it is the only chance you'll get before the party gets into full swing tomorrow. It's a singular privilege."

"I'm not sure about that, Crain," I said. "Something a little more cheerful and… inclusive tonight, eh?" I looked to Melville for support, but he said nothing—in fact, he had become stony faced once again.

"Melville can come too," Crain said.

"I don't think so," the barrister replied. "Actually, I may just retire. I'm feeling rather tired."

"Well, if you're sure, Melville," Crain said. "Come on then, Watson—a quick reading, then you and I can get a drink and talk some more in private. What do you say?"

I could tell Crain was not about to let the subject lie, and so with great reluctance I acquiesced. I steeled myself, for after Madame Farr's little hints earlier, I knew I would be in for more of the same treatment, and perhaps some magic show purporting to be messages from beyond, but I told myself it was stuff and nonsense. I hoped that we could get it over with, and that, when nothing whatsoever came of it, we would be free to enjoy the rest of the weekend.

To this end, I followed Crain, Judith and Madame Farr upstairs, with Simon behind us. I became somewhat hesitant when they approached the Red Tower.

"Really? I thought you said the tower was cold and uncomfortable," I said.

"It is," Crain smiled. "But I don't plan on spending the night. It is the most conducive spot for psychic vibrations—because of Lady Sybille, if you recall."

"Ah," I said, trying not to sound too incredulous. "Of course."

We entered the tower, passing a heavy door which was never closed, and through which a strong draught always blew. Below us, a short flight of stairs ended at a bricked-up arch, which at once conjured memories of Gothic ghost stories I had read as a youth. Crain lit two large candles mounted in a wall-sconce, for there was no sign of gas or electricity in the old tower. He repeated this process three more times as we climbed a winding stone stair. At last we reached a door, which Crain unlocked with an ancient-looking key, and entered a large, icy cold room.

As Crain and Simon set about lighting candles, the details of the tower room flickered into view. It was furnished as a bedroom, as Crain had intimated, although it was old-fashioned in the extreme. The half-wainscoted walls were covered in luxurious, crimson paper, peeling away in places. The four-poster bed was rather small, and draped in a large dust-sheet. The room was bereft of any feeling of comfort, although it was at least clean—someone had evidently dusted recently. The chamber was roughly octagonal, with two small, leaded windows in adjacent facets, which rattled in their casements. There were two other doors, which Crain explained led to a wardrobe and a stairway. The stairs led to the "battlements", but were wooden and so old that they were unsafe.

Simon moved a large antique lamp from one of the nightstands and put it on the floor, pulling the little table to the centre of the room, indicating that I should sit on the bed on one side of it. He then fetched a chair from beside a writing bureau against the wall, and placed that opposite me, where Madame Farr then sat. Judith, Simon and Crain stood about the room, and the audience made me feel most uncomfortable. Crain had taken the liberty of bringing a bottle of brandy and two glasses, and offered me a large one to ease my discomfort.

"Thank you for agreeing to this reading, Dr Watson,"

Madame Farr said. "I feel a great power surrounding you, and hope that in this place, where ancient souls dwell, we might receive some sign from the spirits. But first..." She took a deck of cards from her bag. Tarot cards. I suppressed an inward groan.

"I suppose it will be tea leaves next," I muttered.

Madame Farr did not reply. She handed the deck of cards to me and then said, "I would ask you to shuffle these, Dr Watson, and stop whenever you feel so inclined. Your hands will be guided, I am sure of it."

In silence, I did as she asked. I felt nothing "guiding" my hands, and so stopped presently and handed the cards back to her. She gave me a smile that was perhaps meant to be knowing, but in the wan light of the candlelit chamber instead looked sinister.

She took the top card from the deck.

"The distant past," she said. "But events that have a profound effect on you to this day." She laid the card face up before her on the little tabletop. "The Five of Cups. This represents bereavement—something that has played on your mind of late."

"Only because I have been reminded of it so often," I grumbled.

"Ah, but I sense it is not only your wife whom you miss. I see an 'H'... Henry?"

I tensed. "Go on."

"Father... no! Brother. It weighs on your mind. He fell on hard times before the end."

"So much has been published in my writings," I said. "I have nothing to hide in that regard."

"But the Five of Cups also signifies deep regret. For what, Dr Watson? Do you regret not being there for him, when the time came?"

I said nothing. It was a deduction on her part, nothing more, and she had plenty to go on. When Holmes had made similar observations about my late brother, he'd had only a scratched pocket-watch from which to extrapolate the facts.

"I do not know why it gnaws at you so, Doctor, but I sense something is unresolved. Let us move to the more recent past." She flipped the next card. "Ah, the Three of Pentacles—but it is reversed! A clearer picture begins to form. You have struggled in relationships, both of romance and of fellowship, for there is always the influence of another. A third person in every relationship; one who drains you of energy, but towards whom you always gravitate."

Again, I said nothing. It was plain that she had some familiarity with my stories of Sherlock Holmes.

"This person undermines you. He does not value your expertise, and takes you for granted."

"He?" I asked.

"That is the feeling I perceive. Now, on to the present."

I could almost guess what she would say next, regardless of the card. Was she trying to drive a wedge between Holmes and me? I could not think why, and despite my overarching sense of unease at this performance, I hardly thought she could be successful.

"The Six of Swords," she said.

But before she could utter another word, the heavy oak door of the room creaked open, and the air was sucked out, causing the candles to gutter.

"I say!" exclaimed Crain, and went at once to investigate. He looked outside, and then returned, closing and latching the door.

We were about to resume when a loud knocking sounded from the door behind me, at which all of us in the room jumped. It was the door to the roof. I leapt up, heart pounding.

"The spirits!" Madame Farr cried. "They bring a message."

No sooner had she said this than a series of rapid, quiet taps came from the door, and then from the walls themselves.

"Trickery!" I said, and ran to the door, throwing it open. I was met by nothing but the sight of rickety steps, and near total darkness. Above me, the trapdoor to the roof was closed fast.

"Do you smell that scent?" Madame Farr asked.

"I smell nothing but rotten wood," I said.

"Ah, then you are lucky I am here, Dr Watson, for your wife is with me, and she brings her message clear. Are you sure you can smell nothing?"

I spun around to face her. "What? What can you smell?"

"Fresh flowers. A particular variety… Lilies."

I froze. They were Mary's favourite flower.

"Please, Doctor, sit. These interruptions are commonplace when the spirits take an interest. Let us finish the reading before this auspicious moment passes."

Reluctantly, I took my seat again on the bed, and gulped down the rest of my brandy.

"The Six of Swords represents a regretful but necessary transition. But I sense something prevents you from taking a crucial decision that could bring you happiness. What was that, Mary? Yes, I can hear her now more clearly."

I began to quiver with intense rage. I had been in a similar position once before, in a moment of grief-induced weakness. Madame Farr's little show was more theatrical than my previous experience, and had the benefit of a dramatic setting, but the routine was the same. I despised her for using Mary's name; for putting words into the mouth of my dead wife.

"She tells me that you will not want to listen, Doctor. That you never listened, where *he* was concerned."

I confess she had struck a raw nerve. Mary had outwardly been nothing but supportive of my professional acquaintanceship with Holmes. But there had been occasions when I had felt rather neglectful of her, and though we had rarely broached the subject, in my darkest hours immediately following her passing I had regretted not spending every waking moment with her. Was this merely a simple deduction on Madame Farr's part? Or an assumption? After all, I had rather publicly led a double life; enough to be a strain on any man's marriage.

"Remember the Three of Pentacles?" she pressed. "It is he, Doctor. It is Sherlock Holmes whom you must leave behind if you are to prosper. And if you do not it will lead to..." she turned over the next card, and my blood ran cold. "Death," she finished, in almost a whisper.

I stared for a moment at the painted card, with its skeletal figure in blue-black robes, carrying a scythe and hourglass. And then I stood.

"Madame Farr, it seems to me that death is all around you. You are obsessed with death, such that you cannot truly live. Now if you will excuse me, I have heard enough."

I made for the door. Simon stood in front of it, and made no attempt to move. I looked up at the much taller man, with his bushy beard and suspicious eyes.

"Get out of my way," I growled through gritted teeth.

He looked past me to Madame Farr, and then askance to Crain.

"Watson—" Crain started.

"Not now, Crain," I snapped. I turned back to Simon, and moved so close I heard him gulp nervously. I felt some small satisfaction as he at last relented and stepped aside.

Moments later I was at the foot of the stone stairs. I stormed down to the hall. The front door was locked up for the evening, and so I turned and marched through the rear passages, past the kitchen, and out into the cold night. Gravel crunched beneath my boot heels, and a blustering wind assailed me, though at least the rain had subsided to a fine drizzle. I stopped near the stables, seeking shelter under a lean-to, and brushed the rain from my face.

When I looked up, there was Simon again! He must have followed close at my heels, but made no move towards me. Instead he strode off past the coach-house to some other part of the manor. Was he spying on me? What other cause could he have to come outside at this hour?

Uncertain of the man's movements, I walked around to the front of the house, and climbed the steps to the porch to get out of the rain. I stood there for a moment, until my anger subsided. I turned to the house, to what I thought was the morning room, which should have been in darkness. But someone was inside. By the light of a single lamp, I saw the silhouette of a man, his back to me, his attention fixed on something—no, someone. He was in embrace with someone, a woman, who now pulled away. It was Esther's maid, Sally. He put his hands on her arms, and some words were exchanged, before she left the room with great urgency, leaving the man alone. Eventually, he picked up the lantern and made for the door, and in that moment I gasped.

It was Melville.

I stood outside in confusion—at what Madame Farr had said to me, at what I had seen between Melville and Sally. I gazed across the rain-soaked lawn at the rows of gnarled trees and shadowed statues, where I half expected that sneak Simon to be lurking. This was not a happy place. I was full of regret for agreeing to take this "holiday".

A bolt withdrew behind me, a key clicked in a lock, and the front door swung open.

"Are you all right, Watson?"

Crain had come to find me. I turned and peered past him into the hall before responding, to ensure that the lingering form of Judith was not in sight. To my relief, Crain was alone.

"I just needed some air."

He stood beside me in silence for a moment, and lit a cigarette. I refused the offer of another from his case.

"I understand, Watson, I do. It can be damned tumultuous when the spirits speak to you. Drags all those buried feelings to the surface, you know?"

"I'm not sure that's quite how it is, Crain," I said. It was hard not to feel angry. Crain had put me in the sights of Madame Farr, and I still suspected he had let slip more than a few details about myself and Mary to the spiritualists.

"I see. You are still sceptical. That's understandable—it is an awful lot to ask of you to be otherwise, especially after so long in the company of the rational Mr Holmes."

I sighed. "What is the point of any of it, Crain? I mean, even if there's a grain of truth to it, what good can it truly achieve? I can speak only for myself, but Mary is gone, and I had come to terms with that. This feels a lot like picking the scab from a wound."

"The point?" he asked, looking aghast. "Watson, if you are prepared to accept that there is even the slightest truth to what Madame Farr offers, how could you ask such a thing?"

"I said 'if', Crain. I am speaking theoretically. Because in fact, Mary is surely in heaven, as is your mother, God rest them both."

Crain's colour rose. "There is more than one interpretation of the nature of heaven, Watson, and just how closed it is to other… realms, let's say. I do not doubt for a moment that heaven exists, but we spiritualists take a rather more pragmatic view of the afterlife. Just think of the possibilities! To hear Mary speak once more; to ask if she is in peace, or happy…"

"And if she is not? And there is nothing whatsoever I can do about it?"

"But there is, don't you see? Madame Farr can bridge the gap between this world and the next. She can soothe the living and the dead."

"Do you feel soothed?" I asked. I was feeling less than amiable. Perhaps my colour rose as a result of too much brandy. More likely, Madame Farr's words still stung. "Have you not suspended the very business of living so that you might hang upon the every word of that woman?"

"That is unkind, Watson. She speaks for Mama, and if there is anything to be gleaned from her messages, I owe it to myself, and to my mother, to listen."

I pinched at my eyes. It was no use—Crain was utterly convinced of the spiritualist message. The look in his eyes was evangelical. I saw no point in trying to dissuade him, leastways not at that hour, while we were both intoxicated and with our passions running high. There was nothing more to say than goodnight.

My room was chilly, and I went straight to bed. The servants had left a pitcher of water on the side-table, with a glass already filled beside it, and I drank thirstily to shake away the vestiges of a brandy-induced fug. I pulled the covers high, and soon drifted off. My sleep was fitful, due in no small part to the events of the evening. My mind conjured ghoulish nightmares, of headless shades and bloody chambers; of Madame Farr with her stern, dark eyes and pallid features.

I dreamt, too, of Mary, more intensely than I had at any time since her passing. My overactive mind conjured me to a vast bridge spanning a fast-flowing, black river. Mary was at one end, calling to me. I ran to her, but no matter how fast or how far, I could not catch her. I could only see her outstretched arms, and hear her calling, *"John... Remember... John..."*

I woke with my heart pounding, the sweat freezing at my brow, my stomach lurching as though I were about to tumble from some precipice. My mouth was so dry that my lips stuck together. What had woken me, I could not say, but I had a fearful sense that something was amiss.

And then I heard something in the darkness. A shuffling noise coming from somewhere in the room. It took all my strength to sit upright. My arms shook and buckled beneath my own weight. What faint silvery patches of moonlight fell through the crack in the curtains seemed to shimmer and slide about my vision. The whole room spun around me.

I squinted against the gloom, and what I saw, albeit indistinctly, sent cold creeping up my spine. At the edge of the room was a woman. She was small of stature, slim, and dressed in a long white gown, which extended to her small, bare feet. Her face was covered by a white veil, and her blonde hair tied up in plaits encircling the crown of her head, threaded with flowers. It was the way Mary had worn hers on our wedding day.

I tried to speak, but could not. I was groggy from drink, and now an awful fear came over me, exacerbated when the strange figure began to move.

She skirted the edge of the room silently. The folds of her flowing gown shimmered like marsh-lights; her hair shone from some illumination of its own creation.

"*Remember*."

When the voice came, barely more than a breathless whisper, I almost passed out. I found myself gripping the bedclothes tightly to my chest, holding my breath as though any sound, even exhalation, would cause the apparition before me to vanish.

"Mary?" My own voice was lost in the space of the room, weak and croaking, as though the shadows themselves absorbed the word.

The spirit did not turn, but merely continued on its path, gliding noiselessly from one corner of the room to the other. I squinted again, but my vision only blurred, such that the woman became a smudge of glimmering light against the blackness, iridescent particles reflecting in the weak moonlight.

"Mary!" I said again, this time louder. And as I said it, the shimmering light faded, melding into shadow until there was nought but darkness in the room.

I urged my legs to move, and at last courage came into my heart. I pulled myself upright, swinging my legs over the side of the bed. The room at once swam about me, and I reached for the bedside table to steady myself. If there was any doubt in my mind as to what I had seen, or even if I had still been asleep, and dreaming, those doubts were dispelled as a familiar scent reached my nostrils. A floral scent, which had once filled our home when dear Mary was alive.

I fumbled for a match with shaking fingers, finally sparking one to life and lighting the lamp by my bed. The shadows were dispelled, chased from sight by the golden glow of the lamp. I carried it into every corner, searching every nook and cranny even though my head swam and my limbs quivered. Finally, I returned to the bed and sat down. My throat was dry as the Turkestan Plains, and I reached for my water jug, pouring glass after glass until finally my thirst was quenched, and whatever terror had seized me began to subside.

I felt sick to the pit of my stomach, and fumbled in the drawer of my nightstand. Amongst my handkerchiefs and cufflinks was a silver locket, which I pulled out at once and clicked open. Within were two small photographs, of myself and Mary taken on our wedding day. I could barely focus, and squinted in the dim candlelight. Mary's hair fair shimmered, and there were the plaits wrapped about the crown of her head, threaded with flowers.

I forced my shaking legs to bear me on a circuit of the room, carrying the candle to every shadowed corner. I opened the door and looked both ways along the corridor—the landing and stairs were just a short distance left, while a long row of guest bedrooms extended right. The corridor swam, as though I viewed it through aged glass, and I felt again so nauseous that I retreated to my bed in haste.

Satisfied that there was no mortal soul in the room, I sank back into bed, where finally I noticed upon the pillow beside me a single-stemmed flower. Its scent was delicate, and its appearance was markedly unusual for the time of year.

It was a white lily.

CHAPTER FOUR

AN UNUSUAL GATHERING

Over breakfast, I seethed.

Indeed, Crain, Melville and Lady Esther all ate in silence. I gathered that Esther and her fiancé had had some disagreement, for the occasional looks they exchanged were pregnant with agitation. And through the whole awkward affair, Judith sat beside Crain, her manner as impassive as ever. The only comfort I could take at all was that Madame Farr had left early, repairing to her home in the village to "gather her strength", according to Judith.

It did not help that I still felt groggy and tired. I eschewed tea in favour of strong coffee, and followed that with glass after glass of water for my parched throat—enough to draw bemused looks from my fellows.

After breakfast, Lord Berkeley, Lady Esther and Melville set out to church. Esther made some show of trying to persuade her brother to go along, but he refused rather flatly. Esther explained to me discreetly that the local vicar was most disapproving of spiritualism, and had taken so many opportunities to preach against it from his pulpit that Crain now preferred to pray alone.

I opted to stay at the manor, hoping to engineer some time alone with Crain, but it proved nigh impossible. Crain took himself away to a crumbling old family chapel for an hour as promised, but upon his return Judith took every opportunity to inform him of some "presence" or "vibration", or else to sit with him and mutter some elaborate prayer to the spirits. Eventually, I had no option but to interrupt, and took it upon myself to be blunt.

"Crain, might I have a moment of your time?" I asked.

"Of course. Is something the matter?"

Judith looked at me somewhat blankly.

"As a matter of fact, there is. Shall we take a stroll?" I indicated the front door. I had noted that the drizzle had stopped, and thought perhaps the gardens would be the most private venue for our interview.

"Very well. Judith, you had better fetch an umbrella, just in case it—"

"Actually, Crain," I said, "this is a private matter."

"Well, Watson, I don't need a sixth sense to feel the negative energy around you. This is exactly the kind of thing that Judith excels at."

"I'm sorry, Crain—and I mean no offence to the young lady—but I really must insist we speak alone."

Did Judith's eyes narrow, just a touch? I looked at her anew in that moment. Her build, her movements. If there was trickery involved last night—and I certainly preferred to think it so rather than the alternative—then Judith was the most likely culprit. Yet I found her a rather dull-witted girl, and I saw little malice behind her eyes. An act? Or was she merely a puppet of the far more cunning Madame Farr? But what a risk it was! I did not think I ever gave the impression that I could be trifled with, but my long acquaintanceship with the recently returned Sherlock Holmes should have given any villain pause for thought.

As Crain dismissed Judith, gently, I watched her leave. She was, in truth, most unlike the spirit I had seen, but then, I had encountered a fair number of masterful disguises in my time. And yet I had searched every nook and cranny of my room by the light of morning, and had found no trace of ingress or egress. Whatever, or whomever, I had seen, had vanished into thin air.

Crain walked with me across the gravel drive, along a rough path that twisted between ancient trees. The gardens were still and quiet, but for the occasional cry of a peacock permeating the last of the low morning mist.

"What's got you so rattled, Watson?" Crain asked.

I did not know how to explain, or how much I should say. As I searched for the right words, I felt anger rising within me.

"You have!" I blurted. "You and your blasted spiritualist friends. Holmes told me I shouldn't have come, and I think he may have been right."

Crain stopped, his face a picture of surprise. "He did? You never mentioned that. But honestly, what have I done?"

I was furious with Crain, and blamed him for my state of confusion. Old emotions, long buried, bubbled within. I knew I should approach it rationally—give Crain the chance to explain, to defend himself—but I could not.

"Those things Madame Farr said to me last night. Not every detail is a matter of public record—she could not have gleaned them from my stories alone. So, logically, it follows that someone close to me—someone I trust—told her." I glared at him angrily. Me, a humble London doctor, growling at a wealthy heir like a terrier squaring up to a mastiff.

"And you think I…? No. Watson, you must calm yourself."

"Calm? How can I be calm, when there are tricks being played upon me? Cruel tricks at that!"

"There are no tricks," Crain said, his own tone becoming

sterner. "Certainly not on my part, and I very much doubt on the part of Madame Farr—who, as you say yourself, is my friend."

"And am I not then your friend, should my cause be at odds with Madame Farr's?"

"Don't be silly. You are an old and very dear friend, which is why I invited you here. It is why I want you, more than anyone, to see Madame Farr's work in the purest light. It is why I went to great pains not to say anything to her, or even to Judith, that might in the slightest bias them, even unconsciously, with personal knowledge of you. I swear to you, Watson: what Madame Farr revealed to you last night did not come from me."

"Then swear on something you hold dear, that I might trust in my own senses again."

Crain gave a puzzled frown. "Very well. I swear on the life of my dear sis— No. You deserve a true oath, and you will know better than anyone that what I say now is in good faith. I swear it on Mama's soul, God rest her. I did not knowingly pass information about you to anyone in the spiritualist mission, nor even to anyone in my own house."

I faltered. I knew in my heart that Crain would not take his mother's name in vain, for he venerated her memory more than all the saints and angels in heaven. I nodded. Perhaps Madame Farr had gathered her intelligence solely through my stories and merely guessed at the rest. Perhaps Crain had discussed me with someone else—his sister, maybe—and Judith or that Simon fellow had eavesdropped. I could hardly blame Crain for that. Holmes's warnings still echoed in my mind, and I could not believe I had been visited by a ghost until all other possibilities were eliminated. How I wished he were here.

"Watson, I think you already have the answer," Crain said gently. "You said that someone close to you must have passed information to Madame Farr. And they did."

"Oh?"

"Watson, she is a medium. It is my firmest belief that Mary spoke to her."

I clenched my fists. Crain was sincere. I could see it in his eyes. But still I could not believe it.

"I can see you will need some time to get used to the idea," he said. "Don't worry—many people go through this at first. The early contact is often traumatic. The rational mind rebels against the idea of the supernatural. But it exists, Watson. Madame Farr has convinced me of it, and if you open your mind, I'm sure she will convince you too."

"Have you… have you ever seen your mother? Since… you know."

"Only once. More an impression, really. A sort of figure of light, drifting as though through smoke. It was down by the river on the estate—there's a cottage there where Esther and I used to play as children. Mother would take us there for picnics. It was such a happy place; a happy time. Despite what Sir Thomas thinks…" He drifted, eyes glazing over in some reverie.

"Sir Thomas Golspie?" I asked. "What has he to do with it?"

"It does not matter. Yes, Watson, I have seen her. Indistinct, but I am convinced it was she. And had I not listened to Madame Farr, it may never have happened. But wait… is that what all this is about? Have you *seen* something?"

I felt heat rise beneath my collar as I reddened. "Nothing that cannot be attributed to an excess of rich food and too much cognac before bed," I replied hastily.

"It would not surprise me, you know. A heightened state of awareness, coupled with the location—you realise, of course, that your room abuts the Red Tower."

I glanced over my shoulder at the house. It had not really occurred to me, and now the tower looked more ominous than ever. "Really, Crain, I would rather not speak of this further. It is a trifle. A nothing."

"Very well, I shall say no more. But for the rest of your stay here, I ask that you be as honest with me as I have been with you. Now, won't you come inside? The other guests will be arriving in an hour or two."

"I… I'll just take a little air, if you don't mind," I said. "I shall return presently."

"Good man," Crain said, placing a hand on my shoulder. "Take your time."

I listened to Crain's footsteps recede, and stood alone beside a stone fountain. I stared across the gardens, where statues and saplings stood as dark smudges in the mist. And beside one such statue there was another shape, just for a moment: a figure staring directly at me, before vanishing away like a ghost.

It was Simon.

I had wished several times already that I could consult Holmes on the strange events surrounding my stay at Crain Manor, and so before the family returned from church, I resolved to do something about it. I wrote out a telegram form, and asked a servant to take it to the village and send it post haste. It said simply:

> Holmes, you were right. Madame Farr appears most dishonest, and I fear there is trickery afoot. Unsure of her motives. Should I find evidence of anything more sinister, I will write again. Watson.

It was something and nothing—merely to have told my

friend of my discomfort, in even such vague terms, was somewhat cathartic. Crain Manor felt strangely isolated from the world, but this small act made me feel connected once more to London. I felt better able to face the rest of the weekend knowing that I could contact Holmes if necessary.

At noon, shortly after Lady Esther had returned from church, the first of the guests arrived. I was sitting in the morning room with a book—brooding, truth be told—when Crain came to introduce four newcomers, who had arrived together in the manor's four-wheeler. There was David Langton—Crain's second cousin—and his wife, Constance, and Josiah Cavendish, the family solicitor, with his wife Jane. Langton was amiable enough, a young man, and his wife was all too clearly keen not to stand on ceremony; it quickly became evident that they were not used to the grandeur of the Crain side of the family.

"I was most surprised to be invited to a weekend party," Langton had quipped. "I didn't think the Crains knew what a weekend was, never having worked a day in their lives."

Cavendish, by contrast, was an odd little fellow of advancing years. His rosy cheeks and broad, purplish nose spoke of a love of drink. Garrulous in his manner, he was forever being shushed by his wife who, far from being relaxed in her husband's company, was markedly on edge. I was uncertain whether to feel sorry for the man for being hen-pecked, or to place my sympathies with the woman for enduring her husband's eccentricities. Regardless, I felt at least that Cavendish might prove entertaining.

These arrivals had barely been shown to their rooms when the clatter of carriage wheels sounded outside again, and a small fly drew up before the doors.

"Ah, here's the vicar," Crain said. "The Reverend Cyril Parkin—he was invited on my father's insistence, although he's a decent sort of chap."

"I should hope so, for a vicar," I said, following Crain out onto the porch steps, and noting the ever-present Judith shuffling along at our heels.

Crain shot me a wry smile, the meaning of which I was unable to discern.

A footman helped the Reverend Parkin from his fly, and took his small leather case, while the groom drove the little carriage off to the coach-house. The clergyman approached us with a pronounced waddle, beaming a broad smile made all the more dazzling by his overbite and large front teeth.

"Lives a short ride away, but never passes up a chance to stay at the manor," Crain whispered to me through the side of his mouth. Then he stepped down to greet the vicar with arms outstretched. "Vicar, so good of you to come. I trust you missed the rain."

"Indeed, and we give thanks for it," the vicar said. "If I'm not mistaken the weather may favour us today. I did not see you in church this morning, Lord Beving. I trust you are well?"

"I was… waylaid. Here, come and meet Dr Watson, an old friend."

Crain ushered the clergyman in my direction and introduced us. He was a funny sort of chap, with eyes rather like a pair of toads protruding from their holes, blinking behind thick-lensed *pince-nez*, and lank hair sticking out from beneath a cloth cap. He returned my handshake rather flaccidly.

"We've all heard so much about you," he said.

I shot Crain a look over the vicar's shoulder. "Not too much, I hope," I said.

"O-ho!" the man laughed dismissively, and carried on up the steps. "Do I have my usual room? This way, yes?"

Crain gave a smirk as the Reverend Parkin waddled off, a servant scurrying after him.

"How many more guests are we expecting?" I asked.

"Just Sir Thomas," Crain said. "And Madame Farr, of course. Sir Thomas lives but a short distance away—the next house along the hilltop drive there, and he usually prefers the walk. Hardy old bird, he is."

"I rather imagine so; his reputation precedes him."

"As does yours, thanks to those stories you write. Come, let's gather everyone in the drawing room for some luncheon."

As I turned to follow Crain back into the house, I caught sight of a pair of dark figures from the corner of my eye, and my stomach lurched involuntarily. It was Madame Farr and Simon, striding purposefully along the drive. I could not account for my reaction, and breathed a sigh of relief when I saw them heading not towards me at the front door, but to the rear of the property, towards the coach-house and servants' entrance. I could not postpone an encounter with her indefinitely, but the respite was welcome.

Laughter and light came to Crain Manor, and the gloom of the previous evening was banished.

Lady Esther had joined us all for the afternoon's frivolities, although her fiancé was conspicuous by his absence. Langton, too, made a habit of disappearing, his appetite for tobacco being quite rapacious—too much for the company of ladies, its demands too frequent for all of us men to accompany him each time. He would come back from a walk around the grounds wind-pinched and smelling of bird's-eye tobacco. Constance Langton, meanwhile, attached herself to Esther, the two young ladies clearly being firm friends.

Games were played, and songs were sung. Mrs Langton, it transpired, had the sweetest singing voice, while the Reverend Parkin was a not unaccomplished pianist—though his proclivity for hymns drew several groans in jest, followed by peals of laughter.

Crain, for his troubles, attempted but once to bring the subject of spiritualism to the fore, but was almost immediately quashed by a prevailing atmosphere of gaiety that would not brook the intrusion of sombre topics. Once, however, I did notice a shadow pass the open door of the drawing room, and heard a creeping tread; there I saw Simon peering in at us. No one else seemed to notice him, except for Judith, who exchanged a look with him before he slipped away. I fancied perhaps he was giving a silent signal to the girl, and indeed, just ten minutes later, she set down her sampler and quietly excused herself from the company.

Some hours passed in light-hearted manner, until the door swung open and the butler stepped in to announce a new arrival.

"Sir Thomas Golspie," he proclaimed.

A formidable figure entered the room, and it gave me some thrill to see that he was every bit the figure I had imagined. Sir Thomas was an imposing-looking fellow, broad of shoulder and stoic of feature. His flinty eyes now took in every detail of the room from the deep sockets of his weather-beaten face. He had the complexion of a Cornishman, dark and leathery, and jet-black hair, the white of age only showing at the temples, and in the bristles of his large moustaches.

Lady Esther stepped forward and took both of the man's hands in hers, his face fair cracking as he beamed.

"Esther, my dear girl, you're looking better."

"I feel it, Sir Thomas. It's good to see you."

"Sir Thomas, so glad you could make it," Crain said, striding forward to shake the man's hand. Sir Thomas's smile faded. "The sandwiches are all gone, but there is cake if you are partial."

"And wine!" chimed Cavendish, raising his glass to laughter from the party.

"That's quite all right," Sir Thomas said. He looked over Crain's shoulder, as though counting us all for a second time. "Saw that spindly fellow prowling around outside. Will that Farr woman be joining us?" There was some hard edge to his tone.

"Later, Sir Thomas," Crain said, looking a little abashed. "And I'm sure he wasn't prowling. Come, let me introduce you. You know Cavendish and his wife, Jane, of course. There's the vicar at the pianoforte there. That's my cousin's good lady wife, Constance, entertaining us with her singing. I don't believe you've met. And this here is Dr Watson, an old friend from London."

"A pleasure to meet you," I said.

"Likewise," Sir Thomas replied, gripping my hand firmly in the rough, bear-like paw which it was said had once prised apart the jaws of a lioness to save one of his native porters on an African expedition.

Now that I stood face to face with the man, there was something else about those piercing eyes—a sadness, or even fear. Not of me, but the persistent kind, of a man haunted by some great terror, or perhaps guilt. Certainly, though he was the epitome of politeness, there was no mirth in him; with Melville and the elder Lord Berkeley of a similar disposition, it seemed sternness was epidemic in this house.

"I shall send for more tea," Crain said as the party settled again. "Sir Thomas, would you mind stepping with me for a moment? I must ask you something. Now, everyone else, do not stop on our account. More music!"

The piano struck up again, the Reverend Parkin teasing us with a solemn bar of "O for a Thousand Tongues to Sing", before performing a clumsy segue into "The Fountain in the Park", to much laughter from us all. I could not help but wonder what business Crain could have with Sir Thomas, such that it could not wait. Indeed, a moment later I caught sight of the tops of their heads bobbing past the window.

Lady Esther must have noticed my confusion, and leaned over to me. “Sir Thomas is our godfather, you know. I’m afraid he and James are thick as thieves, and have been since we were small—a young boy must have his heroes.”

I was surprised that Crain had room in his heart for heroes other than his sainted mother, but smiled politely all the same. “He keeps rather a strange collection of friends these days,” I said.

“You probably mean Judith,” Esther said. “He brought her home one day like a stray kitten. He met her out at a cottage on the estate, where he likes to go to… get away from it all. She in turn led him straight into the arms of the mysterious Madame Farr. Don’t be fooled by the girl’s dull appearance. I think she’s clever, and perhaps rather sly.”

“I see.”

“Do you? I hope you don’t, or what must you think of us?” She laughed her musical laugh, and turned her attentions back to the other guests.

Langton returned soon afterwards from another smoking jaunt, this time looking a little flustered, as the wind had got up outside. He sat beside his wife, a frown etched on his face.

“Everything all right, Langton?” Cavendish asked, already swaying somewhat from drink.

“Perfectly, don’t mind me.”

Langton sat, and exchanged very quiet words with his wife. There was something about his manner that bothered me; indeed, I think it was the sense that everyone I had met at Crain Manor so far had been in some way circumspect, or had seemed to be hiding something. All except Lady Esther, whose company was a pleasure. That she had been a little ill recently was telling, but she battled on bravely so as not to disappoint her guests. Or, rather, her brother’s guests.

My unease was likely due to my experience the previous night, which even now seemed to be little more than a bad dream. I was also feeling a little worse for yesterday's drink. I had told Holmes that I was here on a holiday, and so I determined to make the best of it. Even when Crain returned looking unusually buoyant, and Sir Thomas distanced himself from the rest of the company, I refused to let further suspicion and doubt enter my heart. This, I told myself, was Holmes's influence, and it had no place here.

Later that afternoon, I paid a visit to Crain to borrow a white tie for dinner. I had, rather naively, not expected it to be so formal an affair, given the guest list, but I reminded myself just how prominent a fellow Lord Berkeley was. As I returned to my own room, I heard muffled voices coming from one of the bedrooms further along the corridor of the family wing; a man and a woman. I could make out no words, but the man's voice was most agitated. I paused; I was sure it was Melville's room, and I felt aggrieved that the recipient of his ire might be the gentle Lady Esther. Before I knew it, I was gravitating towards the door, with no plan in mind.

I was barely three feet from the door when it flew open, and Melville stepped out, his face like thunder. He paused when he saw me, eyes narrowed, and then wordlessly barged past me. I wanted to say something—at the very least to establish that I had not been eavesdropping—but it was all so sudden that I had no chance. I turned to the door, and saw Lady Esther at the window-seat, dabbing at her eyes with a kerchief. I was about to knock, to offer some comfort—anything—but a slender hand appeared at the crack in the door, and then a face: Sally. The lady's maid looked at me for a moment, gave a very slight curtsey, and then clicked the door closed.

Somewhat red-faced, I went back towards my own room,

and saw Melville's shadow vanish at the end of the passage; I fancied he did not make for the stairs, but for the Red Tower.

CHAPTER FIVE

DINNER IS SERVED

Dinner was a very different prospect from the previous evening. The dining room was aglow with the light from candelabras and chandeliers, and bedecked in the finest silver. Fresh flowers lined the mantel, and trailed along the centre of the long table. There were lilies amongst them, including white blooms, which caused me a moment's consternation. I had not considered that the gardener at Crain Manor might cultivate them out of season, or that perhaps they had been ordered from some nearby florist. In any case, I now had an explanation. If Holmes were here, he would surely deduce that the lily at my bedside the previous night had not manifested as if by magic, but had been placed there by mortal hands. But whose? And how did that account for the other aspects of my ghostly experience?

"Dr Watson."

I had been miles away, and jumped as Sir Thomas Golspie disturbed my wool-gathering.

"We did not have much chance to speak earlier. Young James tells me you are an enthusiast of exploration."

"I am. Your reputation precedes you, sir."

"Reputation is not always a blessing, Doctor."

"Quite," I said, thinking of how my own reputation had served me so far at Crain Manor. "I must say I have followed your exploits in the press ever since Egypt."

"Overrated," Sir Thomas smiled. "I knew little of the world then, and far more famous men than I had already plundered Egypt. I prefer to bring home only that which is freely given."

"Crain mentioned that you have quite the collection of curios, brought back from your many adventures."

"Oh, yes. I have trinkets from all over the world, but South Africa mainly—it is my chief area of interest. I have tribal ephemera, artefacts both archaeological and anthropological. I even have a collection of exotic plants, such as my talents allow me to grow—the African tribesmen use a great many herbs and roots for all sorts of ailments. Does the subject interest you?"

"Very much so."

"Then perhaps if you have time you would like to call tomorrow? I would be happy to show you my collection."

"I should like that very much," I said, trying hard not to appear like a fanatical schoolboy.

"It is always a pleasure to entertain a fellow traveller."

"I was," I said, "though not always by choice."

"Ah, soldier, is it? Can always tell the cut of a man's cloth. I had you as a deal too stout for an academician."

"You are not the first to say so," I replied with a smile. "I learned my trade as an Army doctor, Fifth Northumberland Fusiliers. Though my service was cut a little short." I tapped at my left shoulder.

"Wounded?"

"A jezail."

"Not at Kandahar?" Sir Thomas asked.

"Goodness, no. Maiwand. I had not thought myself lucky at the time, I can tell you. But after what happened at Kandahar, to far braver men than I… well, let us just say I still count my blessings."

"I would toast you, Doctor, but the wine has not yet been served."

"You have seen your fair share of action," I said, brimming with pride at the compliment. "Far more than me, I should say."

"My military service passed largely without incident, Doctor, and all the trials and tribulations that came later were brought on myself."

"Nevertheless, I have read the Mackenzie accounts—your time with the Wasimbu peoples was every bit as hazardous as my scrape at Maiwand."

"Mackenzie exaggerates, perhaps," Sir Thomas said, his face falling a little at the mention. "It just goes to show: I faced far wilder lands than that in a year-long expedition, and it was returning to the relative safety of the Cape colony, the last leg of the tour, which almost did for us." At this, Sir Thomas took a silver snuff-box from his pocket, engraved with an intricate design of snakes in the African tribal style. He did not offer the box, but took two pinches for himself, with what I thought was a trembling hand. He looked at me then, with a manner most changed. "If you'll excuse me, Dr Watson," he said, "I think our host is coming down and I have not yet said hello."

Crain and his father entered together. Sir Thomas turned away from me and made straight for Lord Berkeley, their mutual respect evident. I could not have failed to notice the way Sir Thomas's manner had changed when I raised the topic of the Wasimbu tribe. That he had gone missing from his expedition for some time, and contracted malaria, was well documented. I had assumed he would have grown accustomed to discussing his exploits, but it appeared the memories were still painful. As

James Crain passed Sir Thomas, they exchanged some queer look—certainly, on Crain's part it was a guarded one. I wondered if it concerned whatever matter they had discussed privately earlier that afternoon.

There was no time to ponder further. I was shown to my seat, the middle chair to the right of the host's place—a goodly few settings further up than I'd expected, being an outsider to the family. Lord Berkeley took his place at the head of the table, Sir Thomas to his left. The other guests entered, taking up their seats, so that I ended up with Langton's space to my left and, to my delight, Lady Esther to my right, looking resplendent in a rather unusual high-collared, long-sleeved dress of embroidered gold. Her lady's maid, Sally, fussed around her as usual. Whereas previously I had barely noticed the girl, now I watched her with no small suspicion.

Crain was seated directly opposite me, and I felt a creeping sensation to the pit of my stomach as Madame Farr entered, sitting to Crain's left, opposite Esther.

"Oh, good," Esther muttered.

"An unusual arrangement," I whispered to her. The seating for such dinners usually followed a rather strict plan. Lord Berkeley would always take the host's place, of course, even though the party had been arranged by his son. The female guest of honour was thus Madame Farr, who should sit to Lord Berkeley's right—now Langton's place.

"Father would not brook sitting beside that woman for dinner," Esther returned my whisper with a knowing smile. "I had a word with Eglinton earlier, and he saw to it."

I glanced to Eglinton, the butler, who I'd found to be as efficient a fellow as I ever saw in service.

"But you did not expect to be opposite our friend there?" I asked.

"I did not. But I'm sure Eglinton did his best at short notice."

Across the table, Madame Farr and Crain were already in some deep and sober discussion. Judith looked down at her lap, timid as a mouse. The odd man, Simon, stood beside the butler at the sideboard, drawing the occasional disapproving look. It seemed that Madame Farr liked to have her own servant present to cater to her peculiarities, and for some reason this was permitted.

Lady Esther and I paused our conspiratorial mutterings as the rest of the guests were seated and order resumed. Mr and Mrs Cavendish took up the remaining spaces beside Madame Farr—Cavendish did not seem to mind, given that he was already teetering a little. We waited a few moments too long for the last of the guests. Finally, the Reverend Parkin waddled in, looking rather serious and distracted. It was all he could do to mutter some apologies, appearing notably disappointed when he was shown to the very end of the table, an empty seat between him and Esther Crain.

"Is everything all right, Vicar?" Crain asked across the table.

"Hmm?" Parkin mumbled, staring into space.

Crain caught my attention and rolled his eyes, smirking at the vicar's expense.

"Your fiancé, Lady Esther?" I asked. "I've barely seen Melville all day." The scene I had witnessed between the two of them played on my mind.

"He had some rather tiresome papers to sign earlier, and I'm afraid it has given him a severe headache."

"Oh dear," I replied. "I have some pills in my bag that might help, if—"

"No, that won't be necessary," Lady Esther said, hastily. "He gets them from time to time, from overwork. He told me he would follow me down presently."

Langton now arrived, his hair a little damp from rain. He,

too, apologised to the host, before taking his seat next to me. He passed some silly remark about it being too wet outside even to light his pipe, and I became engaged in small talk with him. As I did, I noticed Lady Esther's maid, Sally, pass by us. She leaned beside Esther, and the two of them conspired in hushed, urgent tones for a moment, before Sally hurried away.

"Eglinton!" Lord Berkeley barked. "We can't wait all evening for Melville. Fetch the soup."

"At once, my lord," the butler said, and scurried from the room.

"I say, Esther," Crain said. "Is Melville all right?"

"Just one of his headaches," she replied. Her smile was somewhat pained, such that I wondered if she had a headache herself.

The chatter continued, and when the servants did arrive with the first course, Melville came in with them, looking rather flustered. His hair was damp, as Langton's had been, and he smoothed it with his hands as he made for his place.

"Been out in the rain, Melville?" Crain asked.

"Just a brisk walk," Melville replied. "To blow away the cobwebs."

"Feeling better now, I hope."

"Very much, yes." Melville reached his place, and bowed briskly towards the head of the table. "My apologies, Lord Berkeley."

The elder Crain merely waved a hand, and took up again whatever conversation he was having with Sir Thomas. Melville was seated, exchanging the slightest nod with his fiancée, and greeting the vicar, who appeared glad finally to have someone with whom to converse more clearly. Lady Esther's demeanour changed as Melville took his seat. There were some whispered words between them, and I fancied she trembled slightly before composing herself.

I knew that, at some point, Crain would try to stamp the

subject of spiritualism upon our gathering. He had assembled this group, and his purpose had been made clear, at least to me if not to the others. Yet the conversation flowed as easily as the wine, and by the time the main course was half-devoured, no mention of spiritualism had been made. Madame Farr had spoken only quietly, and only to Crain and Judith. I took note of the guests: the Reverend Parkin had been subdued since his arrival, and Lady Esther likewise since the appearance of her fiancé. Mrs Cavendish attempted often to converse politely with Parkin, Melville, and even Madame Farr, but was frequently cut off by her husband who, through sheer drunken obliviousness rather than malign intent, turned every discourse into a raucous jest. Langton spoke with me primarily of business—he possessed an extensive portfolio of property in Dorset, like his father before him, I gathered. I could tell he was a serious fellow, hard-working and earnest, and in that respect we had much in common. He bore himself with nobility, not from breeding, but from that drive that some men have to prove themselves the better of those more fortunate than they. Constance Langton was as down-to-earth as her husband, and I sensed she was a little stranded at dinner—the unusual seating arrangements caused by Madame Farr's unwelcome presence had left her surrounded by earnest men, the only other feminine presence in earshot the uncommunicative Judith across the way. As I glanced in Judith's direction, I noted Simon entering from the hall, skirting the room noiselessly and passing Judith's place. I had not even noticed him leave, and his stealth bothered me, perhaps irrationally.

It was as our meat course was being cleared that Lord Berkeley called across the table to his son.

"James, listen, boy. Sir Thomas was just asking about the future of the Crain estate," he said. "I told him that the future is rather bleak, unless you get out there and find a wife. Any prospects in that department?"

This caused rather a number of awkward, downward glances. Crain looked decidedly embarrassed.

"There is plenty of time for that, Father," he replied.

"Time? It's the one thing we don't have, my lad. I'll be dead before long, and what then?"

"Father!" Esther exclaimed.

"Don't worry yourself, m'dear. At this rate, you and Melville will have produced a suitable heir before my only son. Or maybe Cousin David here deserves a turn. At least he works hard."

Langton stretched his shoulders and stared down at his plate, most uncomfortably.

"I work hard, Father," Crain said. "I'm on the estate almost every day."

"Yes, you're out. But what are you doing? Not working, that's for sure. Mark my words, my lad, you need to find yourself a woman who's more interested in the living than the dead, or else I'll change my will. What do you say, Cavendish?"

"Eh?" Cavendish said, almost in a squeak.

"I said I'll change me will. You can see to that, can't you?"

"Of course, Lord Berkeley. Capital idea," the solicitor replied, squinting as he struggled to focus on his host.

Cavendish's wife gave him a sharp nudge, and scowled at her husband.

"There you go. What do we think? Cousin David is next in line—maybe everything goes to him. Every penny!"

"Um… I say, my lord, if I might—" the vicar said, timidly.

"Every penny!" Lord Berkeley repeated, more forcefully, and fixed Parkin with such a look that the clergyman shrank away.

"Father, we should speak of these matters in private," Crain said.

"Indeed we should, yet we have no privacy, do we? This meek little thing follows you around like a puppy." He indicated Judith, who looked suddenly as though she wished the ground would swallow her up. "She'll not do you for a wife, you know. You could have a princess, an heiress."

"Perhaps when I marry, it will be for love," Crain said defiantly.

At this, there was a flicker of emotion from Judith, some half-smile, and those "doe eyes" that Lady Esther had mentioned. I looked to Esther, who was staring past me to her father, with a faint, yet devilish smile on her lips. Was this at her brother's discomfort, I wondered?

Lord Berkeley, however, barked a laugh that turned into a rumbling, phlegmy cough. "Love. Ha! Do you think Agnes and I married for love?"

"My mother—" Crain began, his temper showing.

"Yes, yes, I know all about it. Your dear sainted mother is the only woman you'll ever let into your heart, more's the pity. Let me tell you, boy: yes, I loved your mother, in the end, but it didn't start out like that. It was a good match from the beginning, a smart and practical one. That's all one can hope for when securing a legacy. And I'll be damned if I go to my grave knowing…" Lord Berkeley blustered, and then fell into a fit of coughing, which ended whatever impassioned speech he was about to give. He clicked his fingers, and a servant rushed over with a glass of water. Eventually, he calmed himself, his fit of pique subsiding, and he waved a hand at his son. "The devil with you," he said, quietly. "Maybe when I'm gone, you can ask this one here all the questions you never asked me in life."

"Please, Father," Esther interrupted. "Don't speak so of death. You're strong as an ox—you will outlive me, I'm sure."

"What father would wish to outlive his children?" Lord

Berkeley said, his manner now demure. “I apologise, daughter—to you, at least—for I would cause you no distress. Now, do not mind me. Where is pudding?” He announced this a deal more heartily, and as if on cue, two servants entered with a trolley, and bowls of pudding and custard were served.

“Well, at the risk of sounding a bit morbid,” said Cavendish, with remarkable lucidity for a man who had been drinking wine long before the rest of us had started, “there are a few questions I’d like to ask of the dead.”

“Really?” asked Crain. “What, and of whom?”

“Glad you asked, Lord Beving.” He stifled a belch, and begged pardon before continuing. “First, I would like to ask my former partner, Cruddas, precisely where he mislaid the winnings from the ’87 Derby, because they certainly did not go towards securing our new premises as we had agreed.” There was some laughter, though not from the spiritualists. “Although I do recall he spent a lot of time at rather wild parties in the City that year, which perhaps contributed to his current state. By that, I mean, death. Next, I would ask my first wife…” this drew daggers from Mrs Cavendish, “whether she regrets her strict adherence to temperance, and still believes drink will drive me to an early grave.”

The laughter now was louder, and even Mrs Cavendish tried to hide a smile at her husband’s tomfoolery.

“Finally,” Cavendish continued, “I would ask a general question. More a favour, really. I would request that, when I am gone, I am not summoned to someone’s drawing room to play the banjo. I shall leave such posthumous entertainment to men such as the vicar here, who love a captive audience.”

At this, we all laughed heartily, Lord Berkeley included. Madame Farr, meanwhile, simply looked about, wearing a rather feline expression, observing us all in turn.

"Now, now. Given the present company, this is hardly the matter for jests," Langton said, the smirk on his lips suggesting that he was far from a believer in Madame Farr's practices.

"Quite," Crain said, rather seriously. "Mr Cavendish may joke, but communication with those who have passed *is* possible."

"Do you really think so?" Constance Langton asked.

"I know so. I have experienced it first-hand, with the guidance of Madame Farr."

This drew a wearisome sigh from Lady Esther, and a grumble and shake of the head from the old man at the head of the table.

"I don't know, old fellow," Langton said. "We hear so much talk of charlatanry and fraud in these matters—no offence intended, Madame Farr, I'm sure. It's just that, well, it is a little hard to swallow. I say, don't we have a detective in our midst?"

I felt all eyes turn to me. Crain in particular looked to me in earnest, the hope that I would speak up for him writ large on his face.

"I am no detective," I said. "I am a doctor, and content to be so."

"But your friend Sherlock Holmes *is* a detective," Lady Esther said. "What would he make of all this talk?"

"I know very well what Holmes would say, Lady Esther," I replied. "He would say it was rubbish—indeed, I have heard him say so more than once."

I kept my tone as light as I could, but could see Crain's face fall.

"Hear, hear!" The Reverend Parkin rapped on the table with the handle of his dessert spoon, then looked decidedly awkward at the attention he attracted.

"Surely Mr Holmes would regard the spirit of inquiry as a good thing?" A complete hush descended as Madame Farr spoke at last. A faint smile wrinkled about her lips, while her dark eyes smouldered.

"He would, ordinarily," I said. "But it is the type of 'spirit' that is the problem." Again, I jested, and this drew some laughter from all sides.

"So he would dismiss the evidence of his senses?" Madame Farr persisted.

"The sixth sense, certainly. He is strictly rational in his approach."

"And amazingly knowledgeable," interjected Lady Esther. "If your own writing on the subject is not… exaggerated." She gave me a knowing smile; I believe she was trying to steer the conversation elsewhere, so that I would not need to spar with the rather formidable-looking woman across the table.

"Well… yes, his knowledge and aptitude for the retention of facts is remarkable, but it has to be said that so, too, is his ignorance."

"Oh?"

"Holmes takes little interest in any fact that does not impinge upon his work. For instance, I once wrote that he cares little for the evidence that the earth travels around the sun, and I stand by it. To his mind, it might as well be a ball of fire hanging in the sky. Holmes cares merely that the length and direction of shadows cast by it can be calculated accurately. Only the latter knowledge aids the art of detection. His cardinal rule, therefore, is to acquire no knowledge that does not bear upon his object, lest it crowd out some useful data from his capacious brain."

Crain spoke up next. "Now, Watson, I wonder if you will come clean, so to speak?"

"I don't follow."

"You know my sister has read all your stories, and is something of a devotee of Mr Holmes, but Judith here—though she is too shy to ask it herself—doubts that anyone could be quite so clever as the Holmes you describe. I take you at your word, naturally. So, just between us here at this table, what's the truth?

Is he really the world's greatest detective? Or do you rather flatter his talents for the sake of a good yarn?"

"I understand why you might ask," I said, noting Judith's downcast gaze. "Holmes rarely takes the credit for his cases, for discretion is one of his most prized virtues. Additionally, I always change the names of the clients in my reports, so as to protect them from unwanted attention. And yes, it is true that my literary pretensions lend certain flourishes to the prose that might make one think it was all an invention of my pen. But I tell you in all honesty, and can look you straight in the eye while I do it, that the stories are for the most part true. And the published accounts barely scratch the surface of Holmes's successful cases. If there is a finer detective in the world, I have yet to hear of him."

Madame Farr coughed, and made some pretence of clearing her throat. Most of my audience appeared engrossed in the conversation, but it appeared to me that the spiritualists were rattled. I looked directly to Judith, who still had not looked up. "Does that answer your question, miss?" I asked.

She reddened, and nodded.

Lady Esther clapped her hands together. "I told you so, brother," she said. "Maybe I should secure the services of Mr Holmes myself, to solve the Case of the Impossible Medium. We could all be in one of Dr Watson's stories. What fun!"

"Well, in the absence of Holmes," Crain interrupted, annoyance in his tone, "I think we have enough sceptics here to put the matter to the test."

Hush descended once more.

"What matter, dear brother?" Esther asked coyly.

"The matter, sister, of whether it is indeed possible to speak with the dead." The silence that met this suggestion was deafening. "Well, come on," he pressed. "It is rather the elephant in the room. You all know it is why I invited you here."

"No, cousin," Langton said. "I knew you wanted us to meet your new friends, and perhaps to invest in their enterprise. But dabbling in spiritism is something else entirely."

"Oh, I don't see the harm," Constance said, turning to her husband. "Such parlour games are played everywhere these days, I've heard."

"My gatherings are not parlour games," Madame Farr said, and again her steady, measured tones commanded the undivided attention of the diners, save for Cavendish who hiccupped loudly, drawing a *shush* from his wife. "I would be willing to act as medium between the spirit world and this one, but only for those who commit wholeheartedly. One's whole soul must be given to the séance if it is to succeed."

"I… I would rather not discuss matters of our souls when…" the timid reply came from the Reverend Parkin, "when meddling in matters of the occult."

"Hardly occult," Crain said. "The spiritualist church—"

"Church!" Parkin looked truly outraged now. "This is precisely the problem. We live in increasingly secular times, it seems. Why, the attendance at St Mary's has dwindled, not helped by the church's poor state of repair."

"As you never fail to remind us," Crain said. "What exactly would you have us do?"

"I would never be so crass as to suggest financial assistance—"

"Oh, of course not, Vicar," Lady Esther remarked, with a smirk.

"But some attendance would not go amiss," Parkin persisted, raising his voice slightly. "If perhaps Lord Beving would see fit to attend service at St Mary's more frequently, we could attract the many stay-aways from the surrounding villages and estates. We could make Swinley's church the centre of worship for the area, perhaps even rivalling Bracknell."

"That's as may be," Crain said, "and I dare say such a feat would improve your own standing in the diocese. Our family will, as ever, uphold its obligations to St Mary's. But I have pledged my patronage to Madame Farr's endeavours for now, in the hope that her own church might prosper in time."

"Please forgive me, Lord Beving," the vicar blustered, "but calling it a church is somewhat… blasphemous."

"I say again, the spiritualist church is as godly as any; it merely uses different methods to look for the divine."

"But these spirits—they do not reside in heaven. How can they?" Parkin grew red in the face. I fancied he had come along to impose on his hosts for donations to his own church. Now he looked set to offend them—one of them, at least.

"Heaven, hell, purgatory—these are the constructions of men, who struggle like children to understand the immutable Word of God," Madame Farr intervened. "The truth is beyond any of us; that much I know from my dealings with the spirits. Some of these souls are earthbound, needing our assistance in passing over to whatever place they need to be. Others speak to us from… somewhere. It matters not where. The result for us here—the living—is the same."

"And what result is that?" Another angry voice now, this time belonging to Sir Thomas Golspie.

"Comfort, spiritual nourishment, and the absolute proof of life everlasting. But I think perhaps you do not need proof, do you, Sir Thomas? You have already seen far more than your fellows could ken."

Sir Thomas was a man of dark complexion, whose weather-beaten face was almost the colour of mahogany. But now that face drained, becoming white as a sheet, and his hand trembled around his wine glass. He made no reply. Lord Berkeley glowered across the table, perhaps on his old friend's part, but still held his tongue.

"We have all lost someone dear to us," Madame Farr went on. "Everyone around this table. It is the sheer consequence of life that we all must die. But death is not the end—it is only the beginning."

"A natural consequence. And what good does it do to upset the natural order?" Was that a quiver in Sir Thomas's voice? He seemed strangely rattled for such a formidable man.

"Death is part of the natural order, Sir Thomas. And what comes after is also natural. I can see in your eyes that you understand. A man who has been so close to death must have experienced things that even I could only dream of. Especially in a place of dark magic, where the dead and the living are intertwined in an endless dance. A dance to the sound of drums."

Sir Thomas said nothing more. He leaned back in his chair and turned his face away, wringing his rough hands. Madame Farr's words were cryptic to us, but clearly had some effect on the old explorer.

"Stuff and nonsense!" Lord Berkeley barked.

"Far from it," his son said defiantly. "Since meeting Madame Farr, my eyes have been opened to worlds of possibilities. I have consulted with Mama. She offers me guidance."

"Guidance to what end?" Lord Berkeley asked.

"That, I have not yet determined, but in time Madame Farr will help me interpret the signs and portents, until Mother's purpose is revealed."

Father and son held each other's gaze, and whether or not there was an otherworldly presence, it certainly felt as though the temperature in the room had lowered considerably.

"Since James has already spoken to Mama," Esther ventured, "then perhaps it is time I did likewise. I shall join you, brother."

"My dear..." Melville began, but stopped when he saw the determination in the eyes of his betrothed.

A loud scrape caused everyone to turn, as Lord Berkeley

pushed back his chair and stood abruptly. Everyone rose awkwardly out of politeness.

"I think I've had quite enough for one evening," he said. "My books await. Sir Thomas, might I have a word in my study?"

"Of course."

"Good. The rest of you can do as you like. But, madam," he addressed Madame Farr, "—if you do succeed in talking to my wife, kindly ask her if she plans on cutting her apron-strings to me boy any time soon. This estate doesn't manage itself. Goodnight."

Crain met his father's gaze for but a second before looking sheepishly at his shoes. Everyone else mumbled a good night to the old man, and then sat again. All except Sir Thomas, who followed Lord Berkeley from the dining room.

"Well, I think it all sounds jolly exciting!" Constance said, once we were all seated. "Are we all to take part in the séance? Is that permitted, Madame Farr?"

"Not quite, my dear. There must be an even number of us, and presently there are eleven."

"Ten," said Melville, standing again. "Esther may have decided to humour this nonsense, but I certainly shall not."

"Geoffrey—" Esther said, but Melville marched from the room.

"For obvious reasons, I cannot participate in such a… rite," Parkin said. "And so I am afraid your company is an odd number again."

"Not quite, Mr Parkin," said Jane Cavendish. She nodded to her husband, who was propped precariously in his chair, snoring softly. "I shall join you, to make up the numbers, but my husband would do better to retire."

There was laughter again.

"Eight, then," said Madame Farr.

"Hold on," I said. "I'm not so sure."

All eyes turned to me.

"Oh, come on, Watson," said Crain, not for the first time that weekend. "Surely you'll join in, even if it's only to scrutinise proceedings with a sceptic's eye."

"That's just it, Crain. Apologies to you, Madame Farr, but I see no point—if there is anything in all this 'spiritism', then having a doubter like me will only interfere with your energy, or whatever you call it."

"On the contrary, Doctor," the woman purred. "A séance thrives when opposite humours are in attendance. Positive and negative energies brought by the sitters must, ideally, balance each other out. I have never seen such an auspicious group for a sitting. And after what you have seen here this weekend, I would urge you, of all people, to join us."

I blushed.

"What did you see, Dr Watson?" Esther asked me.

I threw my napkin to the table. "Crain!" I blustered.

"I swear, old boy, I said not a word." Crain spread his hands innocently.

"That fellow Simon then. I saw him in the garden this morning, eavesdropping." I looked about for the man, but he had vanished again, as was his wont.

"I saw him too, Watson," Crain said. "He wasn't close enough to hear anything. And I swear again it did not come from me."

"Calm yourself, Dr Watson," Madame Farr said. "Is this not my business? Is this not my singular gift? I know you have seen something in this house, because I have seen it too. Judith told me that you have the sense, though you may not admit it to yourself yet. The energy of the spirit world surrounds you even now, like an aura. And I see *her*. Not clearly, not yet, but she is here. Mary."

I stared at her uncertainly; suspiciously.

"Who is Mary?" Langton asked.

"My wife," I muttered. "My dead wife."

"Come, Watson," Crain said, gently. "You're a man of science and reason, so what do you have to fear? You will either gain something, or leave in disbelief. But there is nothing to lose."

"He's right, old man," Langton said. "I'm as sceptical as you, but at worst I suppose we'll get a bit cross at the silliness of it all, and at best we get a performance that would cost us a few bob at a variety show."

Crain seemed a touch put out by that, but looked to me again in earnest.

I weighed it up. For all my personal feelings on the matter—and for all that I had been truly unnerved by the events of the previous night—there still pricked at my senses some great suspicion about Madame Farr. My little missive to Holmes earlier was at once recalled to mind: if there was some dark motive, some attempt by Madame Farr to defraud this noble family, then the best thing I could do was to observe, and to unmask it. And if, as a result of my participation, I were to become convinced of spiritualism, then at least I would come to understand what had changed my old friend Crain.

"Very well," I sighed at last. "A séance it is."

With dinner formally over, Madame Farr requested that we give her one hour precisely to "banish negative energies" from the venue of the séance. The drawing room had been chosen for the event, because, as Madame Farr explained, the tower room was too small to seat everyone comfortably, and the energies there were too "tainted with misdeeds". She had displayed no such reservations the previous evening, I noted.

Crain organised the servants to carry out Madame Farr's

instructions to the letter. A large, round table was to be carried in, heavy drapes hung all about the room, and a great many candles arranged. Simon appeared, fetching and carrying, watching every movement of the house staff with quick eyes, and, I fancied, ensuring that none of the house guests intruded upon the preparations.

With the drawing room unavailable, the party had inevitably separated. I stood on the landing, watching the work commence below.

"I see you are employing your own powers of observation." I had not heard Lady Esther approach. "You won't get very far—Madame Farr likes to 'cleanse' the room before the sitting begins, apparently. That means she meditates in there, alone. The windows are covered, so you can see nothing from outside, and James is rather like a bulldog if anyone breaks their silly rules. Believe me."

"Ah, yes. You have tried before," I said.

She smiled. "But this time, there are two of us." And before I could say anything else, she left my company and headed towards her room.

I followed suit, taking a moment in my own room to steel myself, and then went looking for the others. I saw Melville first or, rather, he saw me.

"Dr Watson, might I have a word?" he said.

"Of course." I did not really wish to spend any time in Melville's company, and could only hope that my manner around him was not too guarded.

"I'd like to explain myself."

"Oh?"

"Regarding my behaviour at dinner. You must have thought it strange my storming out like that." I had braced myself for some explanation about his treatment of Lady Esther earlier; this was something of a surprise. "Esther just mentioned something you said at dinner after I'd left, about your wife… I thought perhaps you of all people might understand."

"I certainly understand why a man might not want to put himself through the ordeal," I replied. "Having one's past dredged up, I mean."

"When I first met Madame Farr, she showed me things… things she could not possibly have known. Private things, about my dear wife, Cynthia—you know by now that I am a widower? Yes, of course you do. But you see, it was not merely the details, but the message that accompanied them. You see, Doctor, Madame Farr advised me, in no uncertain terms, that my marriage to Esther would end in disaster. And it was that message, purportedly from Cynthia, that so enraged me. When I calmed myself, I came to a conclusion that has plagued me ever since."

"What conclusion?"

"That these spiritualists are conjurers of the most vulgar order. Madame Farr's messages come not from the dead, but from her own lips, with malice aforethought."

"Malice?"

"Indeed, Dr Watson. That woman has inveigled herself into this family like a worm wriggling into a ripe apple. Her claws are dug deep into James, but she has found Esther a tougher nut to crack. Still she tries."

"To what end, do you think?"

"The family fortune. She has several times petitioned James to beg money to found her 'church', though James's pleas have fallen on deaf ears. And so she plays a waiting game, knowing that when James inherits, she will be showered with gifts, such that she can establish a whole congregation of spiritualists right here in Swinley."

"An odd location to establish such a venture."

"It is not the quantity of believers she requires, Doctor. It is the quality. Wealthy patrons from around the county, and within easy reach of the City. She has her eyes on royalty, I'm sure. Once James becomes Lord Berkeley, he will no doubt make the proper introductions at court."

"That is not the kind of court in which you would like to see Madame Farr, I take it?" I asked.

"Quite right. If I had proof that she is a fraud, I would bring the case against her myself. I imagine this was the motive for Madame Farr trying to sour my feelings for Esther. The last thing that woman wants is for her principal opponent in this house to gain a powerful ally."

"And Lady Esther… you have told her of your suspicions."

"I have no secrets from Esther, Doctor."

I tried my best to betray no feelings on that matter. "This is why she attempted to expose Madame Farr's work previously?"

"You know about that?"

"Crain told me, in his letter. I mentioned it to Lady Esther just now, and she didn't deny it."

"A contributing factor, certainly. But the reason? No. She was worried. She suspected Madame Farr was playing to James's… weaknesses."

"What weaknesses?" I asked. I had my suspicions. Crain's misuse of certain substances in the past was one thing, and had he not been acting strangely earlier that afternoon? But I did not want to give away anything to Melville, lest we be talking at cross purposes.

"You will not hear it from me, Doctor. But there was more than that. The way they used James and Esther's mother as leverage. They tried to do as much to Lord Berkeley, you know, but he would have none of it. But it did affect him strangely. To this day I don't know what was said, but he tolerates the spiritualists in his house in spite of his disapproval, and it has caused no end of aggravation between him and James."

"That much I had gathered."

"I think, for all his talk of disinheriting James, it is the son who wields the power. What legacy for this old family if the Marquess were to follow through with his threats? James knows this—he may be in thrall to Madame Farr, but he is not without intelligence. I think Lord Berkeley is more afraid of losing his son than he is of ghouls and goblins."

"And so Lady Esther took it upon herself to provide proof of Madame Farr's deception," I said.

"Esther sat with them in a séance at Madame Farr's cottage in the village. They brought out a spirit cabinet and other such conjurer's accoutrements. It fooled James, and a couple of small-minded idiots from the village, but not Esther. She was certain she saw that fellow Simon, outside the window of the cottage, pulling on threads to make objects float and what-have-you. She leapt up and rushed to the window, but was stopped in her tracks by Simon himself, in the room."

"Does that not prove there was no trickery?" I asked, surprised.

"No, Dr Watson. It merely proves they are clever. In their own home, with their tricks set up to ensnare the credulous, they are powerful. But here… they may make mistakes. Keep your wits about you tonight, Doctor. I wish Mr Sherlock Holmes were here, to put an end to this nonsense once and for all."

On that we both agreed. "And where will you be, while we are all at the séance?" I asked.

"As far away from it as possible," he said.

"You don't wish to stand guard outside and look for tricks and contrivances?"

"Trust me when I say it would cause the most fearful

trouble if I did. No. If I am present, I shall be unable to contain my temper, of that I'm sure. And after the last time… between you and me, Doctor, there was a period of great unpleasantness between James and Esther, which continued after I first came along. Thankfully, it seems to be water under the bridge now, but for a time things looked damned hard for Esther. I managed to broker peace, it seems. I'll not be spying or trying anything to jeopardise that peace tonight, Dr Watson, you can be sure of that. If you'll excuse me, I have something to attend to."

"One thing, Melville," I said. "You mentioned that Madame Farr had some information about your wife. Something she couldn't possibly have known. Did you ever find out how she came by that information?"

He gave me a rather glum sort of look. "No," he replied. "I did not."

With Melville on his way, and left to my own devices once more, I determined to visit the library. When I arrived, however, I heard stern voices behind the door. At first I wondered if Lord Berkeley was in the room, and began to retreat from the door, but then I recognised the trilling tones of the Reverend Parkin. I paused, wondering with whom he could be speaking so angrily.

"Come, man… a promise… the church… the provision…"

It was all I could make out, and the slurred response that followed identified Cavendish as the other party. It was only then that I decided to enter, for no other reason than to save the drunkard from any abuse. I walked in, innocently enough, to find Cavendish nodding in the library chair, and the vicar standing over him.

"Oh, I'm terribly sorry," I said. "I thought the room vacant."

"It's… no bother," said the vicar, forcing a buck-toothed smile. "I was just discussing this dreadful séance with Cavendish here. Cavendish?"

Cavendish was slumped in the chair, snoring loudly.

"I think the poor fellow has had too much of a time tonight," I whispered. "I say, why don't we find Langton? I think I saw him heading for the billiard room."

The vicar reluctantly agreed, giving the sleeping solicitor a last rueful look over his shoulder as he left. On the way to the billiard room, we passed by Lord Berkeley's study. The door was ajar, and we just made out the old man and Sir Thomas sitting either side of a large desk, each with brandy in hand. The Reverend Parkin appeared as if he wanted to enter, but I continued on my way, nodding him to follow, and he did.

We crossed the landing again, past the yawning entrance to the Red Tower, from which a dreadful chill draught blew. The great windows of the hall below rattled in their frames, rain pattering off them noisily. Flickering candlelight spilled from the drawing room into the hall, shadows flitting back and forth as the spiritualists made their arrangements for what appeared a most elaborate séance. I had no desire to hasten along my attendance in the drawing room, and so with no more than a second glance I led the way to the billiard room.

"Ah, finally, someone to have a game with," Langton said as we entered. He breathed a great plume of bluish smoke from his pipe.

"No sign of Crain?" I asked.

"Went off with that timid girl. A strange one, that."

"And the ladies?"

"Constance and Mrs Cavendish have gone to find some tea—something about having clear heads for the séance. Lady Esther… well, I'm afraid she and Melville were having high words when I saw them last."

"Again?" I said, despite myself. I wondered if this was before or after I had bumped into Melville. In any case, I instantly regretted my careless reaction.

"Again? Sounds like there's a story there, Watson."

"Not really. Besides, I'm sure it's none of our business."

"It's hardly surprising," he went on. "I heard James and Esther have fallen out a great deal over these spiritualists. He's threatened more than once to disown Esther if she continues to cast aspersions their way."

"Why would that cause problems between Lady Esther and Melville?"

Langton shrugged. "Money and title, Watson. Lord Berkeley's estate is a very large pie, and everyone wants a slice. If Esther is thrown out on her ear, she may well keep her private provision, but her children will never inherit any of *this*, or even set foot in it if Cousin James is serious. I can't imagine Melville is happy about that prospect."

I looked to the vicar, whose ears had pricked up at the mention of the Crain fortune. "Melville is independently wealthy, and not without influence himself," I said.

Langton grinned. "There's influence, and then there's *influence*. Do you know Lord Berkeley was received at the Palace four times last year, and attended a dinner at Windsor just last month? There, you see—that's the kind of influence I'm talking about. To come so close to the top table and have it snatched away… It could drive a man to distraction."

"But Melville does not have a high opinion of Madame Farr himself," I said.

"Indeed not—they annoyed him in much the same way they've annoyed you, I gather. But he doesn't have to pretend. Esther, on the other hand…"

I thought of the meeting I had observed between Melville and Esther's maid, which I resolved to say nothing about. At its most innocent, it could have been Melville simply reprimanding a servant, rather too brusquely—although it had not seemed an angry embrace. Perhaps it had simply been an attempt by Melville to influence his fiancée via her trusted companion, although even that was underhand. I thought also of what he had said about brokering a peace between Esther and Crain—was that because he had one eye on her inheritance? I was starting to think Lady Esther's engagement would not make for a felicitous marriage. "It sounds like a family matter, and I for one would rather stay out of it," I said, already embarrassed that I had become embroiled in such gossip, especially with the vicar present.

"Very wise. Now, it will have to be two against one for this game."

"I don't play," said Parkin, somewhat distantly.

"Just you and I then, Watson. Care to make a small wager? Although we'll have to hurry. I expect the dead don't like to be kept waiting."

CHAPTER SIX

A SPIRIT IN SCARLET

I arrived for the séance ten shillings richer after my game with Langton.

The drawing room was utterly transformed. Almost all the walls were draped in black velvet, which also covered the windows and doors—such a curtain was held back for us as we entered, one by one, a room so dark we could barely find our way to our seats.

Smoke hung in the air; thick, sickly incense, burning in a large pot in the centre of a round table that dominated the nearer end of the room. The remaining furniture had been shifted to the far end, near the piano, the outline of chaise and sofa just visible by the glow of the eight candles upon the table—one in front of each guest's chair.

Simon and Judith were on hand to show each of us to our designated place. I noted that, due to the positioning of the candles, we could see little other than each other's faces—I fancied that was deliberate. I was not best pleased to have my back to the expanse of the room, but at least I was able to see

Madame Farr clearly, just two spaces to my right, with only the meek Judith between us. Crain sat to Madame Farr's right, his sister next, directly opposite me, holding a handkerchief to her mouth as surety against the frowsty atmosphere. Then the party went, anti-clockwise, Mrs Cavendish; Langton; and Mrs Langton to my left.

"Please, make yourselves comfortable," Madame Farr said. "It is almost midnight—a propitious hour. I apologise for the gloom, but bright lights are anathema to the spirits. Likewise, the room is a trifle cool, as excessive heat hinders spiritual conductivity. I must tell you all of some simple rules before we begin, so as to give our little gathering the best chance of communicating with the departed.

"First, when the séance starts, we will all join hands, that I might channel the spiritual energy flowing between us. No matter what you see or hear, do not be tempted to break the circle. And do not be afraid—there is nothing that can harm you, so there is no need for the gentlemen to crush the hands of the lady beside them if they take fright."

There was a mild ripple of laughter.

"What might we see?" Constance Langton asked.

"A séance is unpredictable," Madame Farr said. "I must prepare you all for the eventuality that the spirits will not bless us with an appearance. But if they do, it could be as innocuous as strange noises in the room, or as dramatic as a full manifestation. When they communicate with us, we call it 'spirit return'. Often, I can coax the spirits to answer simple questions by means of rapping. One loud rap means 'no'; three invariably means 'yes'. Sometimes you may smell familiar scents. Sometimes a solid object might appear in thin air before you. If a spirit with sufficient force of will appears, it may take momentary control of me: I will speak with its voice. If a spirit should manifest, in any form, under no circumstances be tempted to touch it! To interfere with a manifestation that I have channelled could cause me injury or even death.

"During the proceedings, conversation is encouraged," she addressed us all again, "but no loud or raucous discussion, outbursts, or angry words are permitted. I know some of us have had our differences, and some are sceptical of this process, but I also know that none of you are of a violent or disputatious disposition. If you are at any time overcome by negative emotion, for the good of all, try to contain yourselves. In the opposite situation, you may feel a sudden need to laugh, or cry, or sing—give in to these urges, for it is the spirits acting through them. Likewise, if any member of the party becomes drowsy, or acts as if mesmerised, there is no cause for fear.

"Once we begin, no one will be permitted to leave, or to enter, until the séance is done. This is for my own safety, as sudden interruptions can cause a violent departure of spirits, and this takes a toll on my physical being. Simon will walk the perimeter of the room periodically—pay him no heed. He is merely ensuring that everything is in order, and observing the effects of spirit return upon me, for it can take a heavy toll."

This aroused my suspicions at once, for having an assistant, especially one as stealthy as Simon, prowling a darkened room seemed conducive to trickery. I glanced up and saw Lady Esther by candlelight. I had half expected a knowing glance, but instead I saw her swaying slightly, eyes closed. At first I wondered if she were entering some sort of trance, but then I saw her chest rise and fall rapidly, as though she were struggling for breath, or attempting to control some nausea. Presently she opened her eyes, and saw me observing her. She gave me a faint smile, and then looked back to Madame Farr.

"Now," Madame Farr said, "I want you all to think hard of

one special person no longer on this earth—a person to whom you would dearly love to speak. Let the memory of that person fill you. Focus on the happy feelings that the person evokes. Hold on to those feelings. And finally, let us begin. Follow me in prayer, as we recite 'the Power of Love Enchanting.'"

We murmured the words to the hymn in unison. I found it strange that something so unchristian as to have riled the vicar would be dressed in the trappings of a church service, but supposed that, once upon a time, the same would have been said of the Methodists or the Quakers.

Madame Farr's eyes were closed now, her head inclined. "There is a presence in this house," she said, dreamily. "A strong presence, from a time long ago. A woman..."

"Is it... Mama?" Crain whispered.

"No. This presence is older, much older. A woman in red."

"Lady Sybille!" Crain hissed. I caught Esther giving her brother a look of extreme annoyance.

"Yes!" Madame Farr whispered. "Sybille. This is fortunate indeed. She is a powerful spirit, her energy flows through the warp and weft of Crain Manor. She... yes, she says she will guide me. She has taken my hand. She leads me through corridors. I can hear... laughter. A child's laughter. Oh, I could not have known. Has someone here... lost a child?"

There came a gasp. At first I thought it was Lady Esther, but then I saw the look on the face of Jane Cavendish beside her. A look of expectation, and sorrow.

"The child is elusive, shy," Madame Farr went on. "I cannot catch a glimpse, here in these dark halls. Come forward, child, that I might see you. No? Wait. Listen to me. Is your mother here at this table?"

To my surprise—to the evident surprise of everyone—a sharp rap came from the table, as of something hard and heavy knocked firmly against the wood. It reverberated—I felt it plainly. Another knock came, then a third. Even Judith jumped a little; I felt her small hand squeeze mine a little tighter.

"Charles?" Mrs Cavendish asked. In that moment, I knew there was no catching Madame Farr out if trickery was afoot—the medium had not mentioned the sex of the child, nor any hint of a name, but the shock of the rapping had drawn the information voluntarily from the poor woman.

Madame Farr did not answer, but rather breathed a great, ragged breath. The knocks came again, louder and more rapidly. Three raps for "yes".

"Ask your questions of Charles, Mrs Cavendish," Madame Farr said. "I know not how long he will stay."

"Charles… Are you happy, where you are?"

Three raps came, booming. I studied Madame Farr carefully; I saw not a hint of movement. I felt nothing, either, from Judith. Simon stood over to my right, near the main door.

"Do you grow older? Are you all grown up now?"

One rap. I noted Esther looking surreptitiously around the room, as was I.

"Forgive me, Mrs Cavendish," Madame Farr said. "But the presence is very weak here. Despite that, I am feeling something… The strangest sense of… guilt?" She sounded uncertain.

"Oh. Oh dear…" Jane Cavendish looked crestfallen. "Your father. He's never forgiven himself. And I…" She stopped.

Silence followed.

"Ask a question, Mrs Cavendish, quickly!" Madame Farr urged.

"Was it his fault?" Mrs Cavendish blurted.

One rap. "No."

Weak candlelight gleamed from Mrs Cavendish's moistening eyes. She sniffed loudly.

"Charles is fading," Madame Farr said. "He is trying to get a message to me, but I can barely make it out…"

"Oh, please! Please try!"

"He says… 'Forgive'? Yes! You must forgive your husband, Mrs Cavendish. It was not his fault. Charles… does not blame his papa. He is happy where he is, and he will see you again one day."

Esther gave a muted cry, and seemed to pull her hand from Mrs Cavendish. Mrs Cavendish did not break the circle, but gave a meek apology for squeezing too hard, before breaking down in tears. I was resolutely unconvinced by the performance. Madame Farr had hit upon not a single detail—not the child's age, nor the manner of his passing.

Simon moved silently around the table, behind Crain and Esther, and went to the servants' door to my left, where he stood once more. Only the upper portion of his face was visible in the wan light—the rest of him was hidden by his black raiment, dark hair and unkempt beard.

"We move on through the storied halls of the eternal twilight," Madame Farr said. "Sybille guides me through the darkness, and into the light. There is a familiar face here. Sybille knows her, too."

"Is it… Mama?" Crain asked again.

Three raps, louder and more rapid than ever, shook the table so hard that the candles flickered.

"From where do the raps come?" Esther asked, almost innocently.

"From dear Lady Berkeley. They are the transmutation of spiritual energy into physical force," Madame Farr said.

"But could they not be made by some earthly means?"

"Sister!" Crain hissed.

"Your mother is here, child," Madame Farr said, her address of Lady Esther most impertinent. "Ask her what you will. But first—all of you, keeping your hands together, raise them from the tabletop, so that there is no contact. Six inches at least."

We all did as she asked, our linked hands now suspended half a foot above the table's surface.

"Ask your question."

"Very well. Are you *really* there, Mama?"

To my utter astonishment, the table began to rise. The movement was almost imperceptible at first, but the candlesticks rattled, and began to slide slowly away from Madame Farr. The heavy pot in the centre rattled, moving a few inches in Langton's direction. Everyone gasped as the tabletop met their hands. Then, with a great crash, it dropped back into place. Simon dashed forward, catching two candlesticks before they fell. He scurried around the table, righting the others and sliding them back into place.

"Do not break the circle!" Madame Farr called as nervous chatter filled the room.

When we all recovered from this little fright, we saw that one of the candles had gone out. Esther's.

"Lady Berkeley wishes it known that she bears no ill will to those who doubt her presence here. She always encouraged in her children a spirit of intelligent inquiry, and would expect nothing less of her strong-willed daughter. She wishes to know if Lady Esther has any other questions."

"I… I do." Lady Esther looked less sure of herself now. "I am sorry, Mama. There is something I must know. Do the spirits see the future? Can you see it?"

A long pause. And then three raps, but slowly.

"Lady Berkeley cannot see every possible future," Madame Farr said. "But the spirits have some foresight, for time to them is meaningless."

"Will my marriage to Geoffrey Melville be a happy one?"

The question was direct, and unexpected. I could sense immediately the discomfort it caused, for it had been lost on none of us that Melville and Esther were not terribly happy.

"My… daughter…" Madame Farr spoke slowly, in a voice entirely unlike her own. Her usually dulcet tones were clipped and proper, with a nasal inflection. I guessed from the look on Crain's face that the voice reminded him of his mother's. "A marriage worth anything is worth working for. Your father and I knew this, and were… happy. I see such happiness in your future. I see… long life… children. Two…. No, three children."

Now this was a fine thing, for it was not, apparently, what Madame Farr had told Melville previously.

"I cannot tell you how happy that makes me," Esther said, her voice hoarse with emotion.

"And what of you… my son?" Madame Farr said, her voice still strange.

"Mama," Crain said. "I ask nothing of the future, but only to know that you are here with me. Here in this house, for all the years that follow, until we meet again."

"I am."

Madame Farr's head sank low to her chest. At once, the piano played, a single bar of music, but so jolting in the serene atmosphere that we again all jumped at the sound.

"Mama!" Crain cried.

I realised I had lost sight of Simon. I turned towards the piano, half expecting to catch him in the act, though the room was even darker than before. But then the servants' door opened, and slammed violently. I looked towards it, feeling some dark shape rush past me. Constance stifled a scream, and squeezed my hand hard. The other door opened and also slammed shut. The candles guttered once more; my own went out altogether. Now I saw Simon's shadowy outline, striding towards the door from the direction of the window—had he been there before? He secured the door, and stood beside it like a sentry.

"She always played in here," Crain said. "I can feel her presence now."

"There is another spirit here," Madame Farr said, sounding drowsy. "M? Yes, it is Mary. Mary Watson."

I tensed at once. So far I had seen nothing that could not be achieved by a stage magician—I could not fully explain how it was done, but that did not mean the explanation was a supernatural one. But now I was reminded of the materialisation in my room, and how I had still not discovered any rational cause for it.

"Mary has a message for John."

"Does she?" I asked, hardly concealing my incredulity. "What message?"

"It is about your decision. She says Mr Sherlock Holmes will lead you… oh dear. She says he will lead you to certain death!"

There were gasps from the ladies present.

"She wants you to stay with her. She is not yet ready to leave your home. She waits for you there, and always will."

"Mary would not ask such a thing of me," I said, my defiance drawing stares from the other sitters. "She would not ask me to spend my life in mourning."

Madame Farr squeezed her eyes as though in pain. "No… you misunderstand… She… does not want you to waste your life. She wants to be… part of it, and wishes you all the joy. But if you leave your family home, she fears she cannot watch over you. Mary is your guardian angel, Dr Watson."

"So I must stay away from my friend, and instead live alone? What sort of advice is—"

I could not finish. The window flew open abruptly, letting in wind and rain. The candles all blew out, leaving us in near total darkness but for the faint glow of moonlight from outside.

"Do not break the circle!" Madame Farr shouted again. "Dr Watson's anger has created a disturbance. It will pass. Mary... can you return? Can you give your dear husband a sign that will calm him?"

Simon grappled with the windows as if they were struggling against him, and finally wrenched them shut. I felt something soft brush my cheek, and from the murmuring all around I know the others experienced it too. Simon dashed around, little more than a shadow, until finally a candle was lit. And in its light, we all gasped, as a great cascade of small objects floated dreamily down upon the table.

A snowstorm of white lily petals.

I trembled. Judith squeezed my right hand reassuringly, though it did not comfort me at all. If even part of this séance was genuine, I had allowed anger to become an impediment to communing with dear Mary. And if it were not genuine, then Madame Farr was taking me for a fool.

"Mary's strength is fading," Madame Farr said. "A materialisation can be a terrible strain on the spirit's power. Lady Sybille guides me elsewhere, through the halls of twilight."

I breathed a sigh of relief. Simon came around the table and lit the candles.

Madame Farr spoke again. "I sense a spirit trying to make amends for some slight in life. Someone here lost their father after having harsh words. There was no time to make peace with him before he passed, and it has weighed on this person's mind. No? Does this not sound familiar?"

It could easily have been me again, but I said nothing—more than enough attention had been placed on me for one evening.

"There is... an inheritance involved," Madame Farr went on. "Or rather... an investment?"

Mrs Langton glared daggers at her husband. Langton himself looked as though he really had seen a ghost.

"Surely someone—" Madame Farr began when no one answered.

With a great flash of light and a violent hiss, the brazier in the centre of the table fair erupted. We all cried out in alarm as flames leapt forth, and sparks flashed upwards. Now the circle was well and truly broken, as we all shot up from our seats. Crain called for a blanket to smother the flames, but Madame Farr bade us all stop.

"It is Sybille!" she cried. "The red woman, red from fire. She has always been the mistress of this house, and she wishes to send a message." Madame Farr convulsed, and coughed. When she drew herself upright, her eyes were glassy, her face solemn. When she spoke, her voice was different again—sultry and low, somewhat hoarse. "I am a woman wronged," she croaked. "I am innocent of the crimes of which I was accused. I am a protector of this family. I send a sign, that no harm may come to any who believe in my power."

With that, Madame Farr removed the lace mitten from her left hand, stretched over the table, and thrust her hand and sleeves into the flames. Constance Langton screamed.

Simon reacted quickest, pulling the medium back. Madame Farr blinked, and stared at each of us in turn. Her hand was outstretched to the light, and was entirely untouched by flame!

"What has happened?" she asked.

Her question was answered by a blood-curdling scream, a loud crash, and the sound of shattering glass. It came from the door to my left—the servants' entrance. I was now fully alert, my heart pounding in my chest, and I was first to rush to the door. It was not closed as I had thought, but perhaps six inches ajar. I threw it open fully, and could only gape in amazement, as I am certain we all did.

A maid was upon her knees on the floor of the hall, a silver tray before her, a mountain of broken glassware spilled from it. She quivered in fear, her eyes turned towards a narrow corridor that ran beneath the servants' stair, and which was almost fully in darkness. And in the mouth of that corridor, plain as day, was a woman in red.

Her back was to us, and she swept silently away into shadow. Her gown was large and old-fashioned, like something from a painting by the Dutch masters, with voluminous loose sleeves, and a great bundled-up skirt that trailed behind her. Her hair fell in dark curls down her back, tumbling from beneath a large black veil, and adorned with red ribbons. She was there for but a moment, then was gone. I turned back to the room, and from the looks etched on the faces of the party, I knew they had all seen it. Madame Farr and Simon exchanged a glance, which was hard to discern by candlelight, but which I took for genuine confusion.

"Well, don't just stand about!" Langton cried. "We all saw the ghost. Let's go and catch her!" And with that, he was shoving past me into the hall, leaping over broken glass. There was a cry of glee from the room, and Mrs Langton followed her husband, then Crain after her. I urged my limbs to life, and ran after them.

We squeezed through the passage shoulder to shoulder, almost falling over each other in our haste. There was one store cupboard leading off it, into which a person would barely be able to squeeze, and then the corridor took a sharp left turn, and terminated abruptly at a solid wall. Langton began to press upon the wood panelling, rapping on it for any sign of ingress, but was quickly confounded.

"Where did she go?" he asked.

"There is only one place she could go," came a breathless voice. We all turned to see Lady Esther, the last of all of us to reach the door. "Once upon a time, before I was born, there was a door in that wall. A door to the Red Tower."

CHAPTER SEVEN

THE CURSE OF THE CRAINS

"Would anyone care to explain what we just saw?" Langton said.

"I've never seen her before," Lady Esther said, at last catching her breath, "but I can only imagine that was Lady Sybille."

"The family ghost?" Langton said, incredulously. "Come now, it's just a silly legend."

"Not a legend," Crain said solemnly. "A curse."

"Oh, come now!" Langton laughed. "Enough is enough."

"It's true," Crain said in earnest. "Father never speaks of it, but Mama was always very respectful when mentioning Lady Sybille. Esther and I got the full story from our nanny, who rather liked to scare us silly with such tales. It was only later, when we were old enough to consult the family history, that we learned it was true."

"Go on."

"Lady Sybille was the wife of Edmund, the Eighth Lord Berkeley, during the time of the Civil War. Edmund wasn't a nice fellow by all accounts—legend has it he mistreated his wife terribly, and so she secretly plotted against him with one of Cromwell's spies. One fateful night in 1643, she waited until her husband fell asleep, and stabbed him to death. She attempted to escape the manor, to take secret intelligence to her co-conspirators, but was captured by a royalist patrol. The records state that her white dress was stained entirely red with blood."

"Blood, not fire, as Madame Farr suggested," Esther interrupted, to the annoyance of her brother.

"When they entered Lord Berkeley's bedroom," Crain went on, "they found such a scene of carnage that it resembled a charnel house—as though Sybille had been in the grips of madness when she'd attacked her husband. You can guess, of course, where the bedroom was."

"The Red Tower," I muttered.

"It wasn't called the Red Tower back then," Crain said.

"There has been more than one historian who questions how Lady Sybille could wreak such havoc alone," Esther interjected. "And whether she was fleeing the scene of a crime, or fleeing for her life. Ironically, it was only months later that much of the county fell to the parliamentarians anyway, making her situation all the more pointless."

Crain shrugged. "Edmund Crain had been the highest authority in a region beset by turmoil, and now that responsibility fell to his eldest son—from Edmund's first marriage, you understand. He condemned Lady Sybille as a traitor and murderess, and worked up the guards into a frenzy. She was given a rudimentary trial—if you can call it that—right then and there, at the scene of the crime. She was found guilty, a noose tied about her neck, and then she was thrown from the tower window. Records on the matter are scant, but local lore says she died slowly, and her body was left out for the crows as a warning to any who might sympathise with her. Indeed, in the days that followed, several servants who had supposedly helped her liaise with the parliamentarian spy were rooted out of the household. Anyway, it is said the red ivy that now clings to the walls began to grow the day Lady Sybille's body was cut down, and that it continued to grow despite all attempts to cull it."

"What rot!" said Langton.

"That part is doubtless an embellishment. What cannot be denied is the testimonies much later, of great and sober men, that led to the establishment of the family curse. Our great-great-great-uncle, Godfrey Crain, was a minister, and a well-respected one. One stormy spring evening, on a night much like this, he heard the sounds of a woman sobbing, coming from the tower. When he investigated, he said a ghostly woman, dressed all in red, flew down the stairs of the tower, passed right through him, and fled the house. Several servants claimed to have seen the 'red lady' sweeping across the grounds before vanishing into the storm. That very night, Godfrey's father passed away in his sleep.

"The next time the ghost was seen was in 1775, shortly before a fire broke out in the east wing, claiming the life of our great-grandfather. The fire supposedly started mysteriously, in the cellar of the Red Tower, and it weakened the foundations before it was exhausted. Afterwards, during the rebuilding, Grandfather—then a young man—wanted to tear the whole tower down, but the rest of the family advised against it. Superstition, you see. He decided not to restore the lower level at all, refusing to spend a single penny more than was necessary on it. And so he had it sealed up, as you can see, presumably on the grounds of safety. He wouldn't want his children and grandchildren coming to mischief down there, after all.

"The most recent sighting was by a doctor, visiting the manor to deliver a baby—the child of my grandfather's first wife, Lady Elizabeth Berkeley. Upon entering the house, the doctor passed comment that he had seen a woman in a red dress at the window of the tower room as he had alighted from his carriage. This caused great consternation in the household, and a search was conducted, though of course no one was found. Lady Elizabeth died in childbirth that very night, the baby with her."

After a long and deathly silence, Langton asked, "What are you saying? That one of the Crains is going to die tonight?"

Crain looked very grave indeed, his pallor now ghostly. "That would seem to be the indication, yes."

"Unlike my dear brother, I don't believe a word of it," Esther declared.

"Sister, do not tempt fate. This particular spirit should be treated gently."

"Lord Beving is right," Madame Farr said, her eyes closed, hands raised, as if in prayer. "I sense a great power in this house. I do not believe spirits have the power to kill, not even the most vengeful spirits, but their sudden manifestation can often presage disaster."

"Can't you ask her what she's presaging?" Esther mocked.

"That's enough, sis. This is serious," Crain snapped.

"What? That's why she's here, isn't it?"

"It's true, Crain," Langton said. "We've just sat through an hour of table-rapping, and just when we actually have a ghost to talk to, your friends here clam up tighter than a muckworm's hat-band."

"Then I propose we coax Lady Sybille out of hiding," Esther declared.

"How?" Langton asked.

"I'm going to sleep in the tower room tonight. The room where my great-great-great-great-grandfather was brutally murdered."

"You will not!" Crain snapped. "I forbid it."

"When the ghost appears, someone dies. That's the curse,

isn't it, James? But we've just been told that you and I will live long and happy lives, and that Lady Sybille protects us. So what danger can there be for me?"

Madame Farr looked unsure of herself. "I have sensed nothing of the sort, but..."

"But? I would ask you to be very sure before you say more, Madame Farr. Are you suggesting that my father's life is in danger this very night?"

"I... no. I would not suggest such a thing."

"Well, I do suggest it," Esther said. The sharp intake of breath that followed was Crain's.

"Sis!" he said.

"I know full well what Madame Farr is after. We've all been treated to an extraordinary show tonight, but the game is up. If Watson's friend Mr Holmes were here, I'm sure he would have this lot exposed before breakfast."

"Exposed?" Madame Farr seethed.

"Yes, Madam, exposed. If any ill fate befalls my dear father tonight, it will not be the work of a ghost, but of mortals. Mortals who seek to quicken my brother's inheritance so that they might profit by it."

"Sister, that's enough," Crain snapped. "We have spoken of this before."

"And our disagreement was never settled. So perhaps you and I should make a little wager, brother?"

"That is most improper talk for a lady."

"The circumstances are improper, and I am *Lady* Esther Crain, am I not? I can make the rules."

"Very well. What would you like to wager?"

"That all talk of spirits and curses is utter nonsense. If anything terrible is likely to happen, it is in that room. I shall sleep there, alone, with the only key. None shall enter, none shall leave."

"And what will it prove?"

"That there are no such things as spirits."

"But we have all seen one. We have seen… her!"

"No, we saw *someone*. I don't know how the trick was done, but I am certain it was a trick."

"This is madness."

"Look, James, let me put it another way. If I see a ghost in that tower tonight, then I will wholeheartedly embrace Madame Farr's methods, or may God strike me dead."

"I wish you wouldn't say—"

"But," Esther interrupted, "if I experience nothing, even after everything we've seen and heard tonight… then I shall be for evermore a sceptic, and you will just have to disown me when the time comes, for I shall go to whatever lengths it takes to shake this silliness from your head."

Crain looked angered by that. "Well, damn it all!" He glanced apologetically to the other ladies. "Stay in the room, and see where it gets you. I hope the bally woman in red scares you silly."

"And about that wager," Esther smirked. "Cousin David will adjudicate, I'm sure. I rather fancy you could all place bets on whether I stay the whole night, or whether I run screaming from the room at the first creaky floorboard."

"Yes, we could draw lots on the hour you back out!" Langton said, a little too eagerly for my tastes. "What o'clock are we now? Half past one? We shall start the sweepstake at two."

"Better make it three, cousin," Esther said. "The room will have to be prepared first. No one has slept there for an age."

Much excited chattering erupted, until footsteps creaked on the stairs. We all turned sharply to see Melville approach. I could barely repress a scowl when I saw Esther's maid behind him.

"What the devil is going on?" he asked sternly. "There's a maid down there in hysterics, and an awful mess."

"Geoffrey, dear," Esther said. "I'm glad you're here. I have a lot to tell you, and very little time..."

It took some while to prepare the tower room fit for Lady Esther's habitation, by when we were all weary indeed. We had been given a time to meet at the tower—three o'clock. I took to my room, hoping to snatch a catnap, but my mind was too troubled. There was quite some commotion in the corridor outside for a time, as the guests chattered excitedly, drew their lots for Langton's sweepstake—which I had no interest in joining on the grounds of poor taste—and dashed back and forth. Eventually all fell still again, until some few minutes later, when I heard a faint noise, like a scratch upon wood near my bedroom door. I rose at once, and saw shadows move hurriedly away from the crack of light beneath the door, which shone now upon a folded note.

I went at once to the door and took up the note, which was written in a neat script, in purplish ink. It read:

Dear Dr Watson,

You must have realised by now that Madame Farr wishes ill upon the Crain family. James is in her thrall, and would gladly ruin us to see her "church" rise. I do not think she would be so audacious as to harm my father, for she has proven herself already to be patient in matters of his will. But as for me—if anything should befall me this night, look not to spirits, but to the spiritualists. Remember the opinion of your friend Mr Holmes in this matter, and do not trust them!

I wish there were someone else to whom I could turn, Doctor, but I feel terribly alone. I know at least that you are a chivalrous and constant man, who will not shrink from assisting a lady in need.

In confidence, with regards &c.

Esther

I did not quite know what to make of this. Her signature was accompanied by the words "in confidence", suggesting that I keep the note to myself for the time being. That was a burden indeed, but who really could I trust with this information? No one would surely take it seriously. What troubled me more than anything was the phrasing of those final lines. Was she suggesting that she could not turn even to her own fiancé? Worse, was she implying that he was not "constant"?

I rather wished Sir Thomas were at hand, for he would make an ideal confidant, uniquely placed as he was in the affections of both James and Esther Crain. Unfortunately, he had not been seen since dinner, and when earlier I had asked after him, Crain had informed me that the old explorer had likely walked home already, as was his habit.

I had already been invited to see Sir Thomas, and I did not truly believe Esther was in any immediate danger. I folded up the note, and resolved to set off the next day to see him. If anyone could bash their heads together and make them see sense, I fancied it was he.

I had little time to ruminate more on the subject when I heard voices outside again, and realised the time to wish Lady Esther goodnight was almost upon us.

Not everyone who was summoned to see Esther inter herself in the "cursed room" had been present. Mrs Cavendish and Mrs Langton had retired to their own chambers—I noted that Mrs Cavendish had left her husband snoring away in the library. Lady Esther made a show of asking me to declare her in good health and of sound mind, which I jestingly did, to a round of applause from those few gathered. A few words were spoken, good wishes bestowed, and some rather gloomy prayers muttered by Madame Farr. Finally, Esther closed the door upon us and turned the key in the lock. I could barely keep my eyes open as I dragged myself down the tower stair back to my room, yawning as I went.

I passed Lord Berkeley's study, where earlier I had seen him and Sir Thomas huddled in some private meeting. To my surprise, the Marquess was up still, and peered out into the corridor from a crack in the door as I passed, before closing the door softly. The look in his eyes had been unsettling. Gone had been the sternness and steel, replaced by something else. Bitterness? Wariness? Or had it been fear? A man like Lord Berkeley would surely know all that was taking place in his own house, and although he had seemed not to have a superstitious bone in his body, I wondered now if he was afraid of the family curse. But afraid for Esther, or for himself?

I remembered this time to draw the bolt on my door before repairing to bed, although I doubted very much even a ghostly visitation would wake me, so tired was I.

And yet wake I did! I do not know how long the noise had pricked away at my senses before finally it roused me. I sat upright, listening carefully to what was a whisper in the darkness. Voices, certainly, and more than one. I could not be sure, but I fancied there were two distinct voices, both female. They seemed at first to echo all around me, fading, then coming stronger again. I could not blame drink this time, for I had been moderate through the evening, and felt no ill effects at all.

I lit a candle, and my first instinct was to hold it aloft and shine it around the room. There was no sign of anything, spectral or otherwise. I took up my watch from the bedside table. It was after half past three in the morning. With some small groan, I heaved myself from bed, and carried my candle over to the door. It was still bolted fast. The whispering was quieter now. As I drew back the bolt, it stopped altogether.

Expecting some mischief afoot, I pulled open the bedroom door sharply, and stepped into the hall. It was dark, cold and still. The only movement came from shadows cast by my own flickering candle. I tiptoed along the corridor, first one way and then the other, but heard nothing. I tried the door of the empty room next to mine, but it was locked, and not a sound came from within. I crept along to the main landing, stopping at the door of Lord Berkeley's study as I went. That, too, was quiet. To reassure myself, I tried the door. It was locked. I went thence to the tower entrance and shone my candle up the stair. The draught caused the flame to gutter, and I shuddered. Still I detected not a sound, and surely no mere whispers would carry so far. I was not prepared to climb those stairs and skulk about outside Lady Esther's chamber, but I stood guard for some little time, the contents of the note I had received playing on my mind. Eventually, with neither sight nor sound of anything, tiredness got the better of me; I returned to my room quietly, and it took some time before I could embrace sleep once more.

The scream was so abrupt, so filled with piercing terror, that I could hardly think it real. Even as I leapt from my bed in a cold fright, heart hammering at my ribcage, the sound faded away such that for an instant I thought—nay, hoped—it was but a dream.

A distant shout, a creaking door, and footsteps outside confirmed my worst fears. It was no dream.

I rushed again from my room, joining a press of bodies.

"The tower!" someone cried, and I thought it was Crain. "Esther!"

Candles were lit, casting their light on faces wide-eyed with concern. By the time we ascended the steps, I was only a pace behind Crain at the head of the pack, with Melville behind me. Crain threw himself at the door, pounding his fists upon it.

"Esther! Open the door."

No sound came from within, and the panic from the shadowy gathering behind us rose like a cloud, palpable in the darkness.

Crain wrenched at the handle, but it would not budge.

"There must be another key," Melville said, his voice laden with anguish.

"There is no other," Crain replied. "We must break the door down."

"That door is solid oak, bound and studded," I said.

"Well, what do you suggest, Watson?" Crain snapped.

"We need something to batter it with."

"There's a bench on the landing," Crain said.

"Make way!" I cried, and pushed through the throng behind me, past Langton, past the vicar, past others whom I barely recognised in my haste, back down the stairs.

In a trice, Crain was behind me, and Melville with him. We hoisted up a sturdy monk's bench, and carried it up the stair. Langton joined us now, too, and the four of us heaved the bench as best we could in the cramped space, swinging it once, twice, and a third time, at which the wood around the ancient lock finally cracked, and the door swung open.

We all but tumbled into the room. I scrambled to my feet, only in time to hear an anguished cry from Melville.

Lady Esther was dead.

We stood in shock for what seemed an age, until Melville

suddenly rushed towards the body. Only then did I snap to my senses.

"No, get back!" I commanded. "Do not move her, do not touch anything." Melville knelt by the body, and only when I went to him and placed a hand on his shoulder did he follow my instruction. I looked back; the others were peering through the door, Crain at their head. A woman screamed. There was a great commotion as someone—I think it was Mrs Langton—fainted, and those around her caught her before she fell down the stairs. "Get them back," I said.

I knelt carefully beside the body of Lady Esther and surveyed the room as Holmes might have done.

She lay on the floor in the centre of the room, between the bed and the writing bureau. She was dressed in her nightgown, as white as her skin. There was not a mark on her, as far as I could tell, but her face was etched with an expression of shock and fear, such that her once delicate features were contorted, and discomfiting to look upon. There was no colour in her at all, except for the red rings about her glassy, bulging eyes, which in itself was strange. There was a mild swelling around her throat, consistent with her recent respiratory illness, but certainly not indicative of a cause of death. On closer inspection, this inflammation was accompanied by clusters of tiny red spots—a rash of some sort, already paling post-mortem.

I checked her hands. The fingers of her right hand were bruised yellow—this was possibly from Mrs Cavendish's over-zealous grip at the séance, though it must have been forceful indeed. Her fingernails were blue. The middle fingertip of her right hand bore a superficial impression, as though she had been writing recently. Small purple spots of ink on the heel of the hand confirmed this. I glanced up at the bureau—a lamp, still burning, stood upon it, whereas I remembered that previously it had been situated on one of the nightstands. There was no sign, however, of any writing instruments or even paper. The ink spots could have been from the note she had written to me, but not the indentation. So what had she been writing?

I continued my examination quickly, already acutely aware of Crain and Melville's nervous tension, manifesting as great impatience. There were further bruises on her arms—nothing that would ordinarily suggest anything more than clumsiness, but too many to ignore. I recalled the way Melville had held Sally by the arms, and could not help making the association, despite my displeasure at it. I looked for any signs of poison—there was nothing on her lips, and no odour I could detect. On her left arm, however, were three small puncture marks, scabbed and mostly healed. These were too old to have contributed to Esther's death, but were certainly cause for concern. There might be various medical reasons for such marks, of course, but I could not help but think of Holmes and his occasional dabbling in narcotic drugs by subcutaneous injection. I wondered if Crain still kept the same habit… but his sister? Until I could broach the subject with Melville, I decided for the sake of Lady Esther's reputation to hide these marks, and so I rolled down the sleeve of the nightgown as far as I could. The only other mark I could see was a spot of blood soaked into Esther's nightdress just above the right hip. I could not conduct a thorough examination, but pressed my thumb to the spot, feeling clearly a minor contusion, less than an inch long.

There was nothing more I could do. I stood, and nodded to Melville and Crain. They at once rushed forward, while I tried numbly to continue my investigation of the room, turning my back upon Melville's heart-wrenching sobs.

The windows were shut fast. The door to the roof stair likewise, although I opened it and checked every nook and cranny for possible signs of intrusion. There was not a mark out of place. I returned to the room. The bed looked to have been slept in, at least for a short time. I found a candle in one of the nightstand drawers and lit it, carrying it carefully around the edge of the octagonal room in search of draughts, in case some secret passage presented itself, but the tower was so old and draughty all over that I could detect no particular source. There was no doubt in my mind that the cause of Lady Esther's death was of this earth. Given her age and, supposedly, fine medical care, a natural death seemed most improbable.

I finished my surveillance and returned to the body. The sight of that small frame, that pale skin and flowing auburn hair, was too painful to bear. I turned away, ushering Langton from the room, leaving Crain and Melville united in their grief.

Mrs Langton was sitting in a chair on the landing, fanning herself whilst Mrs Cavendish and the vicar fussed around her. It was probably the shock, but Langton made no immediate attempt to tend to his wife.

"Dr Watson, can you help her?" Mrs Cavendish said.

I blinked, realising that this was the third time she had spoken my name. Shock, it seemed, affected me also.

"Of course," I said, weakly. "My room… I shall fetch my bag."

I did not get far. Around the corner came Lord Berkeley, looking more like a frightened old man than his usual formidable self. His eyes were wide and ringed with shadows. His hair was an unkempt shock of grey.

"My… daughter," he croaked. "Where is my daughter?"

"She is dead." The voice was strong, laden with doom. We all turned to see Madame Farr, fully dressed in her affectations as usual, dark eyes fixing Lord Berkeley with a singular gaze. Only then did I realise that neither she nor her fellow spiritualists had been present on the tower stair.

"Madam, that will do!" I said.

It was too late. Her bluntness rocked Lord Berkeley like a blow from a prize fighter. His legs buckled beneath him, and it was all I could do to catch him before he fell.

"I did not know," Madame Farr intoned, moving steadily towards us like a creeping spectre. "Even I did not foresee the depths of the evil in this house. The curse of the Crains is real. The Red Woman has claimed another victim."

Mrs Langton wailed.

Lord Berkeley clutched at his heart, and tried in vain to speak. He sank to the floor in my arms, trembling and weak; at death's door.

CHAPTER EIGHT

A HOUSE IN DISARRAY

I took Lord Berkeley's pulse once more, as dawn's first light at last pushed its way into the manor. His heartbeat was weak, his breaths stertorous. With great sorrow, I packed up my medical bag and left the old man's bedroom.

"How is he?" Crain was waiting for me in the passage, leaning against the wall, his appearance haunted. Judith stood beside him. Further down the corridor, looking awkward in each other's company, stood Madame Farr and the Reverend Parkin.

I took a deep breath. "It's not good, Crain. I've done all I can for him, but I fear his heart is too weak to get over this shock."

"You can't mean that, Watson! First Esther, and now…"

"Crain, I would suggest you stay with him. I'm sorry to say he does not have much time left. But wait… before you go…" I hesitated, for Crain looked so thoroughly miserable that heaping any further burden upon him seemed too cruel. But who else could I trust? I took out the note I had received the previous night, and handed it to him.

"What is this?" he asked, frowning at the paper for what seemed an age.

"It was pushed under my door yesterday evening, shortly after that business with the Red Woman. Is that Lady Esther's handwriting?"

"It… yes, I think so."

"Then this is evidence of foul play," I said. "She had cause to suspect Madame Farr was plotting her murder."

"Murder? Why on earth would she do that? Why would Esther give you this note?" Crain asked. "Why not just speak to me?"

"She did not mention any such suspicions to you previously?"

"No. I… That is… she made several rather fanciful allegations against Madame Farr these past months. But murder…"

"Crain, your sister has died in the most mysterious circumstances, after having more than one rather public disagreement with Madame Farr, and wrote this note before her death. And yet you dismiss it as fanciful?"

Crain drew himself up to his full height. "Watson, it pains me to say it, but I think perhaps Esther was more ill than I thought. Her behaviour of late has been increasingly irrational, and I have worried for her state of mind. This note is typical of her recent tricks—it was a practical joke, nothing more, and one that was in very poor taste."

"A practical joke? You think it is mere coincidence that Esther died just hours after writing this letter?"

"*Lady* Esther," he corrected me, sternly. "And yes, as a matter of fact I do. Madame Farr is no murderess. What could she possibly have to gain? Look—I would appreciate it if you did not show anyone else this note, for the only evidence it provides in my view is that my sister was delusional. I would not have such a thing known, not at this sensitive time for my family."

"I am not sure I can promise such a thing," said I.

"If the authorities were to obtain this note, it would become a matter of public record. Expert witnesses would have to be called, and should they decide that Lady Esther had concocted this story—that she was… mad… think of the consequences."

I stared at Crain in disbelief. But what if he was telling the truth? What if Lady Esther's illness had not been physical, but mental? Or, more probably, what if she had shared her brother's predilection for opiates, as evinced by the marks I had seen upon her arm, and those red rings about her eyes? It would, perhaps, explain a great many things. I thought also of Melville, whom I had seen arguing with his fiancée the previous day. What if Esther had not written the letter at all, or had been coerced into doing so? I checked myself, for it was a dark train of thought indeed.

I held out my hand. "Give me the letter, Crain," I said. "I shall have to decide what to do with it, as my conscience dictates."

"I shall save you the trouble, Watson," he snapped, and at once flung open the door to his father's room.

I stepped after him, torn between making a scene and preventing Crain from doing anything foolish. I was too late. He shrugged my hand from his shoulder, and threw the note into the fire, standing in the way so that I could not save it.

"There," he said. "Now we can have no more foolish talk, and you and I can be friends again."

I was aghast. I had not for a moment until that point thought that Esther was mad, but now I wondered if madness was in the blood of the entire family.

"Please, Watson," Crain said, more softly, his mood changing like the wind. "I must attend my father, as you advised. You will give us peace, yes?"

Without a word, I backed away from my old friend, and out of the room, whereupon Crain closed the door against me.

* * *

The other house-guests had at least tried to snatch an hour or two's rest, although I doubt very much they had succeeded. Rather than return to my own room, I dragged myself downstairs to find a servant who might avail me of strong coffee. I did not have far to look, for although most of the household staff were awake, drifting aimlessly, stunned expressions on their faces, they agreed to bring some readily enough.

I passed by the drawing room, giving it a rueful glance. I was not tempted to enter, and instead sat in the morning room, where I drank my coffee, took a telegram pad from my bag, and penned the following missive:

> Holmes, please come at once. Lady Esther Crain dead in mysterious circumstances. Lord Berkeley desperately ill. Suspect foul play. Sent for Lestrade. Watson.

I wrote out a similar message, addressed to Inspector Lestrade of Scotland Yard. In truth I would have had any inspector, but his was the first name I could think of. Though he and Holmes did not always see eye to eye, I thought he was just the sort of dogged fellow we needed here at the manor.

I popped into the hall and found a young footman; the same man who had posted my previous telegram. I asked him to repeat the service for me as a matter of urgency.

"The post office does not open until nine o'clock, sir," the footman said.

"Never mind that. Go now, and wake the postmaster. Tell him to send these messages. It is of the utmost importance that they go at once."

The lad went off dutifully, and I rather fancied that the

postmaster would give him no trouble when he saw the livery of Crain Manor on his jacket.

I stood on the front steps, looking across the misty drive, whereupon a black carriage came slowly into view. The undertaker had already been summoned. Two policemen on bicycles followed close behind, not that their presence would do much good, for the mystery was a thick one indeed. But at least now some real investigation could occur—they would at least keep everything in order until Holmes arrived. I would make sure of it.

I drained my coffee cup. It was going to be a long morning.

I heard the wail before I even reached Lord Berkeley's room, and knew that I was too late.

Upon entering the bedchamber, I saw Crain hunched over his father's bed, clasping the old man's hand in his, sobbing uncontrollably. Madame Farr and Judith stood near the door, faces devoid of all emotion, along with Eglinton, the butler, whose haggard face was a pinched mask of English reserve.

For Lord Berkeley was indeed dead.

At the other side of the bed stood the Reverend Parkin, who looked to be in no small distress himself whilst completing a prayer with a tremulous voice. When he intoned "Amen," I muttered it in response, as did Eglinton, though the spiritualists stayed silent; a fact not lost on the vicar.

"Lord Berkeley is gone," Parkin said. "He was the finest of men. A just and true landlord, a hardworking man of the people, and an incorruptible advocate of God's word as interpreted by his servants in the church. We can only hope the new Lord Berkeley will continue the good work of the former. *God's* work."

I shifted uncomfortably. Crain managed to look up at the

vicar, though his shoulders still heaved from his outpouring of grief. He said nothing.

"We do have a new Lord Berkeley," Madame Farr said, flatly. "And God willing we shall receive guidance directly from the former, to understand what has happened here. To understand why such a good man has been so cruelly punished, and what amends must be made to prevent such a terrible fate from being repeated."

I was aghast at these words, but had no time to remonstrate before the vicar snapped shut his Bible and marched around the bed to confront the spiritualists.

"The only sin Lord Berkeley committed was allowing evil into his house, and even that he did through love of his son. If there was a punishment, it was brought upon him by you!"

"Do you agree that God has visited his wrath upon Lord Berkeley?" Madame Farr asked. Was that a smirk on her wrinkled lips? "Come, come. Ours is a merciful lord. If He really did deem it necessary to smite anyone, it would surely be me. No, Vicar. This was not God's doing, but by His grace I shall find out the truth, from Theobald Crain himself."

"Blasphemy!" Parkin cried, and shook his fist at the woman. I stepped forward, ready to intervene lest his anger boil over into violence. Instead he said, coldly, "There is only one way to understand Lord Berkeley's wishes from beyond the grave, Madam, and that is through his last will and testament. And whatever evil you have wrought, I doubt very much that even you would have managed to manipulate a man of such resolute temperament to change his will in your favour."

Madame Farr did not so much as flinch, but merely said, "Such insinuation is beneath you, Vicar. Besides, as you said previously, there is a new Lord Berkeley. It is his wellbeing with which you should concern yourself."

Parkin turned to me. "You heard her, Dr Watson. As good as a confession!"

"Calm yourself, Vicar," I said. "This is a trying time for everyone, but high words, spoken in the heat of passion, will not help."

"Can no one see that a crime has been committed?" the vicar asked.

"Nothing is yet proven. But know that I have already summoned my friend Sherlock Holmes, and if there is any evidence to support your theory, he will find it."

At the mention of Holmes, the vicar's expression changed entirely: he became at once still, perhaps even thoughtful, his toad-like eyes darting about as his mind considered some opaque possibilities. The same could not be said of Madame Farr and Judith, who exchanged a look so uncharacteristically full of worry that my suspicions were at once aroused.

"Y… You are right, of course," the vicar stammered. "Forgive me."

"It is not my forgiveness you must seek, Vicar. In the presence of the bereaved family, such scenes are unbecoming."

Parkin's expression drooped, and he nodded. He was careful to avoid even glancing again at Madame Farr, but instead stepped to the side of Crain. "Lord Berkeley," he said. "Forgive me. Your father was very dear to me, but I cannot imagine what you are going through at this time. Respectfully, I offer the counsel and service of the church, whenever you might require them. I shall leave you to your own prayers now. Good day." Without another word, he left the room.

I stayed some time, but it was clear that Crain would not be consoled, and that Madame Farr would not leave him be. Judith, I thought, was full of hand-wringing angst on Crain's behalf. In the end, Crain commanded that everyone but Madame Farr leave the room, so that they might pray together. Eventually, I had to acquiesce, for all my reservations, and persuaded a reluctant Eglinton to leave the room with me, so that he could speak with the undertaker, and ensure the police were given every cooperation.

Before long, Eglinton had organised the house—it seemed that his sense of duty and the comfort of industrious endeavour kept him from his melancholy. He showed the constables to the Red Tower, where they carried out an inspection even less thorough than my own. Once the police were satisfied, they instructed the undertaker and his man to take away the body. To this I objected strongly, knowing that Holmes would want to inspect the body. But as I could give them no concrete cause of death, the policemen would not be swayed, saying that she must be taken to the police surgeon right away. Given that I had no guarantee Holmes would even arrive today, I was forced to relent. The undertakers carried Lady Esther away, and were given the solemn instruction that they were to return post haste for Lord Berkeley.

I took the two officers aside in a quiet corner of the hall, and in hushed terms told them precisely why I suspected foul play. The older of the two men, Constable Hardacre, stroked his beard thoughtfully.

"You say the lady wrote you a letter, sir? Accusing… what's her name now? Madame Farr?—of plotting against her."

"That's right," I said.

"And where's this letter now, sir?"

"It was…" I checked myself, knowing how it would sound. "Destroyed. Accidentally."

Hardacre tutted, and shook his head in a sympathetic gesture. "And did anyone else see this note?"

I cleared my throat. "Only Lord Berkeley. The new Lord Berkeley, I mean."

"Well, he didn't mention no note, sir. And he's not disposed to speak with us further right at this moment, as I'm sure you can understand. Hold on now, isn't that Lady Esther's fiancé?"

My heart sank as Hardacre summoned a glowering Melville over to us. This was the last thing I had wanted.

Hardacre explained to him all I had said about the note, and asked, "So, Mr Melville, you don't happen to know anything about this note, do you?"

"I'm afraid not, Constable," Melville replied. "Lady Esther was with me most of the time, right up until she entered the tower room. I suppose she could have written a letter, sneaked across the passage and slipped it under Dr Watson's door, but I don't know when. Still, if Dr Watson says it is so, then perhaps it is. He has no reason to lie."

At this he fixed me with the queerest look. His choice of words was not lost on me, nor, it seemed, upon Hardacre, who sucked air through his teeth before thanking Melville for his time.

"There you have it, sir," Hardacre said to me, as though everything were now explained. "We'll be sure to ask Lord Berkeley about it all later, but for now you must leave us to do our duty."

There was little more I could say. They had my statement, and had all the other guests and servants still to interview.

About an hour later, I was looking for Crain when he passed me on the stairs, in a frightful hurry, his face pale and drawn. For once he was alone.

"Ah, Crain, I was—"

"I'm going out!" he snapped.

"But I need to speak with you. The police need to speak with you. And Holmes will be—"

But my words fell on deaf ears. He went swiftly to the front door, snatched an overcoat from the stand, and marched out across the drive. I could not account for his behaviour, but recognised a man in shock when I saw one.

I heard movement on the stairs above me, and looked up to see Simon and Judith staring down from the landing. Judith had been crying. Her eyes were red, and tears still streaked her face. She turned away quickly and scurried off. Simon, however, held my gaze impertinently, turning slowly away only when I took a step towards him. In a moment more, he was gone, probably back to report to his mistress.

What an uncommonly dark shadow had descended upon that house! And what grim circumstance conspired to have me present as a witness to it all. I looked at my watch, praying that Holmes would come, and quickly.

CHAPTER NINE

THE GREAT DETECTIVE

It was ten to one when we heard the sound of a carriage approaching. I followed the footman as he went to the front door, half expecting it to be the undertakers returning for Lord Berkeley. Instead, I saw it was a two-wheeler that pulled up.

I can barely describe the relief I felt when Holmes stepped from it. His tall frame, accentuated by a top hat, cut an imposing figure, and perhaps only to my eye was enough to dispel the oppressive atmosphere of Crain Manor, and raise my spirits. He exchanged a few words with the cabbie, and at last his hawkish eyes alighted upon me.

"Watson! I came as soon as I could. Lucky for you I made the eleven o'clock from Waterloo."

"My dear Holmes! You are a sight for sore eyes. I wasn't sure if you would come."

"Why ever not? Come now, you must tell me everything. Is that a constable I see? You there! My name is Sherlock Holmes. Who is in charge here?"

"In charge, sir?" the policeman answered, looking rather like a rabbit in the lamper's light. "Why, I suppose I am. Constable Hardacre is my name, sir. But there's nothing to be in charge of, so to speak."

"Has not a murder been committed?" Holmes asked.

"Murder? No, sir. At least… I don't think so, sir."

"I shall be the judge of that. Take me to the body of Lady Esther Crain."

"The body?" The constable looked about himself nervously, such was Holmes's commanding presence. "The body is gone, sir. To the police surgeon."

Holmes turned and gave me the most accusing look, which would cause any other man to wither away. "Watson, you let them take the body?"

"If you had taken the time to wire ahead, I should have been able to delay them, but it is done now. Besides, I have already made a full examination."

"And I suppose Constable Hardacre, his cohorts, the undertaker, and an army of servants have already traipsed through the crime scene?"

I sighed. "Not quite so many, Holmes."

"I shall have to make do with what crumbs may have been left by the clumsy boots of well-meaning idiots," Holmes muttered.

"First of all, Holmes, we should seek the permission of the family before launching a murder investigation."

"Lord Berkeley? Is he well enough?"

"He is dead, Holmes."

Holmes looked very grave. "Then your friend Lord Beving is the master of the house. Where is he?"

"I don't actually…"

By sheer providence, at that moment Crain appeared across the lawn, returning from whatever jaunt he had taken.

"Hallo, Watson!" he called, and waved in a remarkably cheery fashion, his earlier disposition much changed. "Who's this?"

As Crain drew nearer, I saw a queer look in his eyes—distant and glassy, though they shot about furtively. It was a look I had seen many times both at home and abroad, in the eyes of men who sought oblivion in the embrace of some mind-altering substance or another to ease their pain. Holmes, being no stranger to such pursuits himself, surely noticed it too.

"Crain, I am happy to see you return. This is my friend, Mr Holmes. Holmes, this is Lord Berkeley."

"Mr Sherlock Holmes!" Crain said, with a twitching smile. He shook Holmes's hand. "I wish we could have met in more auspicious circumstances. My sister..." Crain choked back sudden emotion. "She was an avid follower of your exploits. She devoured every detail of your cases."

"Indeed?" Holmes said, an eyebrow arching somewhat. "And did she ever employ my methods?"

"Why... I suppose she did, yes. At times."

"Times such as...?"

"She attempted to reveal Madame Farr as a fraud, if you must know. It all seems so trivial a thing now."

"Trivial? I doubt that, Lord Berkeley. Presumably she did not succeed in exposing Madame Farr?"

"How could she? Madame Farr is the genuine article."

"Indeed," Holmes said again, his eyebrow completing its ascent to incredulity.

"Mr Holmes, I am quite sure Madame Farr will submit to whatever scrutiny you wish in order that you may satisfy yourself of the facts. You will find nothing amiss."

"Nothing? Then what is your explanation for the two tragic deaths?"

Crain winced, as though his grief had been forgotten and was only now recalled. "The excitement of the evening's events—

the sighting of the family ghost—perhaps it put too much strain on her constitution."

"Family ghost?" Holmes frowned. "Watson, is this true?"

"It is, Holmes."

"You saw it?"

"We all saw it," Crain interjected.

"And was Lady Esther's constitution so poor that she could have died of shock, or of fright?" Holmes asked me directly.

"I would have said not, had you asked me last night," I replied. "But Crain's assessment rather echoes that of Melville."

"Who is he?"

"Lady Esther's fiancé, Geoffrey Melville. He's a barrister."

"Yes, I have heard of him. His word is well respected around the police courts. Watson, it is a chilly afternoon and I rather think, with Lord Berkeley's permission of course, that we should step inside and begin our investigation."

"*Our* investigation?" I asked.

"Certainly. We shall begin by inspecting the scene of the crime, and proceed with a thorough and full recitation of the events of the past two days."

"Again, Mr Holmes, I say there is no crime, and so the tower room cannot be called a crime scene."

"Then my work here will be over and done before you know it. What harm can it do to have a second opinion, my lord?"

"He's right, Crain," I said in a low voice. "I stand by every word I said regarding Holmes. If—and I really mean *if*—there is a villain in this house, he will find that villain. And if not, he will prove that too. You wanted someone to demonstrate whether or not Madame Farr was the genuine article? Well, I give you none other than Sherlock Holmes himself as the tool for that particular job."

I was not being entirely honest with Crain, but my words

appeared to have some impact. Crain was considering things, when there came some motion in the hall behind us, and the sound of footsteps and the dragging of trunks. Within, the Langtons and Cavendishes were heading our way, a pair of footmen bringing along their cases. Behind them, I caught a glimpse of the scarecrow figure of Simon, slipping soundlessly from the hall to the drawing room, but there was no time to halt him.

"There you are, old boy," Langton said to Crain. "I've been looking for you. We have paid our respects, and would do anything to stay with you longer, but I rather think we should get out of your way. Besides, business calls and so on will not wait. I am afraid we must go, although we feel dreadful about it. Cavendish here is in the same predicament."

"Please introduce us, Watson," Holmes said.

"Holmes, this is David Langton, Lord Berkeley's cousin, and his wife, Constance. The gentleman behind him there is Lord Berkeley's solicitor, Mr Josiah Cavendish, and his wife, Jane. This is my friend Mr Sherlock Holmes."

"Charmed to make your acquaintance," Holmes said, stepping into the hall and blocking their path. "I am afraid I must deliver some more bad news, for no one may leave this house while an investigation is ongoing—isn't that right, Constable Hardacre? We don't want Inspector Lestrade of Scotland Yard to turn up, only to find his eyewitnesses departed."

Hardacre looked up from his notebook, eyes darting from Holmes, to Langton, to Crain and back to Holmes. "Scotland Yard? Um… Yes, sir. I suppose that is only proper." He cleared his throat, but said nothing else.

"Lord Berkeley," Holmes said, summoning his most charming manner. "You were about to tell me whether or not I may conduct a private investigation into these matters. If you wish me to stay, I shall do my utmost to clear the innocent and discover the guilty. If you wish me to go, simply say the word and I shall take the very next train back to London. I am, of course, your servant."

Crain stood thoughtfully, his brows gathering as though the very process of thinking were painful. And then he replied, rather weakly, "If Watson swears by your methods, then I am glad to have you, naturally. You have my permission, Mr Holmes. You are in charge of this… 'investigation', if that is what you think is necessary. I shall give the servants the necessary instructions that you might face no impediment."

"Your lordship is too kind. Now, Mr Langton, Mr Cavendish: I shall need to speak to both of you before the day is through."

"Now look here, Mr Holmes," Langton said, straightening. "I am in mourning at the loss of my cousin, and my uncle, and I have little wish to return to the grindstone of work, but I must be in Exeter before the day is out."

"Your business is in Exeter?"

"No, Poole, if you must know. But I have an appointment in Exeter I should like to keep."

"I see. And what about you, Mr Cavendish? Are you set for a long journey also?"

"No, Mr Holmes. I am quite local—Farnborough. I suppose my clerk can take care of things if I must be delayed."

"I am afraid you must. Gentlemen, might you arrange for a servant to send telegrams on your behalf? Besides, in lieu of the presence of a police inspector, Constable Hardacre here is in charge, and given that I am investigating the possibility of a murder, I am sure he will insist on all the weekend guests remaining here until the matter is cleared up. Isn't that right, Constable?"

Again, the constable looked thoroughly out of his depth, and the repetition of the word "murder" brought him visibly to a state of mild panic. "I suppose that's right, sir, yes," he said.

"Capital. Now if you'll find some way to amuse yourselves, I shall come to you in good time. Constable Hardacre, when I say none of the guests are to leave, I mean it. I want everyone accounted for. Lord Berkeley, would you be so good as to give the constable here a list of the guests and their whereabouts?"

"I shall, Mr Holmes. You will find the Reverend Parkin absent already, however. I saw him leave this morning. Probably some church business."

Holmes nodded. "Very well. Perhaps I shall pay him a visit later. Might I also ask the number of domestic staff, so that I may account for them all?"

"I'm not entirely sure," Crain said, looking a little embarrassed. I wondered if perhaps it was true that he had no head for the business of running things, as his father had said.

"An estimate, then," Holmes smiled.

"Sixteen… seventeen, or thereabouts. Ask Eglinton—the butler. He runs a tight ship."

"Thank you, I shall." With that, Holmes handed his coat and hat to the nearest footman with a flourish, but kept a close hold of his bag. "Come along now, Watson. Show me this Red Tower."

"That's a rather small bag you brought," I mused as I led Holmes towards the staircase. "Are you not expecting to stay long?"

"Not at all, if I can help it. It is what you might call my 'bag of tricks'. It was rather hastily thrown together, I can tell you, so we can only hope I remembered everything. Tell me, the Langtons—you say they are cousins of the Crains?"

"Yes, though not close."

"I see they've experienced a dip in fortunes, that is all."

"What makes you say that?"

"As we passed Mrs Langton, I noticed her dress has been repaired several times. There are marks where the lace ruffs around the collar have been removed and stitched, to make last season's fashion acceptable for this one. Her hat, however, was certainly out of style, and her gloves, though expensive, have been allowed to become somewhat worn. Mr Langton, on the other hand, is well attired and groomed; the importance he places on business might suggest that his wife's wardrobe suffers in order that he make a favourable impression on colleagues and clients. And, of course, they are travelling with very little luggage, and have neither valet nor lady's maid in tow. Strange, for such a moneyed family."

"The Langtons are self-made, Holmes. But you must be mistaken about their fortunes—Langton was telling me only yesterday how he doesn't need his inheritance. He seemed rather proud of the fact."

Holmes merely nodded.

As we ascended the stairs, we were met by Madame Farr, Judith standing meekly behind her. The medium froze, and gazed down upon Holmes haughtily.

"Madame Farr, I presume?" Holmes said.

"Sherlock Holmes. No introduction is necessary. Your coming was foreseen as soon as these tragic events were set in motion." Madame Farr's commanding presence met its match in Holmes, and indeed her measured speech and theatrical aspect—which had so cowed me at times these past days—now looked rather ridiculous in the face of Holmes's immutable scepticism.

"A simple deduction," Holmes said. He took a few steps further. Thanks to his height, even though several stairs separated him from Madame Farr, they stood eye to eye. "I shall be interviewing everyone in this house in good time, madam. I must impress upon you the importance of remaining at Crain Manor at least for the remainder of today."

"I would not dream of leaving while Lord Berkeley requires my counsel."

"I think perhaps Lord Berkeley has already sought solace elsewhere. Nevertheless, I shall see you presently. I have many questions for you, be sure of it."

Madame Farr scowled, and as we proceeded past her, I fancied there was something else behind her eyes. Whether her overbearing attitude was practised or natural, her mask now slipped, for but a moment.

She was afraid.

Holmes stood for some time, motionless, in the centre of the tower room, beside the very spot where I had found Lady Esther. I had described to him the events leading up to her death, from the voices I had heard near my room, to the note slipped beneath my door, and then the scene I had witnessed in this very room. I described with no small difficulty the horrific expression on Lady Esther's face; the red-ringed eyes and swollen throat; the blue fingernails and mottled rash; finally, the old needle marks on her arm.

Holmes had paced the perimeter of the octagonal room as I spoke, taking great interest in the locked door to the rooftop. Now he seemed to absorb the atmosphere of the room, recording every minute detail in that great brain of his.

"Who was first to the body?" he asked at last.

"I was. No… Melville was, but only for a moment. I asked him to withdraw at once, and he did."

"Did he touch the body?"

"Yes, but briefly."

"Long enough to conceal something, or tamper with evidence?"

"Unlikely, but possible. His back was to me, my view obscured. But it was a matter of seconds."

"Very good. Who else was present?"

"Everyone but the spiritualists, I think. No, wait a moment—Cavendish was still in his room. Madame Farr arrived later, and she seemed already to know Lady Esther's fate."

"And other than the prescient Madame Farr, they all seemed duly surprised?"

"Constance Langton fainted, so I'd say so. There was one thing… All of us were hastily dressed in robes, although some of us men had pulled on trousers and slippers pretty quickly. Madame Farr was fully dressed; beshawled and bediamonded, her hair immaculate. As I said, she arrived much later to the scene, so perhaps she had taken the time to dress. Or perhaps she had never been to sleep. Either way it is odd."

"Let me see… You said Lady Esther had been ill recently?"

"Yes. Several times I noted she seemed a little breathless, and pale, too—but she was recovering from some chill or other. Come to think of it, her brother commented that she had lost weight recently."

Holmes ruminated for a moment, and then said, "Tell me about the writing desk. You said there was ink on Lady Esther's fingers?"

"Yes, but there was nothing on the desk. I am certain the ink was of the same sort used to write the letter I received."

"Your mysterious letter," Holmes muttered. "It is a crying shame it was destroyed. The handwriting alone may have revealed much. Tell me again what it said, as closely as you can remember."

I recited it from memory. Holmes queried my recollection where it differed from my earlier statement, and I tried my hardest to get it right.

"'Remember the opinion of your friend Mr Holmes in this matter,'" he repeated. "You're sure those were the very words? It is good to see that my name was conjured to ward against the spirits. If you had been able to show the letter to the police, perhaps we would have an inspector here by now. Instead, we shall have to rely on Lestrade. Still, you could hardly oppose Lord Berkeley more than you did—his behaviour is erratic, but he is also the authority here. I wonder what possessed him to burn the letter."

"Men do strange things from grief," I muttered.

"I wish I could have examined the body, Watson—the impression on Lady Esther's finger would have revealed much about when she was writing, and the implement she was writing with. We know that your note was written at some period before Lady Esther was interred in this room, wherefore you believe she sat at the desk there and wrote something else. But there is no sign of any writing material. Melville arrived upon the scene with you, and could not have confiscated it upon entering; so whom? More importantly, when? The door was locked from the inside, and Lady Esther had the only key. She could have admitted someone, and given them the note. Or that person could have been the murderer, and taken the note for some reason. If what we call a note was actually a diary, or some other document that might point the finger at a certain party, that would be reason enough to take it—they would not have known that she had already accused the spiritualists in a secret letter to you. But of course, there would have been insufficient time between Lady Esther's scream and your arrival to make away with ink and pen and paper."

"What if she never wrote anything at the desk?" I asked. "That is an even more obvious explanation for the missing implements. The ink spots I found could well have been left over from the note she wrote to me."

"It is unlikely that a lady would allow such marks to remain on her person after washing and preparing for bed. Unlikely but not impossible. Moreover, it seems a trifle strange that someone so weak would have gripped the pen so hard that it caused a lasting embrasure—unless of course you were correct the first time, in that she was writing only very recently before her death. You said that lamp on the desk had been moved?"

"Yes, Holmes."

"Presumably to provide light for writing the missing letter, you see. Where was it originally?"

"It stood on the nightstand over there when I first saw it."

"And when was that?"

"The first night. Madame Farr and Crain brought me in here for… for a reading. I was rather ambushed, actually."

"These spiritualists again—they are at the heart of everything. Remember back in London I promised that I'd look into this Madame Farr? I am true to my word, Watson, and let me tell you what I found: precisely nothing. A lesser brain would have abandoned the search, but for me, the lack of any mention of Madame Farr prior to her arrival in Berkshire was in itself suspicious. And so I turned to the few published papers by the Society for Psychical Research, and found something most intriguing. A story from Newcastle, of a 'Mrs Mellinchip'—a disgraced and wholly fraudulent medium, whose tricks were only discovered after the revelation of her part in an alleged scheme to poison a client's husband. She fled the city before charges could be brought against her, although the investigators heard sightings of her later in the Home Counties. That was around a year and a half ago, Watson—barely two months before Madame Farr conducted her first séance in Swinley, to wide acclaim."

"You think they are the same person?"

"Without photographic evidence or eyewitnesses, it is impossible to say. I made a few notes regarding Mrs Mellinchip's known tricks, and later we shall see if there is a correlation."

"But poisoning, Holmes! If it is true, then we have our

culprit, though I attest I cannot say how it was done."

"I almost fancy it would be too easy to accuse them immediately and have done with it, but I must have evidence. I shall have to interview Madame Farr presently, but not before I have gathered as much intelligence as possible. I imagine she will be prepared for questioning. This 'reading', Watson—was there anything to it?"

I hesitated, feeling suddenly embarrassed, not just about the reading, but about what had come after.

"I can see by your reaction that there was something to it. Out with it, Watson. Every detail could be of great importance."

I sighed. "Holmes, Madame Farr knew things about Mary that could only have come from me, or perhaps from Crain, though I have his word as a gentleman that he said nothing. And then, afterwards when I retired… I saw something."

"Something?"

"A trick of the light. A dream induced by too much brandy and stirred memories."

"What did you see, Watson?"

"I saw… Mary. In my room."

"Think very hard," Holmes said, his voice quiet and his manner as serious as ever I saw it. "Did you see a spirit in your room, or was it a trick of the light? A stirred memory?"

I took a very deep breath this time. "I think… I saw her, Holmes."

A thunderous look clouded Holmes's sharp features, and abruptly he stormed from the room.

"Come, Watson!" he shouted from halfway down the stair. "Villainy does not rest, and nor shall I!"

I half expected Holmes to hunt down Madame Farr, such was his anger, but instead he asked to be directed to my room. Once there, he bade me be quiet while he swept about with his magnifier, studying every inch. Once or twice he paused, muttering to himself, before continuing. If he found anything of note, he did not relate it. After a while, his temper and restlessness subsided.

"You said you were awoken by voices in the early hours?" Holmes said eventually.

"Yes. Whispers."

"Whispers clear enough and loud enough to be heard from your bed. But when you investigated, you heard nothing further?"

"Nothing. They were quieter when I went to the passage, and gone entirely when I returned to my room."

"Who inhabits the adjoining rooms?"

"The left-hand room is empty. The door was locked that night. To the right is a bathroom, and beyond that is Crain's room. Lord Berkeley—the late Lord Berkeley, that is—has a study opposite. That was also locked."

"And behind—that is the tower stair, is it not?"

"It is."

"And yet the distance from here to the tower door seems greater than the inner dimensions of the tower rooms, don't you think?"

"It had crossed my mind," I said. "But as you can see from the exterior, the tower is ancient, and the walls incredibly thick."

"Let me tell you something, Watson, about my journey to Crain Manor. I hired a cab from Bracknell, rather than venture out to the wayside station that I presume you used. And the reason for that was very simple: I made enquiries at the station, and found a coachman who was born and raised in Swinley. I drew greatly upon his local knowledge *en route*."

"The significance of this, Holmes?"

Holmes smiled. "He told me of several legends regarding this house that he had heard since he was a boy. I know all about this red woman you supposedly saw. I know, too, about a secret passage, apparently last used during the Civil War, and forgotten about ever since. The locals used to say that there was treasure hidden within the house, and that even the family could not find it. Others say the passage contains the bones of royalist spies, bricked up in the walls by parliamentarians. There are other fanciful tales also, mostly regarding mad ancestors and wronged women, but all reference a secret passage as a point of commonality. If the passage exists, many things would be explained."

"I have twice searched for passages, Holmes, and have found nothing."

"If it were easy to find, then it would not be such a mystery. Be so good as to draw the curtains, would you? And then light a candle."

Frowning, I did as I was bidden, whereupon Holmes crouched to one knee, and took his magnifier to the carpet near the bedroom door.

"Look here, Watson."

I went over to Holmes, and got down on all fours to see what he was peering at. A small, silvery crescent shone from the pile of the carpet.

"What is it?" I asked.

"A heel-print, I would imagine."

I gasped. "So it was a human intruder! What is it? Phosphorus?"

"It is too dim for that, and I fancy an actress would baulk at the thought of covering herself in so foul a chemical, not to mention the difficulty of acquiring large amounts. No, this is something less efficacious, but suitable for the effect. Something that requires a modicum of light to work its magic."

"My curtains were open a crack that night," I muttered. "Now that I think on it, I'm sure they were fully drawn before I retired."

"This is luminous paint, concocted using match-heads and other simple ingredients. Any garment soaked in it and left in sunlight for a few hours will appear to glow in darkness when it reacts with a light source, however feeble. It was whilst reading a monograph on the tricks of spirit-mediums that I discovered the formula, as it happens."

"Is there a trail? Can we see where the spirit went?"

"Sadly not. Some decent attempt has been made to clean the carpet—some smudges remain here by the door, but that is all." Holmes stood, and I followed suit. "Tell me again exactly what happened that night. You came to bed feeling somewhat drunk?"

"Yes."

"Every detail. Did you eat or drink anything upon returning to your room?"

"I simply drank some water from the pitcher by my bed."

"You poured it from the pitcher, or it was already poured?"

I thought hard on this. The events were not entirely clear in my mind. "A glass was already poured."

"By your own hand?"

"No… it was waiting for me." I began to feel rather foolish.

"And then you went straight to sleep?"

"I did."

"When you awoke and saw this 'spirit', what then?"

"I was in a terrible state. My legs were like jelly, my head swimming. I could not get up. The spirit was just like Mary—even her hair was styled as it was on our wedding day. I watched the spirit walk from the door, over to the far corner of the room, whereupon it vanished. Only then did I manage to steady myself enough to investigate, but found nothing."

"Did she speak?"

"I… think so. But only in the faintest whisper. And then there were the flowers. A white lily."

"But later you saw these same flowers in the house, as decorations?"

"Yes, and again at the séance. I drew the conclusion that the flowers were placed in my room while I was asleep."

"You carry a photograph of Mary from your wedding day. Was it on your person?"

"It was… but I left it in the drawer of my nightstand after I dressed for dinner."

"So one of the spiritualists could have stolen into your room and found it?"

"Yes, but I think they were all present the whole evening. Judith follows Crain as closely as his own shadow. Simon was in and out during dinner, I think. Even after my reading in the tower, I saw him creeping about in the yard. Unless Madame Farr herself entered my room while I was outside, I don't know who could have done it, or when."

Holmes pursed his lips as he thought. "Before discussing this further, we should find somewhere more private."

"More private than my room?" I asked.

"Oh, indeed—if you heard whispers in the walls, then presumably we can be overheard also."

I felt most uncomfortable at the very thought, but could not fault my companion's logic. "To be honest, Holmes," I said, lowering my voice, "I have felt rather… observed… since setting foot in this house. Madame Farr's assistant, Simon, skulks about always. He seems to be everywhere at once."

"This was the fellow creeping around the hall when I first arrived?"

"You saw him?"

"Little escapes me, Watson. Now, lead on."

I led Holmes downstairs, poking my head into a couple of rooms before settling on the morning room. Holmes insisted on leaving the door ajar so that we might see or hear anyone approach, and we conducted our conversation in hushed tones.

"Did you drink any more water before retiring?" Holmes asked.

"Yes… I poured it from the pitcher. I drank almost the whole damn lot, I can tell you."

"Then I think we have our answer."

"We do?"

"It is unusual for servants to decant the water from a nightstand into a glass."

"Yes, but not entirely unheard of. And this family has so many eccentricities I hardly thought anything of it."

"Ah. But as it stands, there is a fair chance that there was some drug in the glass already—something odourless and tasteless, although even that would not be completely necessary if the victim were the worse for drink. During the ghostly visitation, your senses were clouded, and your strength sapped—you could not confront the spirit, nor could you identify her with any certainty, and thus you were left entirely open to the power of suggestion. When the ordeal was over, you poured several glasses of clean water from the pitcher, thus destroying the evidence of the laced glass."

"It sounds more plausible than the alternative," I said.

"After breakfast the next morning: presumably the room had been cleaned, and the nightstand cleared away?"

I nodded.

"So now we must ascertain what drug was used on you. Any ideas?"

"There are a good many possibilities, Holmes."

"I wonder if, in a far higher dose, the same poison could have been used on Lady Esther," Holmes mused.

"Doubtful," I said. "I was stupefied. With a higher dose, I

don't think Lady Esther could have called out, or left her bed to be found how she was." I paused. "Holmes… Madame Farr has played me for a fool, hasn't she?"

"She has identified your weakness, and used it to her advantage, just as I shall do to her. There is no shame in being hoodwinked, Watson—just be proud that you remained incredulous even after all that. Your friend Lord Berkeley could learn a lot from you."

"Who do you suppose the actress was?" I asked. "Judith is the obvious choice."

"Yes, but rule no one out. It seems everyone has secrets of some sort in this house. It might have been a maid, paid off by Madame Farr. It might have been Lady Esther herself."

"Esther!"

"Why not?"

"What motive could she have?"

Holmes shrugged his angular shoulders. "To incriminate the spiritualists by staging an obvious ruse? And don't forget this is her house—if there is a secret passage, perhaps she knew of it already. And she could certainly organise the servants to set up and clear away such a trick."

"I can't believe it, especially after what became of her. And what if she'd been caught in the act? What good would it have done her?"

"That does make her an unlikely culprit, Watson. Unless… What if she was caught, but by the spiritualists, and killed because she was trying to discredit them?"

"Lady Esther was already trying to discredit them," I said.

"Quite, albeit unsuccessfully. There is much that does not add up, Watson, and we need further data upon which to draw a conclusion. The similarities between your visitation and the appearance of the 'red woman' are presently our best correlating factors. Why don't you show me where this second ghost was seen?"

I guided Holmes out into the corridor, and around to the servants' passage behind the drawing room, where he carefully inspected the sealed portal that had once accessed the tower.

"Crain told us some ghost story about the lower parts of the tower being sealed after a fire," I explained. "Something about the foundations being unsafe, and a good deal more about a curse… it didn't make much sense to me, I'm afraid."

"No matter. It is another avenue to investigate."

We doubled back through the narrow passage, with Holmes tapping on the walls periodically. When we emerged into the broader corridor, Holmes peered towards the rear of the house, where a few servants could be seen flitting back and forth between the kitchen and the scullery.

"That fellow Simon we spoke of earlier," Holmes said. "When I saw him, he was entering the drawing room—heading in this direction. Would he have any business in this part of the house?"

"Presumably he is sleeping in the servants' quarters, just down there."

"Then he has freedom of movement around the house. Servants go by ways untrodden, and move about unnoticed. If the walls have ears, then perhaps we should take a stroll around the grounds, and you can avail me of every detail. I want it all laid out for me, Watson, in the order it occurred, as clear as you can recall it. In my experience the smallest trifle may yield the most profound result."

We took in a good deal of the grounds, which had so far been closed to me due to inclement weather and social obligations. The Crain estate extended far beyond what I had seen, encompassing walled gardens, orchards, and a boating lake fed by a fast-flowing stream that cascaded from forested hills. We took in the great expanse of deer park, which stretched for a hundred acres or more until it reached the distant enclosures of Crain's tenants. My friend James had inherited a generous slice of England's green and pleasant land, under highly unpleasant circumstances.

As we walked, I told Holmes everything I could remember, from the moment I had stepped from the coach to the moment of his arrival. Holmes took great interest in my assessment of each guest's character, but more interest still in my observations of their activities and my recollection of things they had said.

"It is clear to me," he said, "that your opinion of Geoffrey Melville is rather low."

"What I observed outside the morning room window on Saturday night…"

"I see. You therefore think Lady Esther ill-used at Melville's hand?"

"I do. It was not an isolated incident. It only confirmed what I had already suspected."

"That is a common mistake," Holmes said. "If you had already drawn a conclusion, then you would be tempted to confirm that conclusion through observation, rather than allow the observation to guide you to other possibilities."

"Really, Holmes! The man was compromised if you ask me, and with his own wife's maid. Yesterday I saw the three of them together, and Lady Esther had been crying. Add to that the note… What other possibility could there be?"

"That is the only question you should be asking!" Holmes said, almost with a smile on his thin lips. "For now, I shall take from you only that which you describe from observation, and without meaning any offence, set aside that which I consider conjecture and inference."

I mumbled some objection at Holmes's lack of faith in my

judgement, but in truth I knew he meant nothing by it. His methods were his own, as he so often told me.

"Melville was late for dinner yesterday evening?" Holmes asked.

"He was, and was wet from the rain too. The vicar was also late, and looked equally flustered."

"Then let us next consider the absent vicar," Holmes said. "From your recollections he seemed rather single-minded on the matter of the late Lord Berkeley's will."

"To the point of being unseemly," I said. "When I passed St Mary's church on Saturday, it was indeed in a state of disrepair, but I think it is more than simply caring about the maintenance of the property. Even Crain joked that the Reverend Parkin concerns himself rather too much with social climbing, and I saw nothing to convince me otherwise."

"There was a suggestion that Lord Berkeley might not leave a stipend for the church in his will, despite some former agreement?"

"That was the impression I received. And the vicar was being something of a bully towards the drunken Cavendish when I encountered them after dinner, trying to extract the details of Lord Berkeley's will from the solicitor."

"Who invited Cavendish? The younger or elder Crain?"

"I don't recall. I can't imagine he's the sort that Madame Farr would need as a patron."

"Nor are you, if you don't mind me saying," Holmes said. "But he is just the sort the spiritualists might need to witness changes to the will."

"If any changes were to be made, they would not be in Madame Farr's favour," I said. "If anything, Langton was set to benefit."

"Ah, now that is an interesting case. You say he seems like a decent sort of fellow, who makes a living through property?"

"Yes, but there was that queer business at the séance that

seemed to have him rattled. Something about a bad investment that would have met with disapproval from his late father. I'd have paid it no mind if it weren't for his wife's reaction—she positively seethed."

"Madame Farr's knowledge of a person's secrets is not unusual—I would expect the amanuensis, Simon, to be entrusted with gathering intelligence. What was insinuated at the séance may have been intended only to convince Langton of Madame Farr's powers. Or it may have been intended to frighten him."

"If he's in trouble with his finances, he's hardly worth blackmailing."

"That depends entirely on the kind of trouble he is in. And you say he was a keen gambler at the billiard table?"

"He was, Holmes. He was eager to stake money on a friendly game even without seeing the measure of the opposition."

"He would have done well to, given that you're the very devil of a billiards player." Holmes turned along a left fork that wended its way back towards the house, past a small grotto that would have been far more pleasant in fine weather. "Now, something else puzzles me, Watson. Explain to me the tarot reading again." Holmes stopped, closed his eyes, and pressed his fingertips together, as he often did when wanting to absorb every detail.

Though I was not well disposed to reliving that episode, I went through the details of the reading once more, to the best of my recollection. The four cards: the Five of Cups, the reversed Three of Pentacles, the Six of Swords, and finally Death.

"And the final card was revealed after the interruption with the rapping sounds?" Holmes asked.

"It was."

Holmes began to walk again, and I went with him.

"Watson, I do not like to reveal my theories ahead of time, as well you know, but in this particular matter I would not wish to keep you in the dark for longer than is necessary, so I shall tell you what I think. First, it is uncommon in this day and age for spiritists to employ tarot cards at all, for they are representative of the very occultism that the modern 'spiritualist church' eschews. Second, Madame Farr either cannot read the tarot, or was suitably confident of your ignorance that she was able to foist upon you any old rubbish to suit her whims. Tarot readings generally follow one of several patterns, or spreads—a four-card spread is most unusual, unless the first card is to signify a burning question. I have never heard it used to recall the 'distant past.'"

"How do you know so much about tarot readings?" I interrupted.

"You forget how far I have travelled, and how much I have learned about various superstitions. I understand the methods well, just as I understand how easily each card is open to interpretation—an important facet of the trickster's art.

"Now, you chose the cards yourself, yes? I do not think she needed to resort to any trickery to force the selection, as the cards themselves can be rather ambiguous, and her conclusions are suspect at best. Let us look at the cards. The Five of Cups is said to represent loss or sadness, but not specifically bereavement. Madame Farr made a stretch there, in order to push her agenda. As I said, I do not think she manipulated the cards, otherwise she would have chosen a more suitable one."

I stood in awe of Holmes's encyclopaedic knowledge. He seemed to note my wonder and, in all honesty, admiration, for he managed the slightest smile before continuing.

"What was next? Ah, yes, the reversed Three of Pentacles, for the recent past. Now, it does not matter which way up the cards were placed; I am sure Madame Farr would have had an interpretation ready. In this case, she seized upon the number three to make it appear that you devoted too much time to me, rather than to Mary. Do not frown so, Watson. Marriage is one of the few subjects upon which I can claim no authority, but in my observation Mary could have asked for no more dutiful a husband. It is well recorded that we embarked on adventures while you were married, but did not Mary herself encourage you to assist me?"

I nodded. She had not always been happy about my involvement with Holmes's investigations—particularly the more dangerous ones—but she always supported me. Nothing Mary had ever said sustained Madame Farr's accusations that I had neglected my wife due to my loyalty to Holmes. Yet the words had stung, perhaps more because of some intangible feeling of guilt I carried.

"In any case," Holmes went on, his tone softening, "the Three of Pentacles has nothing to do with 'interlopers', and more to do with a lack of effort in one's work, or something to that effect.

"Next, the Six of Swords. A positive card in many respects, and Madame Farr was truthful in her interpretation, that it signifies a necessary change. And yet she added that rot about an obstacle in your path. She was merely watering the seed of doubt already sown in your mind, I'm sure.

"And finally, Death. She offered no explanation, but I imagine you yourself gave the card undue significance in hindsight, after what happened to Lady Esther."

"That is fair to say."

"It is one of the most positive cards in the tarot deck," Holmes said. "But it is often used in plays and sensational novels, I understand, to presage some literal death. And that is precisely how Madame Farr used it. I imagine she concealed the card up her sleeve, and when you were distracted by the rapping noises, she slipped it onto the table. The mental association your own mind made between her dire warnings and the image of the grim reaper on the card would have had the desired effect."

"If the desired effect was to make me deuced cross, then you're right," I grumbled.

"She took a great risk," Holmes said. "Warning you away from my company would only ensure that—in the event of some dramatic occurrence such as, say, the death of Lady Esther—I would be the first person you summoned. She must be very confident in her own abilities."

"I received the impression that she did not believe you to be deserving of your reputation," I explained. "Certainly Judith said as much the next night—or, rather, Crain said on Judith's behalf, as the girl rarely utters a word."

"It stands to reason that Madame Farr would be foremost in our suspicions in the event of any crime committed at the house. This makes me wary indeed, Watson. She is not as clever as she thinks she is, but she is also no fool. After performing those tricks upon you, the best she could have hoped for was a quiet evening, with no unscheduled ghosts and no mysterious deaths. You would have gone away, pondering her words, and possibly returning as one of her regular clientele.

"Ah, there is the house up ahead. There is just time for you to explain to me the details of the séance again. Leave nothing out..."

CHAPTER TEN

PARLOUR TRICKS

"Please, humour me, Lord Berkeley," Holmes said.

Crain shifted on his feet, looking more restless and nervous than ever. His eyes were ringed with red, almost as his sister's had been when I had found her body. He rubbed at his nose, and sniffed, before finally replying, "It's just… how much longer will this take? My guests are not used to being treated this way, and you are making me look like a dreadful host."

"Under the circumstances, Lord Berkeley, I am sure they will understand. Now can I count on you for this favour? Soon you will see for yourself the necessity."

Crain looked to me for support, and I nodded encouragingly.

"Very well," he sighed.

"Excellent!" said Holmes. "I shall need half an hour at most. In that time, I would have all of the guests, save for Watson and I, gathered in the drawing room. I would ask that the servants contain themselves to the back rooms, all except Simon and Judith. You may keep the butler on hand, should you wish—he seems a trustworthy fellow."

Crain looked unsure of himself.

"Is something the matter?" Holmes asked.

"No… well, it's just that Simon… I'm not sure he's here. That is, I think he left this afternoon, about the time I went out for my… stroll."

"No," I said. "He was here when you went out, I remember it quite well."

Crain pinched at his eyes with thumb and forefinger. "I must be mistaken," he said. "It's all been so confusing."

"Might I ask where you went this afternoon?" Holmes asked, brightly.

"That is my business!" Crain snapped.

"Come on, old fellow," I said. "Holmes is trying to help. It might be important later."

"Oh well, if you must know I went to see Sir Thomas, to break the news. He… he took it rather hard."

"I see," Holmes said. "Thank you, Lord Berkeley."

"I… Never mind. It's just that everyone keeps calling me that—Lord Berkeley, I mean. And my father not yet cold in his… well, you know."

"Apologies, my lord," Holmes said, with surprising kindness in his voice. "I suppose people only want to show due respect, you understand. Now, as I said, if you could help the constable here gather all the guests, and I shall make certain arrangements. Half an hour!"

I supposed Holmes had given the instruction to stop Crain brooding so, and it seemed to work. Crain reluctantly went to find Eglinton, shadowed by Hardacre.

Whatever Holmes was up to, he had been planning it from the moment we had finished our walk. He had insisted on making a thorough study of the drawing room, alone. He had scoured the flower beds outside for the impress of footprints, though if he had found anything he had not seen fit to tell me. Then he had made me walk him through both wings of the house, upstairs and down, pointing out every room as far as I knew, taking particular note of who occupied each of the bedrooms. Finally, he had met Crain to organise his little gathering.

"Watson, I want you to find out if any of the maids tidied the drawing room this morning. If so, bring them with you in half an hour."

"And what will you be doing?" I asked, rather put out that Holmes was keeping me in the dark.

"Something that might ordinarily be considered illegal. Which is why I'm going to take that young constable with me, and leave you to bask in the glow of glorious ignorance."

With that, Holmes summoned the other policeman, who had been stationed outside the front door by his more senior compatriot. With a few words of the most authoritative sort, he strode upstairs, the constable in tow, passing the first of the guests as he went.

I waited in the drawing room with the others. Madame Farr, Simon and Judith sat together, away from everyone else. Langton and Constance sat to my left, Langton's foot tapping incessantly. The Cavendishes sat beside the Langtons, while Melville sat to my right, stern-faced and silent. Eglinton stood solemnly near the door, a young maid beside him—the same maid, Polly, who had first seen the Red Woman. Crain paced back and forth. I knew I ought to confront him about whatever it was he had taken earlier, but at such a sensitive time I could not see how to broach the subject.

The traces of the previous night's entertainment had been mostly cleared from the room. The round table was still present, though it was now bare. The drapes that had hung all about the room were gone, and the high windows were exposed, allowing light to flood in.

At last, the door opened and Holmes entered, carrying a large cast-iron pot from which dark smoke belched, mingling with the aroma of incense that still lingered from the séance. Holmes was followed by the two policemen. The younger constable carried a large box, which he set down on an empty chair at Holmes's direction. The older man, Hardacre, closed the door and stood in front of it, arms folded. Holmes placed the burning pot in the middle of the table.

If any of our number now looked agitated, it was the spiritualists, and I rather relished the prospect that Holmes might be laying a trap for them.

"I thank you all for your patience," Holmes said. "I have gathered you all here to conduct a séance in reverse."

"Oh dear Lord…" Melville groaned.

"Do not worry yourself, Mr Melville, for I think this is one demonstration of the spiritist art that should interest you enormously. You see, before my arrival I exchanged notes with a new professional society in London—the Society for Psychical Research—whose members are devoted to the scientific study of spiritualism. Whilst they count amongst their number many true believers in psychical phenomena, they are all men of science, and take an especial interest in uncovering fraud and charlatanry, in order to remove obvious trickery from their serious studies. By this, I mean of course the study of psychic mediums, like our friend Madame Farr here.

"From the society—the 'SPR', as they call themselves—I received a great many case-notes, including all manner of techniques employed by fraudulent mediums in reproducing 'séance phenomena'. Table-rapping, materialisations, strange noises, and even fire-walking."

At this, a good many eyes turned to Madame Farr, who remained impassive.

"By the end of this little demonstration, we should know whether or not Madame Farr is a true conductor of the spirits, or a shameless fraud."

"Really, Mr Holmes," Crain said. "Madame Farr is an honoured guest in my home."

"I understand, my lord. But it is also essential that we establish the facts, for at present I am aware of several unexplained occurrences this weekend that have a direct bearing on your sister's untimely passing, and many of those occurrences begin and end with Madame Farr. If she can be proven a genuine medium, then it is the first step on the road to eliminating Madame Farr from our inquiries."

Crain pondered this for just a moment, a worried frown on his face, then nodded. "The sooner this is done, the sooner you can look for the real culprit, if any physical culprit exists," he said.

"Thank you, Lord Berkeley. Now, Watson has provided me with a full and detailed account of the séance, with each incident described in the order they occurred. If I make any mistake, please do correct me, and I shall take it up with my friend later." Holmes gave a wry smile; he was enjoying this moment, and I knew it must surely bode ill for Madame Farr. I kept my expression as even as possible.

"First," Holmes said, "let us examine that most ubiquitous tool of the medium's trade: table-rapping. All of you heard this phenomenon—and indeed felt it, as I shall come to later.

"Before I can examine the evidence, I must first ask our butler, Mr Eglinton, whether this room was cleaned this morning."

"It was, sir," said Eglinton. "This is Polly—her duties each day include cleaning the drawing room and dining room."

Polly gave a nervous curtsey.

"And did you notice anything unusual this morning, particularly about the furniture?" Holmes said to the maid.

She looked to Eglinton, who gave an encouraging nod. "Yes, sir," she said. "I told Mr Eglinton straight away, in case he thought it was me that done it."

"Would you explain what you found?"

"Scratches, sir, on one of the chairs. That one." She pointed to the empty chair beside Holmes.

"Where are the scratches?" he asked.

"On the left front leg," she said. "Mr Eglinton was going to send for a French polisher before it was noticed."

"Thank you," Holmes said. "Watson, was this the chair on which Madame Farr sat during the séance?"

"I believe so, Holmes."

"Then any scratches would be consistent with a very famous trick, used by mediums to produce rappings upon a table. In its most basic form, the method requires a small contrivance on the knee, hidden beneath the medium's skirts. By flexing her knee, she creates raps of varying power, seemingly emanating from beneath the table, or downwards upon the floor. A more complex form, used for more powerful raps—and other, more sensational phenomena—requires a larger device, comprising a series of rods fixed together with leather strips. When contorted into the correct position, these can become rigid, producing very loud raps, or even levitating a table. The problematic factor in this magic trick, however, is that the rods must be supported against a sturdy object, such as a chair, the result often being that physical evidence is left behind. As séances are normally conducted in the medium's own home, this is of no matter. But here… Well, might I ask for a volunteer?"

"I will!" Constance Langton laughed.

"Very well, Mrs Langton. Please come over here, that's it."

Holmes moved the chair aside. "Now, I would ask you to feel beneath the tabletop for scratches, dimples and dents."

She ran her hand under the tabletop. "Yes," she said. "There is a whole little cluster of circular marks—little dents, I think. How curious!"

Holmes helped her up. "Thank you, Mrs Langton; if you would take your seat again. There you have it, ladies and gentlemen. As verified by an independent witness, we have evidence congruent with a simple trick—one which the SPR have documented several times." At that, Holmes shot a knowing glance to Madame Farr. "The marks indicate that a larger device was used, which would have allowed Madame Farr, at the crucial moment, to align the rods and levitate the table. A flick of the knee, and the whole thing would come crashing down. I take it you all recall being reminded several times not to break the circle? This was to allow Madame Farr time to wriggle free whilst you recovered from the shock of the crash, and kick the device beneath her chair, where her amanuensis, Simon, could bundle it away under cover of darkness."

"Surely even with such a device, Madame Farr would require free hands to complete the deception," Crain said. "Yet her hands were linked with us the whole time. I myself held her hand, and I swear on my honour that I did not break the circle."

"And I believe you, naturally, Lord Berkeley," Holmes said. "But on Madame Farr's other side was, I am afraid, a willing accomplice. Miss… Judith, is it? Might I ask your full name?"

Holmes fixed Judith with a firm stare.

"Just Judith," the young woman replied, an air of defiance in her small voice.

"Please, Judith, your family name, for the constables," Holmes demanded.

"I have none. I rejected my family when they rejected my

beliefs." For the first time, her eyes shone with remarkable strength, and I sensed a degree of pain behind them. I wondered now at how genuinely Judith held her beliefs.

"Very well. You will, at some point, have to answer to a higher authority than me," Holmes said, "but for now 'Judith' will do. You see, ladies and gentlemen, Judith is a true believer in spiritualism. From all I have seen and heard, I have no reason to doubt her sincerity. But she also knows that the spirits themselves do not deal in theatrical flourishes and sudden manifestations. She has come to accept that the spiritualist church will never thrive without the patronage such sensations bring. She assists in small deceptions, because she thinks it is in the greater interest of her beloved movement."

"No… I…" Judith almost choked on the words.

"Releasing Madame Farr's hand occasionally when no one was looking was a minor subterfuge. I am afraid Judith has done worse in the name of her faith. I present to the room one pair of carpet-slippers." Holmes took a pair of slippers from the box and held them aloft. Judith's cheeks flushed. "You recognise these, Judith?"

The girl scowled.

"Under the supervision of Constable Aitkens here, these slippers were taken from Judith's room. They are of singular interest to me, because of a testimony given to me by my colleague Dr Watson. Out of embarrassment, Watson did not relate this story to any of you, but now is the time for transparency."

I cringed, for I knew what was coming next.

"On Saturday night, Watson was visited by a ghost." Holmes let this sink in, and mutters rippled around the room.

"So *that's* what they were on about at dinner," Langton said. "I'm glad someone has finally explained it. Another ghost, eh?"

I felt several pairs of eyes burning holes in my head.

"Now, now," Holmes said, holding up his hands to call order.

"This was not a real ghost, of course. But it was convincing enough to have even the staunch Dr Watson doubting his senses. There were two reasons for this—first, thc illusion conjured by the intruder in his room that night was most effective. Second, Watson was drugged."

"Drugged?" Crain stopped pacing now, and looked at Holmes in shock.

"Yes, Lord Berkeley. At the moment, I can prove the former, but not the latter, though it is a matter of time. Let me explain. At some point on Friday evening, after Watson dressed for dinner, someone crept into his room and went through his things. There they found a small portrait of Watson's late wife, Mary, and used it as a point of reference to deceive him. Dressing up a slender young woman in as close a fashion as possible to his wife's likeness, in garments and wig soaked in luminous paint, these cruel tricksters set about tormenting the good doctor. In his drug-addled state, head swimming, he could not rely on his own eyes, and due to a lack of evidence, he kept quiet about what he had seen until pressed at dinner the next night.

"The ghost—a real, living person, naturally—vanished from sight. I believe through a secret passage located somewhere in the vicinity of the Red Tower."

"Pish!" Crain said. "A family legend, but no more than a legend."

"A family legend well known in the village, and one that Madame Farr would doubtless have heard before even meeting you, my lord. Indeed, rumours that the passage leads to hidden treasure would be enough of a motive for unscrupulous types to search for it, and search thoroughly."

"I resent the implication," Madame Farr said.

"I am very sure you do, madam," Holmes said, "just as I resent my good friend being used as a pawn in what amounts to an elaborate confidence trick. These slippers—"

"Finally, we get to the point," Crain said.

I could tell Holmes was annoyed, but he retained his immaculate manners. "These slippers," he resumed, "belong to Judith. And inside them is a faint residue, particularly around the heel of the left foot. I shall pass it around that you might see it better for yourselves." Holmes passed the slipper to Melville, along with his magnifying glass. As Melville inspected it, Holmes continued. "The residue matches, in both size and shape, a small mark found in Watson's room. It is the sediment from thinned luminous paint. I have a small chemist's set in my bag, and when my tests are complete I am sure the results will be conclusive."

I was certain Holmes could not have brought his chemist's set in his small bag, but naturally held my peace.

"Wait!" Melville snarled. "Are you saying this girl disguised herself as a ghost? So… she was also the Red Woman!"

"No!" Judith cried. She leapt up, and turned to Crain. "Sir… James… don't listen to them!"

"Sit down!" Holmes commanded, and Judith obeyed, shaking all over. "Judith was at the séance table with you all, remember? She may have contrived to drive poor Dr Watson out of his wits, but she was not the Red Woman. Now listen, Judith—you would save us all a great deal of time if you would show us the entrance to the secret passage you found."

Judith hung her head, and said nothing.

"Mr Holmes, these accusations are baseless and false," Madame Farr said, her accent bordering on the exotic, her voice gruff. She rose from her chair like an apparition in black.

"How so?"

"This dear girl is devout in her beliefs, and would not take it upon herself to commit a fraud that might bring shame upon us. Not only that, but none of us were in a position on Friday night to enter Dr Watson's room. He was with us all evening, except for those moments during which Lord Berkeley can personally vouch for us."

"Of course, Mrs Mellinchip, I would expect nothing less."

For just a moment, Madame Farr looked too shocked to be outraged, but that outrage did indeed follow.

"What did you call me?"

"Mrs Mellinchip. That is your real name, is it not? Your theatrical skill at masking your Newcastle accent no doubt comes in very useful when mimicking spirit-voices from beyond the veil."

"I have no idea what you're talking about, sir, but I shall not be insulted so." Nevertheless, Madame Farr sat down again, looking somewhat rattled.

"I say again, Mr Holmes," Crain said, "Madame Farr is my guest. I am as cross as anyone about these parlour tricks, but I'm sure she has her reasons. Produce some facts or put an end to this exhibition."

"Very well, Lord Berkeley. But to do that, we must return to the night of the séance. Where was I? Oh, yes, we have explained the table-rapping, and the great levitation. The contraption used by the so-called Madame Farr would have been disposed of before anyone left the room, and I shall presently reveal how. In the meantime, let us examine what happened next.

"Lady Esther herself received some wisdom from the spirit world, although as a sceptic she had cleverly gained an advantage. She asked our medium a leading question about the future of her relationship. Few people realised, I should guess, that Lady Esther and Geoffrey Melville were experiencing some… difficulties."

"Rot!" said Melville. "How dare you?"

Holmes held up a hand. "Mr Melville, indulge me this once. Lady Esther asked if your marriage would be a happy one, to which Madame Farr responded positively, mentioning several children. A trite and pointless prediction about events long in the future, which Madame Farr knew would only be proven true or false long after she had moved on. She was not to know, of course, that her predictions would be proven false in the most immediate and violent way.

"Seeing his mistress in difficulty, forced onto a topic for which she had not prepared, Simon signalled for a distraction. The playing of a piano seemingly by itself."

"No, Mr Holmes," Langton spoke up. "I remember that part. Simon was not standing near the piano. No one was."

"I said 'signalled' for a distraction, Mr Langton. I assure you that someone was there. And that someone possibly was Simon, as it happens."

"What?" Langton laughed. "Were my eyes deceiving me?"

Holmes smiled. "You there, Simon," he said. "Do you have a family name, or is your situation much the same as Judith's here?"

Simon said nothing, but held himself haughtily, bearded chin tilted upwards.

"I thought as much. You see, ladies and gentlemen, Simon chooses not to speak, for his skill with accents is less deft than Mrs Mellinchip's. He, too, came down from Newcastle to set up this new scheme. His family name, I shall inform you, is Cole. Though I know not if we speak to Simon, or to Arthur. His twin."

"Ludicrous!" Crain said.

I met Holmes's gaze and gave him a quizzical look.

"Sorry to keep you in the dark, Watson," Holmes said, "but I had to be sure. Lord Berkeley, you left the house around midday, did you not? You saw the Reverend Parkin leaving, but you also saw Simon."

"I…" Crain looked most uneasy. "I think I did."

"Did you, or did you not?"

"I did, yes."

"This was directly upon leaving the house?"

"Yes. Actually… Simon was taking the path towards the village. And I thought it was curious, because the vicar was following behind, on foot. I received the impression that Parkin was following Simon, because he wasn't driving his fly, and he looked awfully circumspect."

"Valuable information, my lord, thank you," Holmes said. "And was 'Simon' carrying anything?"

Crain looked crestfallen. "A sack," he said.

"A sack," Holmes repeated. "The point of the matter is, Lord Berkeley, that the moment you left, Watson saw Simon on the stairs. And rather than leave the house, he went back upstairs with Judith. A fellow really can't be in two places at once. This puts me in mind of something else Watson told me, about Friday night. After Madame Farr conducted a private reading for Watson in the tower room, the good doctor went outside to take some air. He saw Simon heading across the lawn, from the direction of the stable block. But why? He was not going back to the village. It seems to me that his only intent was to be seen, because that would mean someone else could be rifling through Watson's belongings whilst our celebrated medium and young Judith kept Lord Berkeley busy."

"I'm sure there is some other explanation…" Crain said, rubbing at his temples.

"Wait a minute," Langton said. "I saw him shortly after arriving yesterday, when I went out for a smoke. But when I got back to the party he was already ahead of me. I thought it a trifle strange, but assumed he was simply fleet of foot."

"That assumption has many times worked in Mr Cole's favour. That first afternoon, as you were all gathered downstairs, the Cole twins were probably taking it in turns to search your belongings for anything they could use in the evening's séance. I would wager that the brother seen by Lord Berkeley this afternoon was disposing of valuable evidence, carried in a sack. A ghostly costume, perhaps? Luminous paint?"

Simon for a moment glanced left, then right, and then bolted for the door opposite Constable Hardacre. Holmes was before him so swiftly I barely saw my friend move. They struggled briefly, before Constable Aitkens hauled the bearded man away. Mrs Cavendish cried out in alarm. Madame Farr was shouting, "No, you fool!"

Finally, Simon was subdued, and calm was restored.

"And now we truly come to the solution to the séance. And rest assured, Lord Berkeley, there will be evidence. Might I have some witnesses follow me to the piano? Lord Berkeley, Watson, Mr Melville. If you please?"

We followed. The lid of the piano was open as always, but now Holmes lowered it so that it was almost closed.

"Peer in, and tell me what you see," he said.

We all looked. Inside the piano, tiny blobs of glowing, greenish paint adorned five of the strings. They were barely visible until our eyes had adjusted.

"Luminous paint, again," Holmes said. "During the day, those small dabs absorb enough light to glow in the dark, and yet are barely visible at all when exposed to light. I observed them earlier, because I knew to look for them. The bars of music were played on the piano by Simon's twin, Arthur—let us, for now, assume that I have the names the correct way around. The string with the left-most daub of paint is the first to be plucked, and then the other four follow, in order, left to right; thus!"

Holmes reached inside, and plucked the strings. The piano resounded with the rather crude tune we had heard at the séance. Satisfied with this demonstration, he returned to the table and bade us do the same.

"When the piano played, everyone turned towards it," Holmes went on. "All dressed in black, and crouching behind the piano, in shadow, 'Arthur' could not be seen—yet if you were allowed to examine the piano for too long, your eyes may have adjusted, and the illusion would have been broken. And so another distraction was required."

"The two doors slammed shut!" Constance exclaimed.

"One at a time," said Holmes, "and that is the crucial detail. You see, it was Simon who slammed the first door, and doubtless stepped away quickly. Everyone turned their attention away from the piano to the door, at which point Arthur darted around the edge of the room to the other door, and slammed that one behind him. This allowed Simon to stride to the door and pretend to secure it dutifully."

"It all seems so obvious now," Constance said. "But at the time… I feel so foolish."

"These tricks are tried and tested, madam," Holmes said. "Do not fret over it—deception is the primary occupation of Mrs Mellinchip and her cronies."

If looks could kill, Madame Farr's icy glare would surely have struck Holmes stone dead. As it was, he met her gaze with a wicked smile.

"Next, our medium turned her attention to Watson. Her earlier encounters with my friend had already given her confirmation of his weaknesses, and now all she had to do was exploit them in order to reinforce her position. She attempted to drive a wedge between Watson and me, in order to prevent him consulting me about her when he returned to London. What she could not have known is that Watson had already given me her name before departing, allowing me to conduct my own research.

"She must have known Watson would challenge her, and thus arranged for something special. Arthur Cole, having slipped out of the house, now ran to the window—remember the curtains were closed, so no one would see him outside. Evidently the window had been left on its latch, and now Arthur pulled it open suddenly, causing the inclement weather to disturb proceedings and blow out the candles. You were warned, presumably, not to break the circle?"

"Yes, we were," Langton said. "Madame Farr, or whoever she is, was adamant about that."

"Simon went to the window and made a show of fastening it shut, though the room was now in near darkness. What he actually did was pass the end of a fish-wire through the window to his brother. Even with the window closed, this could be pulled. It was attached to the chandelier above you."

We all looked up.

"Balanced carefully within the crystal of the chandelier were many dozens of lily petals—a flower Mrs Mellinchip had already established as being special to Watson, and which were plentiful in the house. Their scent would have been masked by the thick incense smoke. When the wire—loosely tied—was pulled free of the chandelier, the petals fell. The wire was then forcefully yanked through the gap in the window-frame, and Arthur made good his escape."

"This is how they fooled Esther at Madame Farr's house!" Melville said. When all eyes turned to him, he explained, "I was telling Dr Watson just yesterday. Esther attended a séance at Madame Farr's house months ago. She was certain some of the tricks were performed by someone pulling on a wire outside the window, but she was unable to prove it."

"And now, if we look to the window..." Holmes said. He marched past the glowering spiritualists, and opened the window, then held out his magnifying glass. "If anyone would care to inspect this area of the window-frame," he said, "they shall see for themselves."

Mrs Langton stood. "May I, Mr Holmes?"

Holmes nodded, and handed her the magnifier.

"My, he's right," she said. "The paint has rubbed away in sharp lines."

"You notice the larger chip on the inner edge?"

"Yes."

"That is where the hooked end of the wire snagged before being pulled free." Holmes took back his magnifier and showed Constance to her seat again. "Constable Hardacre, earlier today I made a thorough inspection of the earth directly beneath the window there. The rain has washed away much of the evidence, but the impression of a large boot, pointing towards the window, was clear. No one would have business there unless they were peering in, or waiting for someone at the window. I took accurate measurements—assuming this Cole brother has identical feet to his identical twin, the shoe should fit, as they say."

"We shall certainly check, sir," Hardacre said, looking less browbeaten and more impressed as the minutes passed.

A sudden fizzing noise drew our attention, and we all gasped as the pot in the middle of the table now flared brightly, flames licking over the top.

"A little early," Holmes shouted over our commotion, "but planned all the same. Behold, Mrs Mellinchip's grand finale!"

Before our astonished eyes, Holmes thrust a hand into the flames, and held it there. When he withdrew his hand, he held it to the light so we could all see it was unharmed. He then rubbed his hands together, and peeled away a rubbery coating from his skin, silvery and translucent. For this, he received a small round of applause.

"First, the fire trick," Holmes said. "The brazier burns by means of charcoal discs upon which incense is thrown. Flames crackle and spark through each disc in turn, with a short delay as each subsequent disc ignites. It is possible to time this process, give or take a few minutes, as you have just seen. Had I not been interrupted quite so often, I should think I would have given a perfect cue to the eruption of the secret ingredient—a layer of phosphorus, which ignites in somewhat dramatic fashion.

"The medium prepares for this trick by coating her hand—the hand that was held throughout the séance by Judith here, I should add—in a thick, fire-proof solution. I used a recipe provided me by the Society for Psychical Research, and packed my case accordingly: one half-ounce of camphor gum dissolved in two ounces of Scotch whisky, with one ounce quicksilver and one ounce liquid storax, mixed, applied to the hands and allowed to dry. The sleeve of Mrs Mellinchip's dress was soaked in a solution of salt and soda to stop it catching."

"How can you be sure of the solution?" Langton asked.

"Because when I visited Judith's room to find evidence of luminous paint, I also searched Madame Farr's room."

"Outrageous!" the woman wailed.

"It certainly is," Holmes retorted, and reached into the large box beside him. From it he withdrew one of Madame Farr's black dresses, and passed it to Crain. "My Lord Berkeley," he said. "Could you examine the left sleeve, please, and tell us what you find?"

Crain quailed as he took the dress, looking as though he might be sick. "A crust of salt," he said, very quietly.

There came from the medium an outburst of a most unseemly nature, after which Madame Farr—or Mrs Mellinchip, as Holmes insisted on calling her, to her chagrin—reverted to a state of uncooperative silence. Gone was her aura of mystery and power, and in her place was a very ordinary woman of middle age, looking uncomfortable and out of place in somewhat ridiculous attire.

"There is one event remaining," Holmes said, "and as yet I

can find no satisfactory explanation for it. The arrival of the Red Woman does not entirely suit Mrs Mellinchip's purpose, as far as I can ascertain. And the method of the trick so far eludes me."

"Maybe Judith has a twin, also," Mrs Cavendish posited, drawing a sullen glare from the girl.

"Possible, Mrs Cavendish, though the odds are against it. I have theories, of course, but no data. Evidence must be uncovered if we are to establish the guilt or innocence of these spiritualists."

"Surely their guilt is already established?" Melville snarled, standing abruptly.

"Only insofar as they have tried to trick you all, and perhaps swindle you of donations to their cause. I believe we could arrest these swindlers right now, on a charge of fraud. What you imply, Mr Melville, is that they are guilty of murder, and that cannot yet be supported.

"Lord Berkeley," Holmes went on. "I have not yet had the time to conduct a search of Mr Cole's quarters. With your permission I should like to do so now, in your presence."

Crain looked crushed. He could not speak, nor meet Holmes's eyes, but only nodded.

"Constable Hardacre, you will be so good as to accompany us. Constable Aitkens—that man must not leave this room, and nor must 'Madame Farr'. I trust the gentlemen present will assist if either of them try to escape?"

"Too right!" Langton said. "All that nonsense at the séance—all trickery. These cads were dipping into our private business all along. Yes, I for one will help the constable."

Hardacre stood beside Simon, a burly hand on the tall man's arm. Crain reluctantly swung open the door to the man's meagre quarters, and Holmes stepped past him into the room.

It was a small room, with nothing more than a small bed, cupboard and washbasin, beneath a single small window. Still, Simon was not on the house staff, and such accommodation was adequate for visiting servants. Everything in the room was arranged immaculately. Shirts were folded in a neat, square pile atop the cupboard. The bed was made with military precision, a spare blanket and towel folded on top of it as neatly as the shirts. Toiletries were arranged in a precise row behind the basin.

"Such attention to order," Holmes said, making the same observation. "It is a drilled habit, usually born of a life in service, in the army… or of time spent at Her Majesty's pleasure. Let us see what's in here…"

Holmes opened the cupboard beneath the washbasin, and poked around within. Finally, he produced a large brown glass bottle.

"A curious thing," he said, showing the label to me.

"Benzene," I said. "What is so curious?"

"Come, Watson, you can observe as well as I. What is benzene used for?"

"Commonly as an aftershave balm," I said. "I always have a bottle on hand myself."

"Simon here has a rather messy beard," Holmes said. "There is no razor in this cupboard, no shaving kit of any kind—not even a mirror. The bottle is large; it is not the kind supplied by your common-or-garden chemist at the counter. It is half empty. Tell me, Watson—if one were to imbibe a small amount of this, diluted in, say, water, what would the effects be?"

The penny dropped at once. "Drowsiness and lethargy. A dullness of the senses akin to extreme drunkenness. Nausea and dizziness. At higher doses, a weakness of motor function and uncontrollable trembling."

"And how easy is benzene to detect when diluted?"

"Difficult—it has a peculiar scent when neat, but diluted… it is negligible."

"In your medical opinion, Dr Watson, could your condition on Friday evening be described as consistent with benzene poisoning?"

"Yes," I said, anger building within me.

"A near-perfect method," Holmes said. "Benzene is common enough that the idle observer would overlook it. Mr Cole here might have found some in the house, no doubt, but brought along his own supply to be sure."

"I never," Simon said, the first time I had heard him speak, and indeed it was in an accent clearly of the north-east. "It were given me. It's not mine."

"I am sure you will keep to that story in court," Holmes said. "But when your identity is confirmed with the Newcastle-upon-Tyne constabulary, and a testimony of your previous drugging plot is brought forward, I am sure a judge will be as incredulous as I am. Watson, tell me—could benzene have been used to induce the effect you saw post-mortem in Lady Esther?"

"If her heart was weak, and a sufficient fright administered… perhaps."

"A fright, such as the sudden appearance of a ghost?"

"Now 'old on…" said Simon, pulling anxiously against Hardacre's grip.

"Death could not be certain," I said, "and the poisoner would have to administer the dose expertly. But… I confess it is not impossible."

Before more could be said, Crain screamed an unearthly cry of anguish and grief and rage, flying at Simon like a man possessed, overcome at last by the succession of shocks to his system.

"Watson!" Holmes shouted.

I leapt forward, wrestling Crain away, as Hardacre pushed Simon back along the servants' corridor.

"Calm yourself, Crain!" I said. "If he is indeed a murderer, he'll swing for it."

Crain fought against me, shouting unintelligibly. Several servants popped their heads from side-rooms to see what the commotion was, and hurriedly vanished whence they had come upon seeing their master's state. Finally, Crain's struggles ceased. The strength palpably drained from his limbs, and he broke down in heaving sobs.

"That's a good fellow," I said, soothingly. "Come on, let us go somewhere to talk."

No sooner had I released him, than he stood bolt upright, and looked at me with wild eyes, like a cornered animal.

"No. I've had enough," he said. "Do you hear me? Enough!" He turned and ran.

To my relief, he pushed past Hardacre and Simon, and fled in the direction of the back door. I was about to follow, but Holmes put a hand on my arm to stay me.

"Leave him, Watson. I estimate he is in no fit state to reason."

"I daresay you're right, Holmes," I muttered. "I daresay you're right…"

CHAPTER ELEVEN

ULTERIOR MOTIVES

Holmes asked the policemen to keep a close watch on the house, ensuring that the spiritualists in particular did not leave. Many of the house-guests grew more agitated at their confinement.

"Beggin' your pardon, sir," Hardacre said, "but this case is a deal too thick for us. When is that inspector due?"

"Do not worry, Constable, everything is in hand," Holmes said. "Assuming that the mystery is not solved before he arrives, we should have one of Scotland Yard's finest with us by nightfall. Now, Watson, will you walk with me? We must sift through the details, for there is surely something we have missed."

I followed Holmes to the morning room. With the spiritualists under watch, there was less need for circumspection as we discussed the intricacies of my experiences over the past days. We again went over the manner of Lady Esther's death, though I could shed no more light than I had the first time. Through it all, Holmes pressed his fingers to his temples and squeezed his eyes shut, as though he might summon the answer through sheer force of will.

Eventually, he said, "There are two possibilities for the circumstances of Lady Esther's poisoning. Either someone entered her room by means of the elusive secret passage, or she was poisoned before entering her room, but only felt the effects later. But the latter scenario does not account for the scream, nor for the terrible fright she seems to have received moments before her death. Then there is the writing desk, and the question of what she had been writing before she died; but there was no sign of a letter, a diary, or anything else in the room. As you suggested earlier, it may be that we are looking for something that never existed, and that there was no letter. But then why move the lamp? It makes no—" He stopped abruptly.

"Holmes?" I prompted.

"Watson, what a fool I've been!" Holmes stood up, and flew from the room, so swiftly it was all I could do to chase after him.

When I caught up with Holmes, he was striding with purpose towards the nightstand nearest the door to the defunct stair.

"Lady Esther did not move that lamp to provide light for her writing," Holmes said as I caught my breath. "She moved it to get at something behind it, and the bureau was the most convenient place to put it."

"There is nothing behind it," I said. "I checked all along the wall for a secret passage, and found nothing."

"It is not a passage I am looking for—not exactly."

Holmes rapped along the wainscoting all around the nightstand, then began to prod and poke at it with his long fingers. Finally he set his hands on two points on a small wooden panel, and pushed.

There was a soft click, and a panel around eight inches square swung outwards. Holmes reached into the cavity that had been revealed and pulled on something, and then pulled again, harder. A louder click echoed from somewhere behind the wall.

“The entrance to the passage is not in this room, Watson,” Holmes said. “But the release mechanism is. It is an old chain pulley, which opens a door in that side-room.”

“The tricks during my reading…” I muttered. “This is how they were done. One of those blasted twins was lurking in the passage!”

“Quite so. And now that we have found one, we shall find the others.”

“Others?”

“I would stake a wager even against our inveterate gambler Mr Langton that there are at least four entrances to the secret passage. One must be in your room, a second downstairs where the Red Woman mysteriously vanished, and a third right here.” As he said this, Holmes threw open the small door to his side, stepped into the dark space beside the stair, and pulled at part of the timbered wall behind the old staircase, which opened upon aged hinges with a grating creak. “There should be a fourth door leading outside, because what purpose would such a passage serve if not as a secret means in or out of the property? Now, light that lamp, Watson. It’s time to walk in the footsteps of ghosts.”

I followed Holmes into a cramped space, which he negotiated well enough, though I had to turn sideways to manage it. Steep, winding stairs descended sharply, threading around the tower’s circumference. Dust and humidity made the simple act of breathing unpleasant, such that I had to press a kerchief against my mouth and nose to keep from wheezing. Finally, the ground levelled out at a small landing, before more steps circled down again into darkness.

“If I have my bearings correct,” Holmes whispered, “we should be standing right by your room. Hold the lamp higher, Watson. Ah, here you can see signs that the floor has been hastily swept. A-ha! And here is the reason why. You see that, Watson?”

“I do,” I replied, rather angrily. As we neared the end of the passage, smudges of luminous paint shone along the floor, and here and there the unmistakable forms of small, bare footprints were evident.

"They vanish before reaching the stairs," Holmes observed. "Either our ghost put on her slippers, or the paint rubbed off before she got any further. But here on the wall are hand-prints. The spiritualists did their best to clear traces of paint from your room, but there was no need to clean this filthy old passageway. Their carelessness will be their undoing, for later I may be able to capture a clear thumb-mark from this cluster, and that will identify the ghost with near certainty. Now, let me see... here we are."

Holmes reached into a gap revealed by some missing bricks, and yanked on another chain. There followed the click of a lock, and as before a slim section of the wall, perhaps two feet wide by five feet tall, clicked open. Holmes pushed at the newly revealed door, and sure enough my bedroom lay beyond it.

The door bumped against something, and would not open fully. Holmes poked his head around to see what caused the obstruction.

"The wardrobe," he explained. "Whoever used this passage was slight indeed, for I could barely squeeze through there. The position of the furniture was sufficient to throw me off the scent, and it all but confirms the story that the current members of the Crain family likely did not know of the existence of this door. Passages like these are invariably used as escape routes, so we may assume that the release mechanism can be reached from a panel, as in the room above, but it is hidden behind the wardrobe."

"So the door must have been opened from this side in order for my ghost to escape."

"Very good, Watson. Someone—Cole, I imagine—would have waited for Judith to finish her performance. When her act was over, Judith would have changed into slippers and robe, and handed the luminous clothing to Cole to dispose of. The sack containing the costume was probably left here, to be reclaimed earlier today by one of the twins. It is possible there were other props stashed here, too, but my arrival put an end to further games of that sort. On the night in question, however, Cole and Judith would have been able to hide in here, or in the tower room, but more likely they made their escape through a third secret exit, near the servants' quarters. And that, I imagine, is where they were seen."

"Seen?" I asked. "By whom?"

"By the Red Woman, of course," Holmes said facetiously. "But that revelation, my dear Watson, requires a further examination of evidence. Come, let us seal this door and continue down."

We closed the secret door, and Holmes bade me follow him down the second staircase. I had taken only two steps before cursing as I snagged my jacket on a nail.

"Wait," Holmes said. "You've found something here, Watson."

"I can't think what," I grumbled, "other than the need to have my jacket mended."

"In such a tight space, you are not the first to catch yourself here. Look: a fragment of cloth. Blue silk, by the looks of it."

"What does that mean?"

"I am not entirely sure yet, but a hypothesis is beginning to form in my mind. Come, let's finish what we started, and we can discuss this later."

The stairway was even narrower than the first, and markedly rickety and uneven. At the bottom was a dirty, musty chamber, with a low ceiling and rotted, broken floor revealing the foundations beneath. The brickwork was blackened with soot, the smell of which still hung thick in the dusty air, causing us both to cough.

"It looks as though Eglinton was correct," Holmes said. "This chamber has not been used for a long time. There is a bricked-up door which must have once led outside, and beside it… yes, there is a cavity in the wall there, suggesting another passage. This has to lead into the servants' wing. That is where the Red Woman disappeared—presumably, like the others, it must be opened from this side. Ah, look over there."

By the light of the lamp, we observed a selection of tools, from picks and shovels to a large sledgehammer. "The spiritualists, I take it?"

"Most likely. If they really were hunting for buried treasure, they would have been disappointed. That much is surely a legend, or else it would have been discovered after the fire. I imagine the Cole twins brought these tools down here, piecemeal, although they would not have been able to work overmuch for the noise it would create. If they had found anything, the spiritualists would hardly be here still."

"But perhaps the discovery of the passage alone provided inspiration, to use the legend in committing a deadlier crime," I suggested.

"Inspiration, yes. But again, you jump to conclusions, Watson. I think the passage itself is treasure enough for our charlatans, for by means of its very existence, Madame Farr is able to bring patronage and belief to her little 'church', through fraud. I still assert she has no motive for any greater crime than that. Now, there is one more door, and that is the one used by the Red Woman."

I turned about to the right-hand door, holding up the light.

"A simple catch this time, Watson," Holmes pointed out. "There is no need for a mechanism, because the door opens only from this side. If one were seeking escape, and the outside exit was not safe, one could steal through here and try to escape through the back door."

"But that would mean… the Red Woman had an accomplice."

"Right again."

"So the method of both materialisations was identical. They both used a woman in costume, and both had someone on hand to assist them. And yet you don't believe thc same culprits were behind both?"

"Once more, Watson, a capital summation. But shall we leave this rather unwholesome environment, rather than stand around in it all day? I'd like some fresh air."

Holmes twisted the catch, and a large panel came free, sliding aside to reveal a small opening. There came a sudden scream, causing me to jump. We stepped out of the passage to see Mrs Langton and Mrs Cavendish, their nerves clearly frayed.

"Mr Holmes! Dr Watson!" Mrs Cavendish exclaimed. "We half thought you were… well…"

"Ghosts?" Holmes proffered. "Not we, not yet."

Holmes took out his magnifier and examined the walls around the passage door, which had been perfectly disguised as a tall, thin panel in the wainscoting, in the cavity between my room and the neighbouring one.

"We came to see the place where the Red Woman vanished," said Mrs Langton, in some embarrassment. "Then we heard voices from behind the walls and… well, you gave us such a fright!"

"For that, I apologise, dear ladies," Holmes said. "You must also forgive me, but we must discourage further exploration of these passages until needs require it. They are most unsafe… I am afraid your ghost hunting must be confined to the more conventional portions of the house."

The ladies did not look terribly disappointed by this, for the passage was not in the least inviting. Instead they watched as Holmes shut the secret entrance; even though we knew where it was now, it was still impossible to detect with the naked eye once closed, and when Holmes pressed upon it to ensure it was secured, it did not give an inch.

With that, we left the ladies to discuss this exciting development, and met again with Constable Hardacre, who was remonstrating with a somewhat bad-tempered Langton in the hall. Langton ceased his arguments as we approached.

"We have found the secret passage, Constable," Holmes explained, ignoring the scene we had interrupted. "We now know how the Red Woman made her escape, and where the spiritualists were hiding their theatrical props. We shall need to venture soon to the village to find the evidence, but I think there is more that we may have missed here at the house."

"You still think the spiritualists innocent of murder?" Langton said.

"I would not say that yet, Mr Langton; only that they have no solid motive for the crime, beyond ensnaring James Crain even further in their fantasies. Still, I cannot rule out that the motive was a financial one, though I cannot yet see how or why. The elder Lord Berkeley's sudden demise has rather muddied the waters, for now suspicion naturally falls on the beneficiaries of his will as suspects."

"Look here, Mr Holmes, I have already told you—"

"Calm yourself, Mr Langton. If I were accusing you, I would do so directly. I do not accuse you of anything—not yet. But so many threads in this case appear snipped off at the ends whenever the matter of money is raised. The threats Lord Berkeley made at dinner—people have been murdered for less; Melville's admission that James Crain had threatened to disavow his sister of her title; the argument between Cavendish and the vicar. And it is the Reverend Parkin who intrigues me the most right now."

A figure appeared behind us, a cigarette smouldering in a trembling hand. It was Crain, looking most agitated; almost haunted.

"Parkin?" Crain asked. "Why?"

"Because, Lord Berkeley," Holmes said, "of an observation you yourself made. You say the Reverend has his own fly, which he drove to the house yesterday afternoon presumably? But he did not take it this morning? He was following Cole, you think?"

"I… I think so," Crain said.

"And Watson tells me that there were two people late for dinner last night, and both of them were flustered upon their arrival. One was Melville, apparently nursing a headache, and the other was the vicar."

"I hardly see the importance."

"Perhaps we soon shall, if there is anything to see. Might I ask, do you have the key to your father's study?"

"Of course."

"Then may I take a look?"

Crain nodded nervously. We parted company with the others and followed him up to the study. Crain inserted a key into the lock, frowned, and pushed open the door.

"That's strange," he said. "It wasn't locked."

"Are you sure it was locked to begin with?" Holmes said.

"Father always locked it."

"And are there other keys?"

"This one, Father's, and Eglinton's."

"Could the room have been left unlocked by the maid this morning?"

"The maids never enter Father's study unbidden."

Holmes nodded. "And where last did you see your father's keys?"

"By his bedside when… when…" Crain's voice cracked.

I placed a hand on Crain's shoulder. "It's all right, Crain. We'll get to the bottom of this."

"Lord Berkeley, if it is not too difficult a time, could you please check that your father's keys are where they should be. It is of great importance."

Crain sniffed, nodded, and hurried at once down the corridor.

Holmes entered the study and beckoned me in. It was a large room, though surprisingly gloomy, with only a single window, before which stood a grand pedestal desk. A glass-fronted bookcase against one wall, I noted, was filled with accounting ledgers, finely bound and meticulously ordered. The opposite wall was dominated by a large tribal mask of African design, adorned with feathers and grasses, around which were hung a collection of photographs of Lord Berkeley in his younger days, with his wife Agnes, their two young children, and Sir Thomas Golspie.

"I doubt he will find the keys," Holmes said. "Because if what I suspect is true, the person who took them left the house in a hurry, and was not in the right state of mind to replace them."

"You suspect the Reverend Parkin of breaking into Lord Berkeley's study, don't you?" I asked. "A man of the cloth?"

"I always find it remarkable just how the human mind can rationalise any misdeed if the cause is important enough. I hear tell even pious men are not above such folly."

Holmes strode to the desk and looked through the few papers present. I peered over his shoulder, but saw nothing more interesting than bills of lading and orders for agricultural and building supplies.

Holmes next opened each drawer in the desk. Every one had its contents arranged in the most orderly fashion, as if it were part of a Chinese puzzle, with everything fitted perfectly in its place. All, that is, but the last drawer. This one was crammed with papers and ink bottles and ledgers, as though they had been tipped in carelessly. Even as I tried to grasp the significance, Crain returned.

"The keys are not there, Mr Holmes. I have searched Father's room. I only hope the undertaker has not… What is this? Who has done this?" Crain looked accusingly at us.

"We found it this way, Crain," I said. "I take it this is not normal?"

"It most certainly is not! Father was the most fastidious man I knew. Look around you!"

"That much is clear," Holmes said. "No man who ordered his work so painstakingly would keep a messy desk. There is a lock on this drawer—why is it not locked?"

"It should be," Crain said. "The key is on Father's bunch."

Holmes began taking the contents out of the drawer, arranging them neatly on the desk. He stopped only when he removed two folded parchments, bearing illuminated mastheads that read "Last Will & Testament".

"Both blank," Holmes said. "Was your father truly planning to change his will?"

The door to the study creaked open, and a thin voice said, "He had considered it." We looked up to see Cavendish, approaching timidly, wringing his wrinkled hands before him.

"Mr Cavendish, how good of you to save us the trouble of coming to find you," said Holmes.

"Yes, well, I was just passing, you see, and I… well. Yes." Cavendish swayed just a fraction; I fancied he had already taken a tipple or two this afternoon.

"You supplied these forms to the late Lord Berkeley?" Holmes asked, holding up the blank wills.

"I did. At his request, I should add."

"When?"

"On Sunday, before dinner. He wrote to my office a few days earlier, stating that he was considering making a codicil to his will, and he would like me to bring some forms along. I… I rather think that's why he invited me. I don't pretend to be on close personal terms with the Crain family." Cavendish looked in embarrassment to Crain, and then back to Holmes.

"How many forms did you provide for Lord Berkeley, Mr Cavendish?" Holmes went on.

"Three, sir."

"There are only two here."

Cavendish shrugged. "Perhaps he used one."

"We should make a thorough search of the office to be sure," Holmes said, then paused. "Mr Cavendish, did anyone else know you were supplying these forms? Or of Lord Berkeley's intent to create a codicil?"

Cavendish mumbled something indistinct, and looked to his feet.

"Speak up, man," Holmes prompted.

"The Reverend Parkin," Cavendish said, loudly, looking terribly guilty as he said it.

"You discussed this matter with the vicar?" Crain spluttered.

"No, my lord! When I left this room, I bumped into the vicar. He said he was just passing, but I had the oddest feeling he'd been eavesdropping. Then later… although my memory is indistinct, you understand…"

"That is why you were arguing in the library," I said.

"You saw? Oh, yes, of course you did. I had forgotten you were there."

"Not to be indelicate, Mr Cavendish," said I, "but you were rather the worse for drink. I led the vicar away and left you to sleep it off."

"And I appreciate it, Doctor. To my great shame, I remember very little from last night. But I do remember the vicar asking me to witness and sign some letter to the archdeacon. I honestly cannot recall the exact contents, but it seemed important to him, and so I signed his letter and was about to settle back to my nap, when the vicar's tone became a little… how shall I put it? Forceful. He became most insistent about knowing the contents of Lord Berkeley's will, and his intentions to change it. Parkin was consumed by the subject; he was most anxious to discover if the church was to receive an increased stipend. Something about a promise made quite recently."

"Was there any indication why this promise was made?" asked Holmes. "Think carefully; it may be important."

"I… yes. Well, it's rather delicate, I suppose. But the vicar was worried about the dwindling numbers at church. What with the state of St Mary's, and the rising fortunes of Madame Farr, Parkin thought Lord Beving—I mean, the new Lord Berkeley, so sorry—would, um…"

"Go on."

"Would squander the family fortune on… and these are his words… 'charlatanry and devil worship.'"

"Good heavens," said I.

"Thank you, Mr Cavendish," Holmes said. "You have been most helpful. Lord Berkeley, did you notice this morning if the vicar had a bag with him?"

"No, he didn't," Crain said, with a distracted air. "I thought he would have returned by now; his things must still be in his room."

"And would you object if we examined his room?"

"No, I would not object at all."

Thus we went next to the vicar's room. I saw at once why he had been so eager to claim it as his own, for it had perhaps the prettiest aspect of all the rooms I had seen so far, with a broad bay window overlooking many acres of forests, fields and hills. It was light and airy, compared to the rather fussy and dark décor of my own quarters, although the bed was small and the furnishings sparse.

Holmes noted that the small table near the bed was arranged with ink, pen and blotter.

"Not violet," Holmes said of the ink. "The vicar favours a sepia blend. The blotter is interesting." He held the page up to the light. "There is little to go on, save the uniform arrangement of blotches. This is suggestive of a repeated pattern, as of someone practising a particular flourish, like the handwriting samplers at school."

He turned now to the rest of the room. The vicar's clothes were folded neatly on the bed, which had been made, and beside which was his brown leather bag, open. Holmes looked to Crain before searching the bag, and Crain nodded assent. Holmes dug around inside, and soon withdrew a slip of paper. It was a note, composed of what looked like newspaper clippings. Holmes read it aloud:

SIR

I HAVE INFORMATION OF GREAT IMPORT TO OUR MUTUAL GAIN. THE CHURCH WILL RECEIVE NOTHING FROM HIS WILL UNLESS YOU ACT. MEET ME IN THE ORCHARD AT SEVEN. COME ALONE.

A FRIEND

"Who do you suppose it is from, Holmes?" I asked.

"Let us see what clues can be gleaned from the composition of the note. Each word has been carefully clipped from a newspaper with a small pair of scissors. Some of the words have been pasted together from several sources. Some of them are taken very obviously from the *Financial News*. Look here—'mutual gain' is a single piece. Page two of the *Financial News* on Thursday last contained an item on the stock market gains of the

South Africa Mutual. If I recall correctly, the headline was the clumsily worded 'South Africa Mutual gains exceed expectation'. The bulk of the words come from *The Times*—you recall we saw a note very much like this in the Baskerville case."

"I remember it all too well," said I, with a shudder.

"There are some words whose type is a mystery to me. 'Orchard', for instance. One might expect such a word to be more common in a local paper, particularly in a rural community such as this. This blend of recent London newspaper and local might point us towards the person who constructed the note.

"Lord Berkeley, does anyone in the household read the *Financial News*?"

"Not that I'm aware of. Father might do—have done."

"But there were no newspapers in his study."

"Nor in his room, that I noticed, when I went for the key."

"Very good." Holmes took a last look at the note. "One more thing springs out. The vicar is not specifically named. One might first wonder if he was indeed the intended recipient, or if he merely came by this note some other way. However, observe that Lord Berkeley is also not mentioned by name. Now we can deduce that matching up clippings to form names proved too difficult in the time available. Therefore this note was pieced together hurriedly."

"Why?" I asked. "What could have been so important?"

"If we knew the answer to that, Watson, we would likely solve the whole case. The note has about it a sense of urgency. I would posit that the vicar received it shortly before dinner last night, which was why he was late. But did the vicar really meet someone in the orchard? Or was this note contrived to get him out of the house? Perhaps that is the answer..."

"What do you mean?"

"The vicar drove himself to the house, you said. And he left on foot… I would like to see his conveyance."

"I don't follow, Mr Holmes," Crain said, frowning hard, as though merely speaking were a struggle. "The note requests the vicar's presence in the orchard. The coach-house cannot be seen from the orchard."

"Precisely, Lord Berkeley," Holmes smiled.

He turned about and strode from the room. I followed at once, with Crain lagging behind. When we reached the hall, Holmes seized on the butler.

"My good man! What newspapers are delivered to this house?"

"We take *The Times* and the *Abingdon Herald* daily, sir; the *Ascot Weekly Journal* each Wednesday, and the *Pall Mall Gazette* each Friday, so Lord Berkeley can keep abreast of London affairs."

"And there are no other London papers? The *Financial News*?"

"No, sir."

"Do you have the *Pall Mall Gazette* to hand, by any chance?"

Eglinton went to the rack near the door and searched through several days' worth of papers. He came back, shaking his head. "No, sir, Lord Berkeley must have taken it to his study."

"It is not there," Holmes said. "If you happen to find it, I should like to know."

Eglinton looked somewhat confused, but agreed that he would tell Holmes as soon as the newspaper turned up. With that, we went out to the coach-house and stable block.

By the time we reached the coach-house, I was deeply concerned about Crain's state of mind. He twitched constantly, and seemed incapable of staying still for more than a few seconds. He looked about himself with a frightened expression, as though he expected to see some assailant leap out at him at any moment. The after-effects of whatever drug he had been taking recently, combined with his grief, were exerting a heavy toll.

We summoned the groom, Benson, to show us the vicar's fly. The man brought a lamp up, for it was now quite dark.

"Benson," Crain said, "this gentleman is going to ask you some questions. Answer him as best you can."

Benson nodded.

"This fly has not been moved all day?" Holmes asked of the groom.

"No, sir. It's not been moved since yesterday, to the best o' my knowledge."

"You mean, when the vicar arrived?"

"No, sir, yesterday evenin', before dinner. I wasn't expectin' any more work that night, so's I was surprised when I heard a carriage leavin'."

"And was it the vicar?"

"Who else, sir?"

"Who indeed?" Holmes said. "I take it the vicar's horse was gone also."

"Why, who else's?" the man asked, wearing a puzzled expression.

"And at what time did the vicar return?"

"Well, that's a funny thing. I 'eard a carriage pulling up… oo, must be shortly 'afore seven. Well, I was in the middle o' my tea, wasn't I? Been interrupted once already, and a man's got to eat. So I pulls on me boots and comes running out, only to see the vicar on the other side o' the courtyard, cutting through the gardens."

"Heading into the house, or away from it?"

"Into it, o'course, sir. He was late for his dinner, wasn't he? I know 'ow he felt…"

"And where were you stationed, my good man?" Holmes asked.

The groom pointed to a collection of sheds and outbuildings, about a hundred yards away across the courtyard.

"And you say the vicar came from the gardens, behind you? So he would have walked around to the front of the house from the east side?"

"Aye."

"He got there awfully quickly, don't you think?"

"Well… I s'pose he did, sir, yes. And him a real neck-or-nothing sort of nag. Like I say, must have been in an awful hurry for his dinner."

"And here we are, keeping you from your meal, I expect," Holmes said.

The man gave us a look suggesting that Holmes was correct.

"You mentioned you had been disturbed once already last night," Holmes said. "By a house-guest?"

Benson only nodded.

"Mr Langton?"

He nodded again, clearly reluctant to speak of it.

"Answer the man," Crain snapped.

"Yessir," Benson mumbled. "Mr Langton came out for a little chat about the horses. Keen on the races, he is."

"Very well," Holmes said. "I need nothing more for now, Benson. That will be all."

The man sidled off, and once he was out of sight I turned to Crain, who had begun swaying, and muttering to himself.

"Crain, are you quite all right?" I asked.

"N… no, Watson, I'm not. Mr Holmes, what does all this mean? Are you saying… are you saying that the vicar had something to do with my father's death?"

"I would suggest no such thing, Lord Berkeley," Holmes replied. "There is something strange afoot, and the vicar is involved, but beyond that I cannot say."

"He was late for dinner last night. Where could he have been?"

"That I cannot say. But if he was preparing for any misdeeds, my lord, why would he not have prepared everything in advance? Why leave at all?"

"To fetch poison?" Crain queried, his voice rising in pitch almost hysterically. "To fetch poison to kill my sister!"

"Do you really think him the type, Lord Berkeley?" Holmes said, calmly. "And from where would a simple vicar obtain this poison? We have not even established what, if any, substance was used on your poor sister. And I still maintain that your father died of a heart attack, brought on by shock."

"The vicar knew about his weak heart," Crain said, his voice now dripping with malice.

"Lord Berkeley, I believe I am very close to bringing our case to a successful close. I ask only for a little more patience."

"Patience!" Crain blurted. For a moment he looked at me as if seeing me for the first time. His eyes were glazed over and bloodshot, underlined with red. His lips were cracked and dry. I guessed that the effect of whatever substance he had taken was wearing off.

"I say, Crain," I said, trying to sound cheerful, "why don't we go back to the house? I think I should take a look at you… it's been a frightful shock."

He pulled away from me angrily. "No," he said. "I think I should like to be alone."

"Lord Berkeley," Holmes said, gently. "It is my view that none of us should be alone just now."

"Hang your view, Mr Holmes! I have tolerated your intrusion, and extended you every courtesy, but any authority I have vested in you does not extend to me, in my own home. Now you keep to your business, and I shall keep to mine."

"Very well, my lord, and I apologise wholeheartedly if I have caused offence. But still I must request that you remain here at

Crain Manor, at least until our friend from Scotland Yard arrives."

"Bah!" Crain growled petulantly, and with that, he stormed from the coach-house.

"His behaviour grows more erratic," Holmes said, rubbing his chin thoughtfully, but otherwise unrattled. "It is likely to deteriorate before it gets better."

"You know?"

"I would guess that whatever he has taken has some kind of hallucinogenic side-effect. Not the usual type of thing one might seek for peaceful oblivion, but some men cannot see sense when their craving calls."

I thought that perhaps Holmes would know that as well as anyone, and perhaps sensing my disapproval he quickly changed the subject.

"These little mounds of white ash on the wall here," he said. "Pipe ash. Bird's eye, if I'm not mistaken."

"That will be Langton," I said. "Bird's eye is his preference."

"A first-rate observation, Watson. Some of these mounds are recent, others older, others still dispersed due to wind and rain. How frequently does he smoke?"

"As if the world's supply of tobacco might soon be exhausted. He comes out here because it's really too much to expose the ladies to."

"There are rooms in which he could smoke."

"I think he's just being polite, Holmes."

"One can think too much," Holmes said. "I must ask Mr Langton just a few more questions, before you and I go in search of the Reverend Parkin."

"I don't know what you mean. I didn't see anything," Langton said, but he kept his voice hushed lest anyone overhear.

"You saw Simon yesterday afternoon—or perhaps Arthur—and it's fair to say he didn't see you, otherwise he'd have been a trifle more careful. A man making such frequent visits to a concealed spot must be privy to all manner of interesting observations. Think hard, Mr Langton, for we are dealing with a case of fraud and probable murder, in which every guest at this house is in some way implicated."

Langton shifted uneasily at this suggestion. He looked about furtively, drew nearer to Holmes and said, almost in a whisper, "Perhaps I did see something, but if a word of this reaches my wife's ears I shall have a bone to pick with you, Mr Holmes."

"She will hear nothing from me unless it is pertinent to the crime, for justice cannot hinge on gentlemen's agreements. Your wife would not approve of the reasons you were loitering in the servants' area rather than the courtyard?"

Langton reddened. "You could say that, yes. Look, Mr Holmes, please keep this between us. I have made some rather poor investments recently, which has made rather a dent in my fortunes."

"I see. At my little show earlier at the expense of Madame Farr, you were outraged that the spiritists had been 'dipping into your private business'. I take it by that you meant your finances?"

Langton wiped a hand over his face. "I have a few letters—final demands, actually—in my bag. It was my intent to speak with Uncle about them; see if he could help me out, you know? Damn it all. My father was a self-made man. We never needed the Crain money, and now a few mistakes have knocked me all out of sorts."

"You understand this gives you motive for murder?"

"What, because Uncle Theobald threatened to name me his heir? But he didn't, did he? He couldn't have had time. It would have been deuced stupid of me to do the old man in before he changed the will. And senseless entirely to harm a hair on

Esther's head. She was the best thing about this family by a long chalk. Dr Watson understands—I saw the way he looked at her. A breath of fresh air, and now…" Langton sniffed, and rubbed at his face again. "Look, Mr Holmes, I'm guilty of a good many things, but murder is not one of them. I'm ashamed, more than you can know. My wife is no longer being kept in the manner to which she has become accustomed, and I think it is only the promise of my inheritance that reassures her of our future. Not that she would wish ill on the Crains, you understand. It's just that, well, if money is tight, we can always call on 'position', so to speak."

I felt a pang of guilt at taking money from Langton over billiards, even if it were just a few shillings.

"And yet you still like to make the odd wager," Holmes said, apparently reading my mind. "These investments, I take it, were not all of the business variety."

"Look, a chap has to speculate to accumulate, Mr Holmes. A few good wins and I'll have recouped enough to settle some bills, maybe even enough to reinvest."

"Your important meeting in Exeter," Holmes said. "Presumably this was not a business meeting, but a race meeting? There is no sport at Ascot this week, just a stone's throw from here, but the afternoon races at the Exeter tracks are noted for their prize coffers."

"You have me again, Mr Holmes. Yes, and yesterday I was meeting the groom, Benson, for some inside information. He stabled some of the runners here over winter; knows the ones that'll defy the odds. All wasted now, of course."

"You have my apologies, but this investigation must take precedence until the killer is exposed."

"You keep talking about murder, Mr Holmes. I still can't bring myself to think my sweet cousin was killed. I mean…

why would anyone do such a thing?"

"That's what I am here to find out, Mr Langton. Now, back to your various smoking sessions…"

"All right, but when I tell you what I saw yesterday afternoon I hope you'll understand why I was reluctant. It has nothing to do with Esther's death, but rather a lot to do with Cousin James's behaviour."

"Go on."

"Yesterday afternoon, shortly after we arrived, I went out to find Benson. I met him last time we visited, and his knowledge of the horses is as good as any Irishman's. Anyway, he was pretty busy at the time, but promised to meet me later. So I had a smoke, and saw Sir Thomas arrive. That put my hackles up a bit, because there's some family history there, the sort we don't speak of."

"Will you speak of it now?"

"If I have your word it is in confidence."

"You have it," Holmes said.

"Well then. Sir Thomas keeps a rather impressive glasshouse at home, in which he grows all manner of… exotic plants, if you take my meaning. And rumour has it he's a dab hand at using said plants to make various potions and preparations—tricks he learned in Africa from some shaman or other. Anyway, after dear Aunt Agnes died, Cousin James went to pieces, and Sir Thomas was the dutiful godfather, very supportive, you know? James must have been desperate indeed, because Sir Thomas furnished him with some root, which is as powerful as any opiate, and it got him through the dark times. But he was hooked, you see; couldn't give the stuff up without an awful time of it. I thought that was ages past, but it looks as if Cousin James has succumbed to temptation again."

Whilst Langton spoke, Holmes's eyes lit up like lamps, and I knew he had gleaned something of great significance.

"You think Sir Thomas has provided more of this African drug to your cousin?"

"Certain of it, Mr Holmes. Minutes after Sir Thomas arrived, I saw him and James take a stroll. They didn't spot me. I was going to greet them, but they began to remonstrate over some private matter. Sir Thomas thrust a small bag into James's hands, and then they walked off in opposite directions. Unfortunately, I wasn't the only one who saw this—that's when I noticed Simon. But he saw me, also, which is what I didn't mention before, and he gave me the queerest smile, as though he had caught me in some illicit act and might use it against me later."

"Did he try to?" I asked.

"I suppose he didn't get the chance, but I half expected him to."

"And you say your cousin had defeated the addiction once?" Holmes said. "But succumbed again?"

"I think so. Madame Farr was a good influence on him in that respect. But with everything that happened…"

"That's just it: Sir Thomas arrived *before* anything happened. Which would suggest your cousin had need of the drug before the death of his sister."

"Oh yes, in all the confusion that hadn't occurred to me. It looks as if he rather pulled the wool over our eyes, then. There is none so wily as an addict." There was something in Langton's eyes that suggested he spoke from personal experience, and I reckoned his own gambling habit had the potential to cost him as dear as any opium fiend's dependence.

"And what about last night?" Holmes asked. "You were smoking before dinner, and met Benson again. He was awfully reluctant to reveal your name."

"I did, and he's a good fellow, though I'm damned if I deserve much in the way of loyalty. To answer your question, I did not see much at all. I had a smoke, and then went to rap on the foot of Benson's hut. He'd promised to find out if Rascal's Crown was still running in the 3.30 today. Ten to one, and to hear Benson talk it was a sure thing. Alas! Anyway, we heard a carriage approaching, and Benson was going to run out, but I kept him from his duty a few minutes longer. When he went outside, I saw him scratching his head because the vicar's fly was in the coach-house, and there was no sign of the horse. He made some remark about it being a strange state of affairs, when we both looked up and saw the vicar fair running around to the east wing. I realised I had tarried too long—that was my cue to leave. I cut through the back door and beat the vicar to dinner—I expect he had to freshen up first after all that running about. Not in the best physical condition, our man of the cloth."

We were interrupted by a noise from outside, the crunch of boots on gravel. Holmes dashed at once to the window, threw it open and looked outside.

"Who was there, Holmes?" I asked.

"I only caught sight of a boot heel and trouser leg, but I think it was Lord Berkeley," Holmes said, closing the window fast. "Confound it all, Watson! The walls really do have ears in this house."

"Well we all know what's got into Cousin James," Langton said. "I say, you don't think he'll tell Constance any of this?"

"Who can tell," Holmes said, though his thoughts were patently elsewhere.

"I'll go after him," Langton said. "It's about time someone talked some sense into him."

"I would appreciate that very much, Mr Langton," Holmes said.

Once Langton had gone, Holmes turned to me. "Watson, did you know about Sir Thomas's botanical interests?" He sounded as serious as ever I had heard him.

"Yes, Holmes, but not in such a euphemistic fashion. A passing mention of his collection, that is all."

"Watson, your failure to mention this fact has hindered the investigation more than you could know. But you are not wholly to blame: I should have summoned Sir Thomas and the Reverend Parkin as soon as I arrived, and questioned them earlier."

"Sir Thomas supplied some addictive drug to his godson," I said, "but I cannot believe him a murderer."

"Nor I, Watson; you do not follow at all. Whoever left the house last night in the vicar's carriage may well have gone to fetch poison. A very exotic African poison, one that would provoke an agonising death, and doubtless be undetectable by any but an expert."

"Someone entered through the passage and poisoned her..." I muttered.

"Most likely."

"But how? Presumably she was asleep. Those needle marks were too old for it to have been injected. Was she forced to imbibe it? Is that why she screamed?"

"All possible. I think it is past time we paid a visit to Sir Thomas. I believe in doing so we will not only find the cause of your friend's strange behaviour, but also at last reveal the cause of Lady Esther's death. Come, let's disturb that fellow Benson again, and see if he will drive us."

CHAPTER TWELVE

SIR THOMAS GOLSPIE

"If you've come to see my collection, Dr Watson," said Sir Thomas, "I cannot stress highly enough the inconvenience of your timing."

Sir Thomas did not look himself. His hands shook, and his eyes darted this way and that, as though he were seeing some threat in every shadow. And his house, cluttered with trophies and ephemera from his many expeditions, had more than its share of shadows.

"That is not why we have come, Sir Thomas. And I can only apologise for the hour, and the unfortunate timing of our visit. We rather hoped you might be able to help us. It's about Crain… and Lady Esther."

"Ah." Sir Thomas wiped a broad hand across his chin. "Then I suppose you'd better come in."

He shuffled along the carpeted hall, leaving Holmes and me to close the door behind us, and follow. We entered a sitting room, in which every wall was covered almost entirely in mounted animal heads, racks of antlers, exotic weaponry, and tribal masks and shields. An antelope hide hung athwart the couch. The floor before the hearth was adorned with the pelt of a lioness, on which an old, white-muzzled deerhound lay, barely concerning itself with our arrival. I wondered if the rug had once been the lion from the stories about Golspie's feats.

"You keep no servants, Sir Thomas?" Holmes asked. I, too, had wondered why Sir Thomas, perhaps not in the best state of mind at present, had answered the door to us himself.

"Just occasional staff. The maid comes in three times a week, and the gardener lives nearby. Mrs Griggs serves as both cook and housekeeper—she lives here, but she's already abed, I imagine. I've no patience with butlers and footmen and all that pomposity. I am a private man, Mr… Holmes, wasn't it?" He poured himself a brandy, and offered us the same. Holmes declined with a raised palm. I accepted thankfully, for the evening had grown cold. "I never had much time for servants," the old explorer went on, a wistful look in his eyes. "You know, on one expedition, to Fuuta Jaloo, there was one chap—Jago Kettering, Watson will know of him—who would not leave camp without a valet in tow, and a butler to serve us all meals under a silver platter. We weren't halfway up Mount Loura before the valet slipped whilst trying to retrieve Kettering's shaving bag from a precipice. We managed to save him, but his leg was broken in three places. Cost us four bearers and two days' trekking, by which time the butler had come down with dysentery. Bet you didn't read about that in Mackenzie's damn book. This is the problem, y'see. Every man on an expedition is selected for his skills. But servants are there to *serve*, both our whims and our vanity. They don't have the training or the experience for anything beyond service. I found long ago that a bit of local knowledge and the sweat of one's own brow is all a man needs to get by."

So visceral and vibrant were Sir Thomas's recollections—so

personal—that it was hard to see him as anything other than an intrepid, steely explorer, rather than the elderly, troubled man who stood before us now.

I sipped my brandy. Holmes was, in his usual way, taking in every detail of our surroundings.

"I must offer my condolences, Sir Thomas," Holmes said. "I understand you were close to both Lord Berkeley and his daughter, Lady Esther."

"Known them for many years, since before Esther was born," Sir Thomas said, his eyes full of sadness. "Theo was a good friend. One of the very best of men. He helped me through some difficult times… and Esther, that wonderful girl. What a waste."

"You understand that she was murdered?" Holmes said, rather too bluntly.

Sir Thomas glowered. "I don't doubt it. James told me the circumstances, and I damned near marched to the manor at once to arrest those 'spiritists' myself. I trust that Farr woman is in police custody by now?"

"She is, though not for murder. Not yet."

"Why the devil not?" Sir Thomas shouted, setting down his glass so forcefully I thought it might break.

"Because there is yet more to this case than meets the eye, Sir Thomas," Holmes said, unbowed. "You have heard the circumstances of Lady Esther's death, I presume? We believe her unusual condition was caused by a drug of some sort. Something that caused her to pass away in a fit of sheer terror. Unless, of course, you believe, as your godson does, that she was scared to death by the sudden appearance of a ghost."

Sir Thomas's rage faded. "No…" he muttered, though I was not entirely sure he was answering Holmes's question. He took a gulp of his brandy.

"This mask… it is peculiar to the tribes of West Africa, is it not?" Holmes said, showing a remarkable knowledge of African exploration that I had hitherto not known he possessed. "It is from your last expedition?"

"It is," replied the old man. "And it is not only the mask of a tribe. It transcends tribal divisions. It is the death mask of the Tagullah."

"I have heard of them," I said. "A secret society, who transform boys into hardened fighting men. I thought they were just stories told by explorers to frighten each other silly."

"I wish they were stories, Doctor. But then again, if the Tagullah were not real, perhaps I would not be here today."

"This did not make it into the Mackenzie Accounts," I said.

"And few people know the story at all—few living at least. Mackenzie is dead, and he was the last of the men on the expedition to know the truth. Theobald knew, but he's gone now. So I suppose that just leaves young James." He poured more brandy, and took a drink. "It was '67. The last time I ever set foot in that region, as it happens. We'd been nine months conducting our survey, and had been dragged into every conceivable danger. We had found ourselves lost in hostile territory near Angola. We were caught in a rockslide that decimated our supplies. We were almost swept away in flash floods on the banks of the Shiloango. One man was so riddled with Guinea-worm he could travel no further with us. You name it, sir, and it befell us. Some whispered that the expedition was cursed, and it put the wind up our bearers, I can tell you. But we came through it all with great resolve. There are new species of plant and animal in the British Museum that are there because of us. There are treatments for yaws, ophthalmia, and even yellow fever that did not exist before we embarked on our expedition. Ten of us set out in the spring of 1866, and all ten of us made it back in the face of extraordinary odds. I was the only one who almost did not.

"We were skirting the edge of the Kalahari, following

a known track, with good guides at our disposal. Without warning, we found ourselves caught in the middle of a battle. A large number of Wasimbu warriors had tracked a party of slavers—depraved men willing to sell their own kind for a little coin and a few good rifles. They had captured a goodly number of women and children under the protection of the Wasimbu, with the aim of sailing them up the coast and selling them to the Portuguese. It was a daring business, so close to the British Cape, and had it not been for the appearance of the Wasimbu, I expect they would have succeeded.

"The battle was bloody, and prolonged. We fought to defend ourselves, and tried to flee. Our baggage was scattered, our party separated. I was chased into the desert by a horseman, taking a bullet to the shoulder as I ran. In desperation, I shot his horse from under him. The beast fell upon me, and the man would surely have killed me had it not been for the intervention of a Wasimbu warrior. I remember looking up into the eyes of my attacker, certain he would be my slayer, only for a spear-tip to pierce him through the mouth. I passed out from pain, and I still do not know exactly what happened next.

"When I came to—the first time, at least—it was night. I was lying on a hard bed, strapped down, beside a blazing fire. There were trees all around. Drums were beating, men and women were whooping and singing in a tongue I did not recognise. I began to hallucinate—the shadows came alive. Tribal masks took on a life of their own, and I remember being gripped by utter terror. I do not know how many days and nights passed in this fashion—I would wake invariably to find some demon-headed shaman rattling bones about me, or a group of wailing women beside me. Once, a man cut off the head of a chicken and dashed its blood over me. I was fed strange herbs that contorted my feverish visions into nightmares beyond imagining. Those nightmares became as real as anything I could discern. It took a long time before I gleaned the extent of my predicament; that although my wound had been treated, in my weakened state I had contracted malaria, and might well die.

"In my fleeting lucid moments, I found someone with whom I could converse, at least a little. A young warrior named Uuka told me that the spirits had come to the tribe's witch-doctor, and bartered for my soul. I belonged to the 'Hungry Night', and should I die, the tribe would pay a thousand times over in misery. My condition was beyond the witch-doctor's power to heal, and there was only one way he could think of to stave off my death. He named four brave warriors, Uuka at their head, and carried me deeper into the jungle, to find the Tagullah society.

"The journey was arduous, and oft-times my guardians thought I would not last the trip, praying desperately to the spirits to spare me. When finally we reached our destination, we were met by a dozen silent, skull-masked warriors, who materialised from the jungle like ghosts. Uuka negotiated with them for some time, and finally they acquiesced. Only then did I learn the horror of my situation. The other three Wasimbu departed, while my stretcher was hoisted aloft by the Tagullah warriors. As I was carried away, I looked back, and could barely moan in dismay as one of the warriors stepped towards Uuka and slew him. I shall never forget his face. He stood there, accepting his fate with nobility as the knife was drawn across his throat. His sacrifice was the price that had to be paid for the service of the Tagullah, because by accepting me into their embrace, they would face great danger on behalf of the Wasimbu.

"And so, in the weeks or perhaps months that followed, I was inducted into the Tagullah mysteries. I saw more of their ways than any white man has ever seen, or perhaps ever will again. Their shamans conducted intricate rituals over me. They fed me potions, stuffed my infected wound with poultices made of herbs and other, fouler things. They cured me of ills that even our own doctors would have been hard-pressed to treat. But it came at a terrible price.

"As soon as my fever broke, I was put through the initiations usually reserved for the young recruits sent each year to the Tagullah enclaves. I was made to drink poisons, and to sleep naked on bare earth, inuring me to the dangers of the jungle. I received my marks of death…" With this, Sir Thomas unfastened the topmost buttons of his shirt, revealing a small glimpse of a puckered, swirling scar upon his chest. "I took part in a ceremony in which I mixed my own toxic brew, which I then had to drink. If I made it correctly, I would suffer a day-long hallucination filled with terrors, followed by a lengthy spell of torpor. If I made a mistake, I would not wake from sleep. Some of the boys alongside me suffered that very fate.

"When I awoke, it was to the sound of drums. I was told by the headman—the Tagullah Devil—that I had died, and had been reborn, and now my soul belonged to the Hungry Night, that pantheon of a thousand demons ruled by Landa, the crocodile spirit, with his bloody jaws, and Ngatadobi, the limbless messenger. I saw those entities as clearly as I see you now. I was renamed Mahlubandile. I was lost in the customs and ways of the Tagullah for an interminable time. I lost all sense of who I was. I was trained as a warrior, painted like a demon, and I took part in ritual acts that I would rather forget, but which I see every night in my dreams. I spent as much time as I could drunk on *pombe*, wondering if I would ever return to my homeland, until finally I forgot my homeland altogether.

"Mackenzie found me, of course. What seemed like a lifetime under the dreamlike influence of the Tagullah had, in reality, been less than four months. Mackenzie had led the expedition to

Cape Town, and had gathered enough men to come and find me. When he did, I did not know him. He said… he said he could not tell me apart from the Tagullah, at first. He said I was mad, and perhaps I was. Perhaps that is why I remember nothing of my journey to Cape Town, or indeed anything until I awoke on the ship a day's sail from the Cape.

"But I never forgot what I became, or the fate that was decided for me by the demons of that land. I learned of the Hungry Night. I saw the spirits and the darkness they bring. I saw things that no man should ever see; things I wish I could… un-see."

"That is why you wanted no part of Madame Farr's séance," I posited.

"You could say that. I have no belief in her petty spiritualism, Dr Watson. But I have every belief in spirits. Oh, I can see in the eyes of Mr Holmes that he thinks me mad. Perhaps I am; but who could not be, under the circumstances? Madame Farr is a dangerous woman, because she knows not with what she dabbles. In my experience the spirits, even the benevolent ones, require a sacrifice. They do not—cannot—assist mortals through any will of their own. They are bound, and they are bound by blood. A sacrifice, Doctor. I have seen… I have seen young boys slaughtered in order to bring back the spirit of a sainted ancestor. I have heard the voices in the Hungry Night, a cacophony of howls, of demons and ghosts, awaiting the spilling of blood, that one of them might be bound to the service of a witch-doctor, and exert their power over our world just for a moment. It is all the spirits can desire. All they can hope for, if hope is even the right word."

I swallowed hard. "You speak of human sacrifice. An exchange of life for… what?"

"For a service. In order for the chief's great-grandfather, or whoever, to bless the crops or imbue the tribe's warriors with wisdom and strength, they must send a willing soul to the other side. The night requires it. What Madame Farr peddles is a fantasy, a yarn spun by simpletons to assure God-fearing men that there is life everlasting. So afraid are we of our own mortality that we embrace any succour, no matter how ridiculous. But let me tell you, gentlemen: we ought to be afraid. During my ordeals among them, I many times prayed for death. But by the end, I prayed for more life. I will hold death at bay for as long as I am able, because when my light is extinguished, it is not the afterlife of a Christian nation that awaits me. It is the enfolding shadow of the Dark Continent, and the cold embrace of the Tagullah's Thousand Demons."

There was deathly silence for a moment. The room had seemed to grow darker and colder as Sir Thomas spoke, and now I could not repress a shudder.

It was Holmes who broke the silence. "What you have described, Sir Thomas, is a rather unusual view of the world, an understanding of blood sacrifice, dark ritual and, crucially, of poison-making. Beliefs and skills that would make you singularly better placed to poison Lady Esther Crain than the likes of Madame Farr."

"Holmes!" I said, aghast at the accusation.

Sir Thomas did not look at all shocked, or angry; only sad. He buttoned his shirt, and took another drink. "You mistake my sharing of a terrible burden for a confession, Mr Holmes. As you will—it is in your nature to be suspicious. I could never have a family, Mr Holmes. How could I? How could I share this darkness with a wife, and children? How could I risk their souls? It is the destiny of the Tagullah to walk a path alone, for otherwise the demons they serve might claim those they care about. It was not a calling I took voluntarily, but it is a calling nonetheless. I take my responsibility to my tribe—yes, *my* tribe—seriously. I use my knowledge to help people where I can, to cure ills, to give counsel. I have used my contacts at the Royal Society to bring a little of Africa home for me, to surround myself with potions and unguents, and all the trappings of a Tagullah wise man. I have vowed that, when my time comes, I will return to the Tagullah, to die as I have lived. Not as Sir Thomas Golspie, but as Mahlubandile. Do you see? No, I did not kill Esther; how could I have? I loved her as dearly as if she were my own daughter. Theobald understood this."

"But the manner of Lady Esther's death," Holmes pressed. "You recognise what I described? You know what might have caused it."

"I know several potions that could achieve the effect, and one in particular, perhaps. And that one can indeed be found in this house. But it is kept under lock and key at all times, and the number of people who would even know what to look for is few indeed."

"Then let us speak of those few people. Not to be indelicate, Sir Thomas, but you were seen yesterday afternoon handing a package to James Crain. It does not require my powers of deduction to work out that you have supplied him with a potent drug, of a sort not often seen in this country."

Sir Thomas's shoulders sank. "You are right, of course, Mr Holmes. But you must know that I was trying to help him."

"How so?"

"The pills are made primarily of the powdered bark of the iboga, with a few minor additions to aid digestion and reduce the more… chaotic… effects that its use can stimulate."

"Ah!" said Holmes. "So you used your own particular brand of medicine to wean James Crain from more conventional opiates?"

"You are correct, Mr Holmes. The use of tribal medicines has barely touched this land as yet, but I have long been aware of their benefits. The iboga is used in ritual magic in West Africa. It is a powerful stimulant and, in large doses, an equally powerful hallucinogen. Crucially, it does not produce the cravings and sickness that one might experience from misuse of, say, opium. Indeed, it has been known, in my experience, to provide some release from the addictive qualities of opiates and their ilk."

I raised an eyebrow at Sir Thomas's use of "experience", but said only, "So Crain had taken to drugs, and you were hoping to cure him of an unhealthy habit, whilst keeping him under their influence?"

"It was working, Dr Watson. When Agnes passed away, James was beyond consoling. He would spend days at a time wandering in her footsteps, doing all the things alone that they used to do together. He was a young man with his life ahead of him, money and influence, but he began to throw it all away. And he used his wealth to acquire opium, in large quantities. You are his friend—you must know this."

I nodded, now feeling very guilty that I had not intervened to help Crain much sooner.

"He would not quit the habit on my account, but I did persuade him to seek oblivion elsewhere. And as soon as he switched from opium to my own preparation, I gradually began to weaken the formula. Now, he is taking half the potency that he needed at first, and barely notices the difference."

"But Crain is addicted," I said. "We have it on good authority that he has never given up his dependence upon this drug."

"That is more a fault of his character, than of the root," Sir Thomas said, sadly. "I have never seen such despair in a man as when James lost his mother. God, we all took it hard—she was a fine woman. The very finest. But James… it gnaws away at him every day, and has done for years. There's a void in that boy that no drug can fill, though not through want of trying on his part."

"What about Lady Esther?" Holmes interjected. "Did she have need of your… 'medicine'?"

Sir Thomas's entire body tensed. "She did not. Esther was always the strong one. She looked after her father, and helped run the estate while James fell to pieces. She busied herself, learning every aspect of a man's business, and was damned good at it too. She was the glue that held the family together, and now..." He turned away from us, that we might not see how affected he was.

"But the circumstances of Lady Esther's death... they are not terribly dissimilar to your experiences with the Tagullah," Holmes said. "You told us that you brewed the fateful potion yourself. You know what would make a survivable dose, and what would be lethal, correct?"

Sir Thomas nodded.

"Then could it be that Lady Esther was poisoned by that very same poison? That she was driven to violent waking terrors, such that her heart would stop?"

"It is possible... No. What am I saying? How could it be possible? I swear that I was not responsible, and no one else could access my stores."

"No one?" Holmes arched an eyebrow.

Sir Thomas turned to us, looking very pale. "Come, I'll show you."

We followed him through the house, past more displays of African ephemera, mannequins adorned with tribal garb, cases full of weaponry, masks and sinister-looking fetishes. We passed by the kitchen, and through to the rear doors, which Sir Thomas swung open to reveal a large glass-house, of a type most unlike any I had seen in England.

Heat and humidity streamed from within. Sir Thomas entered and turned up the gaslights, and at once we were met by an astonishing array of exotic blooms, including many mature trees, wrapped around with creepers. A fine mist rose dreamily from grates in the stone floor. Sir Thomas beckoned us through the aisles between the specimens, past a row of more familiar flowers including, I noticed, lilies of every colour, and finally to a large shrub. From its base, long blade-like leaves protruded in a fan shape, interspersed with delicate red flower clusters. It was perhaps the least impressive of the flora on display, but had clearly been given pride of place.

"This is it, gentlemen," Sir Thomas said. "Probably the finest specimen in England."

"*Boophone disticha*," Holmes said. "The windball plant."

"Very good, Mr Holmes. The scales of the bulb are used in a variety of medicines that I myself take—they often prove a more effective analgesic than anything prescribed by our modern apothecaries. The rest of the bulb, however…"

"Is one of the deadliest poisons known to man," Holmes finished for him. "Leading to its other common name of 'poison bulb'. It is sufficient to bring down a fully grown lion, it's said."

"It can, I have seen it," said Sir Thomas. "Applied to an arrow or dart, it is the most effective weapon of the tribes of Central and Western Africa."

"And the bulbs… where are they?"

"I harvest them each year, very carefully, and store them under lock and key. I am not a careless man, Mr Holmes."

"Oh, I don't doubt it. But when was the last time you saw your stocks of poison bulb, with your own eyes?"

Sir Thomas frowned. "I can see I shall have to prove it to you. Come along then."

Again we followed Sir Thomas, who led us back towards the sitting room, but instead took a right-hand door into a small library. One wall was adorned with glass cabinets, filled with more relics—save for one, which contained eight shelves neatly lined with jars and phials.

Holmes at once perused the labels on the jars. "Sir Thomas,

whatever the outcome of this investigation, I must commend you on a truly first-rate collection. If I had but a sample of some of these compounds, I could fill a good many gaps in my knowledge."

"If you bring Esther's killers to justice, Mr Holmes, you may take what you like."

Holmes bowed, trying not to show how obviously thrilled he must have been at the sentiment. Sir Thomas took up a set of keys and unlocked the cabinet. He then reached to the middle shelf and took out an iron strongbox, placed it on the library table, and unlocked that also.

"My most dangerous ingredients are here," he said. He opened the lid, and searched around for a particular jar. He frowned, shook its contents, and peered at it again. Then he began to shake, first the hands, then all over. He thrust the jar into Holmes's hands, and pulled out several other jars, filled with various different powders. Finding no comfort in what he saw, he staggered to the nearest chair and fell into it, head in his hands. "My God," he croaked. "It is my fault."

Holmes held the jar up to the light. I saw the label neatly written, *Boophone disticha*. The jar was perhaps a quarter full of a brownish powder.

"The contents are depleted?" Holmes asked.

Sir Thomas nodded. "It should be full."

"Who else knows where the drug is kept?"

"A handful of people. Fewer now that two of them are so recently deceased."

"Let me pose the question another way, Sir Thomas. Who among the weekend party knew about the poison bulb?"

Sir Thomas looked up, brow furrowed. "James, of course. Theobald. Esther herself. And I suppose her fiancé, Melville."

"Holmes—" I began, but he cut me short at once. I felt a great anger and excitement wash over me. I had suspected Melville from the start, and had been dissuaded from that opinion only at Holmes's insistence. Did my friend feel guilty that he had perhaps made a mistake for once? I could not tell from his expression.

"The girl," Sir Thomas added. "Judith? Yes, she came here with James several times. Was it she? That witch!"

"Do not excite yourself, Sir Thomas," said Holmes. "Think—the keys. Are there other copies?"

"None."

"And is this set always carried on your person?"

"Most of the time."

"But not always?" Holmes persisted.

"Not when I sleep, but even then they are in my room."

"Very good. Unless one knows what to look for, *Boophone disticha* is virtually undetectable to English science. A tiny amount might induce nightmarish visions. It could, theoretically, be enough to kill someone with a weak constitution. A larger dose would certainly be lethal. We have already discussed what the most potent dose would do. Presumably you have discussed this poison with others in the past. Theobald Crain? His son? His daughter?"

The old man nodded wearily. "Those three are my family. I have told them my story more than once, and have given them the tour of my greenhouse, discussing the various plants there. I can't believe that James would murder his sister, or his father. But who else? Unless… that Farr woman. Or the timid thing who follows James about. Could they have encouraged him to tell my secrets? Damn them!" He tried to stand, and almost fell back down. "I should have left my secrets behind in Africa," he groaned, his flash of anger now turning to despair. "Oh, what have I done? I am responsible!"

"Maybe, or maybe not," Holmes said. "One thing for which you are responsible, however, is the mental state of James Crain.

And given that he is, at this time, acting most abnormally, and is as well versed as anyone in your particular brand of pharmaceutical remedy, a cloud of suspicion blackens around him."

"I say again, James would never harm his sister."

"He threatened to disavow her more than once, and in his disturbed mental state could have decided to do more than that."

"The pills I gave him were helping!"

"The effect on his behaviour is still profound," I said.

"That is not the drug. He is grieving for his entire family. He has never been the most resilient sort, but now… I did not supply him with those pills knowing that we were on the cusp of this tragedy. I would not advise anyone to take such drugs whilst in a state of intense distress. Who knows what he might be thinking?"

"Precisely. One might wonder if James Crain is in the grip of a temporary madness inculcated by a heady mix of despair and iboga pills. But do I think he murdered his sister? It is difficult to say, but I would rather think not—nothing I have heard would truly suggest his quarrel with Lady Esther was sufficient to drive him to murder. One might, however, think he had cause to do away with his father…"

"His father! Preposterous."

"Was the argument between James and Theobald Crain at dinner not typical of their relationship?"

"Of late, perhaps. Again, it comes to that damned Farr woman. Parts of the estate—mostly property in Swinley—were devolved to James to run. He didn't do a bad job, by all accounts, but when he fell in with that accursed woman he signed over the lease on an old cottage to her. That was the first true falling out between father and son. And can you imagine what Theobald thought when that Judith girl practically moved into the manor? That set a few tongues wagging, I can tell you. But Theobald was terrified of losing his legacy. He threatened and postured, but ultimately James always got the better of him, simply by threatening to leave. The Crain family is incredibly wealthy and influential, yes, but it has not been a lucky one. Hence the next male heir in line after James is David Langton, some second cousin, once or twice removed. He's a decent sort, and Theobald likes him well enough, but he would never sign over the lands and title to a self-made man."

"It is interesting indeed that you raise the subject of inheritance," Holmes said. "Someone else at the dinner party was very eager to discuss the contents of Theobald Crain's will. The vicar, Mr Parkin."

"That does not surprise me, Mr Holmes. As it happens, I spoke to Theobald about his will just yesterday, because he had been planning to make an alteration, and wanted my opinion. But it was far from what you might think. I suspected that the vicar had been eavesdropping, because he is obsessed with restoring his church to past glories, with the patronage of the Crain family. Parkin had nothing to worry about, the blithering idiot. Theobald planned to increase the church provision to spite Madame Farr and her cronies. And he planned to grant a sizeable provision to Esther, too; or, rather, to Melville once they were married. Theobald was no fool. He had heard that James had made threats towards Esther, and wanted to ensure that she would be well looked after should the spiritualists drive an insurmountable wedge between brother and sister. He doted on that girl. He… he doted on them both, as did I.

"Look, Mr Holmes, it seems to me that your culprits are now at Crain Manor, and that is precisely where you should be. To my shame I wish my part in this damned affair had been a lesser one, but I think I have helped you all I can."

"Not quite," Holmes said. "You mentioned your housekeeper

earlier. May we speak with her before we leave?"

"My housekeeper? But why?"

"Because, Sir Thomas, while your testimony in a court of law will carry great weight, we still have only opinion and hearsay, which is not enough to identify any murderer. Your housekeeper, on the other hand, might have valuable information, no matter how trifling it may appear, which will help me point to our culprit decisively."

"I should have to wake her."

"If you would, Sir Thomas, I should be most grateful."

With some slight objection, Sir Thomas led the way to the servants' quarters, which I imagined would once have accommodated a modest but busy staff, yet now were little more than a collection of dusty storerooms in the house of a rather lonely old man.

Holmes had insisted we go directly to the housekeeper's quarters, as time was against us. Sir Thomas held up a hand and bade us wait while he knocked on the door, at first quietly, and then loudly.

"Eh?" a muffled voice called out.

"Mrs Griggs," Sir Thomas said loudly. "Are you awake?" He turned to us and said, "I warn you, she's rather hard of hearing. You'll have to speak up when you talk to her."

It took some time for the door to open. To our surprise, the matronly, middle-aged woman before us was already fully dressed, and still wearing her work apron.

"Sorry about that, Sir Thomas," she said. "Fell asleep in my chair again. What is the matter with me? Something you need?"

"Yes, Mrs Griggs. I am sorry to wake you, but these gentlemen here have some questions for you."

"What time is it, sir? Who are these gentlemen?"

Sir Thomas gave a small sigh, but said patiently and

rather loudly, "These gentlemen have some questions for you, Mrs Griggs."

The woman invited us into a small sitting room, within a comfortable little apartment.

Mrs Griggs threw several blankets off the chair beside a dwindling fire, where I imagined she had just been dozing. Sir Thomas at once poked at the fire, and tipped on a few more coals, at which the housekeeper gave a small curtsey. I wondered just how much the woman looked after Sir Thomas, and how much he looked after her.

"Mrs Griggs," Holmes ventured.

"You'll have to speak up, sir, I'm a bit deaf," she said.

"Apologies. Mrs Griggs, I must—"

"I said I'm deaf," she repeated, loudly and slowly, as if Holmes shared her impediment.

Holmes glanced first to me, then to Sir Thomas, but saw no support forthcoming, He smiled politely and almost shouted, "Were there any visitors to the house yesterday, while Sir Thomas was out?"

"Sir Thomas was out yesterday," she said. "At that party. Oh, are you here about Lord Berkeley and Lady Esther? A rum do!"

"Yes, Mrs Griggs. When Sir Thomas was out, did anyone call at the house? Here, at this house?"

"You know, I thought something was funny yesterday. I had one of those all-overish sort of feelings. Got myself in a bit of a fright."

"A fright?" Holmes asked, throwing me a guarded look. "What sort of fright?"

"I was going about my business, must have been about seven o'clock, when I felt a terrible chill, and a cold draught blowin' through the house. And so I has a look about, to make sure as I haven't left a window open or such. And I only went and found the back door open, when I was sure I locked it. I'm getting most forgetful in my old age. And anyway, I locks the door, and goes to check the windows, when… oh, I feel silly now…"

"Please, go on."

"I thought I saw someone, on the stairs. For a minute I thought it was a man, all dressed in black. But then he was gone."

"Did you investigate?"

"Who?"

"I said, 'Did you investigate?'" Holmes shouted.

"O' course I did. I run an orderly house here. Took the dog, just in case; fat lot of good he is, mind. But there was nothing to be seen. Then I remembered what Sir Thomas said before he went out, that them spiritists were at the manor—that Madam Tar, or whatever her name is. Trumped-up madam, if you ask me. Anyway, I thought if they're up to their funny business again, it's ever likely we have strange goings-on."

"And the dog… you say he detected nothing?"

"Eh?"

Holmes now turned in frustration to Sir Thomas, who positioned himself on Mrs Griggs's other side, presumably at her good ear, and carefully enunciated, "Did Nelson detect any intruder, Mrs Griggs?"

"Oh, him? Well, he was acting all strange, like. He ran back downstairs, left me all alone, and me thinking we might have a burglar in the house! I know he's in advancing years, sir, but really. Anyway, when I came downstairs again, he was just standing by the front door, whimpering. I looked out the window and I saw the vicar driving past. Mind you, I thought that was funny, because Sir Thomas mentioned the vicar was due at the party. He must have been very late for dinner."

"Mrs Griggs," Holmes said, in his crispest tone. "You see this set of keys?" He signalled to Sir Thomas, who took out the keys and held them aloft. “You know where these are usually kept?”

“Yes, sir,” she said. “In the japanned box under the master’s bed.”

“And have you ever told anyone else about those keys?”

“Eh?”

“I said, does anyone else—” Holmes stopped in his tracks, his attention taken by something over the woman’s shoulder.

He at once moved past her and Sir Thomas, to the mantelpiece.

“Mrs Griggs, who is this?” Holmes asked, though not loudly enough, drawing a befuddled frown from the housekeeper.

“Oo, a lovely photograph, isn’t it? A gift from Sir Thomas some two Christmasses past.”

“That is Mrs Griggs’s daughter, Sally,” Sir Thomas intervened.

“What about Sally?” Mrs Griggs asked.

Holmes picked up the photograph and showed it to me, before saying to Sir Thomas, “That is Esther Crain’s lady’s maid.”

“She is,” Sir Thomas said.

“Oh, my Sally will be inconsolable,” Mrs Griggs chimed in. “She doted on that Crain girl.”

“My God, Holmes…” I said.

Holmes set down the photograph. “Sir Thomas, did you not think to mention this earlier?”

“Why should I?” replied Sir Thomas.

“Sally Griggs visits this house, I take it.”

“Of course she does. Any respectful girl should visit her mother regularly.”

“Everything now makes sense, or at least begins to. Sir Thomas, you must excuse us. Mrs Griggs, I know you can’t hear a word I’m saying, but thank you for your time. Watson, we must away, and quickly.”

Holmes marched from the room, leaving me to shrug an embarrassed apology to Sir Thomas. Moments later we were at Benson’s coach.

"Back to the manor, my good man!" Holmes ordered. We climbed inside. I looked back to see Sir Thomas, silhouetted in the light from his hallway. His shoulders were dropped, his head bowed. As he shuffled inside, and closed the door upon the night, I fancied he looked half the man.

"Holmes," I said as the coach pulled away, "you must now see that Melville is guilty of murder. I know you suspect that Mrs Griggs saw an intruder creeping about the house. Melville had enough time to take the vicar's fly to Sir Thomas's house, to find the key in its hiding place, as instructed by Sally, to steal the poison bulb, and return to the manor."

"And the dog?"

"The… Well, the dog knows Melville. It would not raise an alarm, although to hear Mrs Griggs the dog is docile anyway."

"Watson, you are correct on every count. Save one."

"Oh? And which is that?"

"Melville did not kill Lady Esther."

"This is absurd. You admit that it was he who stole the poison. What other reason could there be?"

"None, it would appear. But he is not guilty of murder. I would stake my reputation on it."

I sighed loudly. "I trust we are going to put an end to this affair now?" I looked out of the window as the sky reddened. I could barely face another night at Crain Manor.

"We can but hope, Watson. I almost have everything I need. Almost."

CHAPTER THIRTEEN

A SUSPICIOUS DISAPPEARANCE

As we approached the gates of Crain Manor, we were greeted with an unexpected scene. Three figures were out on the road ahead of us, silhouetted black upon a lane turned blood red by the setting sun. Holmes poked his head from the window as the coach rumbled to a full stop. Presently, two people approached—Langton and, to my surprise, Judith, breathless and worried looking.

"What is going on?" Holmes asked.

"Mr Holmes, thank goodness you're back," Langton said. "We've been worried sick! It's Cousin James—he's gone."

"Gone where?" I asked, at once concerned.

"That's just it, we don't know. After you two left, I tried to talk to him, but we only ended up arguing. He said a great many strange things about murder, and ghosts, and something about Mr Parkin being a worm in the bud, or words to that effect, and then he stormed off. A few minutes later, he drove off in the vicar's fly at a terrific speed, and we haven't seen him since."

The third member of the little search party came up to the

coach, and we recognised Hardacre, holding a lantern against the failing light.

"And you're only just looking for him now?" Holmes said sternly.

"We didn't know what to do, or where he'd gone. That is, until… well, it's going to sound a trifle strange…"

"After everything I've heard today, Mr Langton," said Holmes, "I rather doubt it."

"Very well. Judith here attracted our attention. She'd been confined to the morning room with Madame Farr, and I must say that while that harridan has been wailing and gnashing her teeth the whole time, Judith has been a model prisoner. Indeed, we had all decided that she really didn't need to be held prisoner at all. And so when she started calling to us, we rather thought we should listen. And, well… you tell him, Miss."

Judith looked about, as though she were most unused to receiving attention at all, and said quietly, "I had a premonition, about James—I mean, Lord Berkeley. I think he's in terrible trouble. I can't explain it. I just, sort of… know."

"Some of us were quite incredulous, as I'm sure you'll understand," Langton said. "But none of us could deny how queerly Cousin James had been acting, and when he didn't come back after an hour we all started to worry. Judith here knows a place by the river where James sometimes goes, and so we were just on our way to organise a proper search when you came along. I'm very glad you did, because it'll be dark before long and I didn't fancy stumbling across the fields on foot."

"It seems to me," said Holmes, "that the first place Lord Berkeley would have gone is to the village."

"The village? But why?"

"Because of what he said about the Reverend Parkin. With fragments overheard at the coach-house earlier, he must have assumed that Mr Parkin was the one who fetched the poison and killed his sister."

"My word… he has gone to exact revenge!"

"Yes, and if my suspicions are correct, he will do so against an innocent man. Mr Langton, might I impose upon you to stay here, and help young Aitkens keep an eye on the prisoners? We shall need Constable Hardacre here to come with us, and Aitkens might not manage alone. Judith—you can come with us also, for despite the part you have played in his deception, I fancy you know him better than anyone alive. Come on, now! We must intervene before Lord Berkeley does something foolish."

When we reached Swinley, night had fallen almost entirely, and as the weather was still drear, most villagers had retreated to their homes, or to the local pub. Benson drew our carriage to a halt outside the vicarage. There was a single light burning within, which at first gave us hope that nothing was amiss, but that hope faded when we were greeted by an elderly housekeeper, who informed us that the Reverend Parkin had not returned "Since leaving to visit that Madame Farr woman up the lane."

"Did he say that was where he was going?" Holmes asked.

"No, but you can see the house from here. Look." She pointed vaguely in the direction of a narrow lane that wound uphill. "The vicar must be very busy today on his rounds. And you are the second gentleman to come asking for him today."

Holmes shot me a glance, and said to her, "Who was the other, if I might ask?"

"Why, Lord Beving of course. Or is it Lord Berkeley now? Oh, I do get confused with all this Lord this and Marquess that. Anyway, you must know that his father and sister both passed away today. And considering what a terrible shock it must be, he came personally to bring Mr Parkin his fly. Don't know why Mr Parkin left it behind. He doesn't often partake too much of drink, but perhaps last night he had one or two sherries too many and thought it best to walk. Anyway, I said—"

"I'm terribly sorry to interrupt, madam," Holmes said, as the woman had barely taken a breath, and seemed as though she would launch into another diatribe at the drop of a hat. "We really must go, our business is most urgent. Goodnight."

He doffed his hat and we both returned to the coach, the housekeeper's mouth working silently as she tried to work out whether or not Holmes had been rude to her.

Moments later, directed by Judith, we drew up outside Madame Farr's abode, which was also apparently the headquarters of her fledgling spiritualist church. It was a modest cottage, of the kind reserved for labourers from the estate workshops—I wondered now if Crain had made a gift of the dwelling to Madame Farr, and whether this had driven a further wedge between him and his business-minded father.

We alighted from the carriage and approached the house. The curtains of the neighbour to the left twitched.

"I feared we would have to break down the door," Holmes said, "but it appears someone has beaten us to it."

Holmes pushed the front door, which swung open with a creak into a dark passage. With no gaslights to be seen, Holmes lit his dark-lantern and stepped over the threshold, sweeping his light to and fro, before settling on the room to his right, which he entered.

"Watson!"

I hurried into the house, Judith almost pushing in ahead of me despite her slight stature, and Hardacre close behind. Holmes was standing in the centre of a living room, lantern now unshuttered, casting its yellow light over a scene of great disturbance.

Furniture was overturned. One of the curtains had been

torn from its pole. The coal scuttle was toppled, its contents spilled across the hearthrug. Papers, books, cushions, broken ornaments, cups and bottles were strewn across the floor. Near the fireplace, a tall, black cabinet lay on its side, coffin-like—I recognised it as a medium's "spirit cabinet".

That there had been a struggle here was obvious; whom it had involved, less so.

"We must search the house at once," Holmes said, "lest there be enemies lying in wait. Here, Watson, I took the liberty." Holmes drew from his pocket a revolver. He handed it to me and said, "You go upstairs. I shall look down here. Constable, do not disturb anything in this room."

I ran upstairs at once, flinging open each door, but finding not a soul, alive or dead. In what I assumed to be Madame Farr's room, however, I found a bookcase, stuffed to bursting with ledgers and papers. I took one out and flipped through the pages, and my stomach lurched.

The book contained page after page of neatly rendered biographical data. Each included a name, followed by age, physical description, significant family members, the dates of readings and spiritualist meetings, and sundry notes. Some pages were partly blank, others filled with minutiae.

I was overcome by a sudden epiphany, and pulled out more of the ledgers, flicking through the pages of each, scouring them for familiar names.

"Watson!" The voice of Holmes came from the stairs, but I was too engrossed. "Watson," Holmes said again, and now he was in the room with me. "What have you there?"

No sooner had he said it, than I found what I was looking for. A fresh page, headed "Watson, Dr John H." I scanned the few details, and turned the ledger to Holmes.

"This is how it was done," I said. "She keeps a record of all her victims, past and future. Every scrap of information she can use is written here."

Holmes looked at the page intently. "Brother, Henry. Father, deceased; name? And here: these are conversations with Crain. 'Ordered flowers for Watson and Mary's wedding. Two-score white lilies; Mary's favourite.'"

"I had forgotten those flowers had come from Crain," I said, glumly. "Mary was always so good with that sort of thing, writing thank-you cards and what-have-you. I never really paid attention to the details."

Holmes flicked through the books as I had done, his brow furrowing more deeply with each turn of a page.

"Oh dear, Watson. This will have to be seized as evidence, but it is rather like prying into people's most private thoughts. The section on James Crain is copious. Of particular interest is his closeness to Sir Thomas Golspie. Many visits to Sir Thomas are recorded—that will be Judith's intelligence, I'm sure. It says here, 'James's dependency on Sir Thomas grows. Must stop.' What do you suppose that means?

"And here are notes about Mr and Mrs Cavendish. It says Mr Cavendish had some quarrel with his now deceased former partner-at-law. And here, ah… they lost their child in a boating accident. Madame Farr has written in the margin, 'Boy or girl?'"

"That's right," I said, still reeling. "She asked Jane Cavendish rather leading questions to that effect. She established it was a boy, Charles. She spoke of guilt… Good God, Holmes, this is wicked!"

"Wicked indeed. Is there anything else of import here? I am loath to delay, but this is an opportunity to gather evidence in case that Cole fellow returns. Ho, what's this?"

Holmes had crouched to look under the bed, and now dragged from beneath it a metal box. It was locked, but that had not stopped Holmes before. The lock was a simple one, and a strong blade and the right technique soon had it open. Within was paper money amounting to some fifty pounds, and a bundle of letters and folded documents.

"There's no time to sift through all this now," Holmes said, "but I think I see at last what Mrs Mellinchip's plan was. She has fooled us all, it seems."

"Whatever do you mean?"

"I mean, we have here correspondence from some relative in the United States—the names are disguised, but the salutations would suggest sisters or perhaps cousins. And here we have a variety of steamer timetables. Look, Atlantic crossings from Liverpool, Bristol and Halifax. Everyone assumed that the mysterious Madame Farr was trying to found a spiritualist mission here in Swinley, to grow wealth and influence and spread the word of her cause. What if her motives are even more selfish than that? We now know she is a criminal evading justice—and analysis of these letters could well help me prove that beyond any doubt. Why would she risk staying here, even under an assumed identity, and remain in the public eye? Better to flee, as far away as possible, to the home of spiritualism."

"You're right, Holmes. I expect you've squared the circle there."

"I expect so, too." We both looked up to see Judith, trembling, eyes moistening with tears, her mouth set most tightly. "You are right, Mr Holmes. You have been right about everything. Madame Farr persuaded me to pass on everything that James told me in confidence. And, for the most part, I did, not out of any desire to defraud the Crain family, but out of love. By assisting Madame Farr in her readings, I helped bring comfort to James, don't you see? The more convincing she sounded, the more consoled James was. But I never knew any of this. I never knew about this… Mrs Mellinchip. And I only helped her because I believed she had some real power, and wanted to form a church for the good of the community. Never for a moment did I think she was… was…"

"A common thief?" I snapped.

Judith nodded.

"Well, now you know," Holmes said to her, and less unkindly than I felt she deserved. "Let's gather these things up and hand them to the constable. Watson, I need you to come with us now—there is quite the scene downstairs."

Holmes led me back to the sitting room. He stepped carefully over the detritus and righted every candlestick he could find, lighting them to further illuminate the scene. He moved around the spirit cabinet, and peered inside momentarily.

"Melville mentioned that spirit cabinet to me," I said. "It was used in the séance that Lady Esther tried to upset. She was deceived by the Cole twins, and never knew it."

I looked to Judith, who said nothing, but only dabbed at her eyes with a kerchief.

Holmes stooped to snatch up some small, gleaming item of polished silver that I had not noticed. I had no time to ask what it was, before Holmes strode directly to a door in the corner of the room, where what I had taken for a pile of laundry lay in a heap. Holmes picked up a large, lumpen sack, and two pieces of torn, crumpled paper beside it, and brought them over to us that we might see.

"It is strange," he said, "that we entered via an open front door, while at the back of the house there are clear signs of forced entry. Two people clearly fought in here, though neither thought to remove this evidence. Evidence which was earlier seen by Lord Berkeley himself being carried by Mrs Mellinchip's associate, Mr Cole.

"I believe I can predict the contents of this sack without even opening it, for its singular incongruity with its surroundings mark it as the very item Mr Cole was seen carrying from the manor this afternoon. But, for the benefit of Constable Hardacre, I shall not rely on stage tricks to reveal the evidence herein, but rather on the credulity of our own eyes. So!"

Holmes tipped up the sack, and out tumbled what resembled the contents of a theatre's costumery. I felt sick to the pit of my stomach, even though I had already guessed what we would see.

A white dress, shimmering luminously even now; another dress, this one of brightest scarlet; a black veil; a bizarre contraption of springs, straps and metal poles, resembling a calliper; an unruly coil of fishing wire; and finally, assorted rags and scrubbing-brushes, some of which sparkled in the candlelight.

"Surely now, Holmes, you will admit that you were wrong," said I. "The Red Woman's dress, plain as day! The spiritualists must have an undisclosed accomplice—another woman. Didn't someone suggest earlier that Judith herself might have a twin?"

"And I said before that it was unlikely. Besides, she is a local girl, is she not? It would be a trifle to ascertain the truth. As for another accomplice, it would be difficult to come and go in and out of a busy household like that. Not impossible, but nearly so. Cole only managed it because of his identical twin. Another girl would have to be almost a ghost herself. What say you, Judith?"

"I have never seen that dress before," she answered meekly, "save for the night when the Red Woman appeared. And there is no one else in our circle, save for Madame Farr, Simon and Arthur, and myself."

"A likely story," I grumbled, ignoring the girl's glare.

"No, Watson—set aside your personal feelings for the moment. I have a theory about this, which even now takes shape in my mind. And I tell you that, on balance, it is unlikely the spiritualists were responsible for the appearance of the Red Woman."

"Holmes, please forgive me, but I think you are now guilty of clinging to a theory in the face of overwhelming evidence."

Holmes smiled. "Then I shall, ultimately, be guided by every immutable fact that science can provide. From chemical testing of the luminous paint on the dress against that found on Judith's slipper, to the certain residue of paint from the window-frame of the drawing room left behind on that fishing line. I shall comb every detail, and no court in the land will be able to ignore such forensic scrutiny of observable evidence. Mrs Mellinchip might like to ask the spirits for advice on this matter, but I imagine she will find them rather wanting in the face of sound logic and rational deduction. But that evidence, Watson, will also show some irregularities, I am certain. And in those irregularities, we shall get to the bottom of this mystery."

I sighed at Holmes's stubbornness.

"Beggin' your pardon, sir, but what about this mess?" Hardacre asked. "What happened here?"

"The clue lies with this," Holmes said, unfolding the torn papers he had found on the floor. He smoothed them out, and held them aloft together, to reveal two parts of a whole parchment, upon which was printed "Last Will and Testament: Codicil". "Whoever was involved in the fracas here doubtless fought not over the evidence, but over this. And I believe that our friend Mr Cole was not involved—not unless he was somehow subdued. Otherwise, the sack would not have been left in plain sight for us to find. No, Constable, I think I know what has happened here, and by the time we return to Crain Manor I shall have a full explanation for you. But first, we must locate Lord Berkeley." At that, Holmes handed me a small, silver box. Its lid was engraved with a pair of intertwined snakes, crudely rendered in bold, zig-zag lines.

I opened it, and although it was empty, there was some

powdery residue, with a strange, herbal scent.

"You recognise it, Watson?"

"It is identical to Sir Thomas's snuff-box." I spun the little box around and saw on the underside the engraved letters "J. H. C." "Crain's initials," I muttered.

"Yes. And therefore it is not used as a snuff-box, but as a pill-box."

"Yes, I suppose it is. I do not recognise whatever this is within though. I expect it is a residue from the iboga pills that Sir Thomas made." I passed the box back to Holmes.

"So you see," he said, "we can now place both Crain and Parkin here. The vicar was last seen following Mr Cole. And we know that he was snooping around the late Lord Berkeley's study. I think this codicil is a forgery, and a rather hasty one at that. Look." Holmes held up the paper to the light from the window. "The document has been recently drawn, and although the penmanship is very fine, it was done with no real eye for detail. A learned hand, but not that of a master forger. The signature of Lord Crain is close to the hand I observed in Lord Berkeley's study, but the flourishes are all wrong. The curves have been made slowly, by someone copying a signature too carefully, without the requisite practice—you can tell by the uniform concentration of ink—a sepia blend, such as we found in Parkin's room. Lord Berkeley would have made this mark in a quick sweep. I could make a comparison with those bills of lading back at the house, but I am as certain as I can be that this is a forgery, and a poor one.

"The second signature is Cavendish's. Another forgery, taken from the letter that Parkin asked him to sign last night. It is too blatant a deception to hold any water at all in court, for Cavendish would surely deny ever having signed it. We shall of course ask Cavendish later to compare this document with Lord Berkeley's real will, and such a direct comparison will doubtless be required by a court. For now, it is a trifle to assume that this was written by the Reverend Parkin, and the amateurishly direct stipulations would support the theory. Look here: 'In recognition of the great service done to my son, James, Madame Adaline Farr, of Swinley, is to receive fully half the provision formerly reserved for the Church of St Mary's, as stipulated in my Last Will and Testament.'"

"Why on earth would the vicar demand such a thing?" I asked. "Does this not run counter to his desires?"

"Of course it does, Watson. Why else would it be here? If it were genuine, the precise sum would be listed, not some oblique reference to the master document. Parkin knew that the codicil would be found a forgery. He wanted to hide it here in Madame Farr's home, to be discovered by the police."

"Really? But the struggle... perhaps he—or whoever forged the document if not he—merely dropped it during some fracas."

"Let us assume for now that this codicil did belong to Parkin. Why would a document in the possession of the vicar, and a bag of incriminating evidence carried by Mr Cole, both be left behind in this house?"

"I don't like to think Crain could be involved in such a sorry business, Holmes," I said. "For all we know, the two men chanced upon each other in the house, and the vicar bested Cole. He might have left before Crain even got here."

"Do you think that possible? The description you gave of the vicar was indicative neither of athleticism nor belligerence. And then what? Did he kill the man and drag the body away somewhere?"

"I suppose he could have..."

"Watson, I fear you are allowing your loyalty to your friend to cloud your powers of deduction. There is a simple way to find out for certain. Did you see the neighbour spying on us as we approached?"

"I did."

"Then let us see what she has to say."

Moments later we were standing outside the neighbour's cottage, waiting for the hesitant, shuffling footsteps on the other side of the door to reach us. Soon a bolt was withdrawn, and the door opened to reveal a beady eye fixing us warily.

"Madam, I am Mr Sherlock Holmes, and this is my friend Dr Watson." Holmes tipped his hat. No response was forthcoming. "We are here on a matter of the utmost urgency, as part of a criminal investigation," he continued, unperturbed. "We believe you may be of singular assistance to us."

"Me? Why?" The old woman's voice was thin and sharp as a blade.

"Because, madam, you strike me as an observant and shrewd woman, and a good neighbour, who might take an interest in the comings and goings hereabout. One never knows when there is mischief afoot."

The door opened a trifle wider, revealing more of the woman's wizened features, and the dingy cottage behind her, the mirror of Madame Farr's.

"Living in such proximity to Madame Farr, I suppose you cannot fail to have overheard a commotion earlier today?" Holmes said.

"Always queer sounds coming from next door," the woman said. "Rapping and bumping—it's the spirits, so they say."

"And what do you say, Mrs—?"

"Dallimore. I say I'd rather not court such things, for good or for ill. So I keeps me own counsel on the matter, 'n' that's that."

"Very wise. But earlier—something perhaps even more unusual. A fight?"

"Aye, I heard it."

"But you did not report it to the police?"

"I did not. And if it's all the same to you, I'd rather not be involved now, neither."

"I understand entirely, Mrs Dallimore. But trust me when I say that this is of the utmost importance. You will suffer no recrimination for helping us."

"How can you say that?" The woman scowled. "There's higher powers round here than the law."

"You mean, perhaps, the Crain family?"

I glanced askance at Holmes, and Mrs Dallimore looked rather caught off-guard.

Holmes adopted a more soothing tone. "Mrs Dallimore, please. A great tragedy has befallen that family, as you may well know. Passions are running high, and even the best of men might be driven to rash action. We wish only to help restore order, and you may speak to us in the utmost confidence. Please, Mrs Dallimore, we would be indebted to you for any information you could share."

"How indebted?" the woman asked, brazenly, her eyes narrowing rather slyly.

Holmes sighed, and fished around in his pocket. "I can offer the sum of four shillings."

"Make it five."

Holmes nudged me, and with an even greater sigh I handed over a shilling from my billiards winnings.

"Start at the beginning, Mrs Dallimore," Holmes said. "Leave out no detail."

We stood on the doorstep, the door providing a barrier between us and the reluctant witness, as she recounted the facts according to her recollection. She had seen "that queer fellow", meaning Simon, return to the house shortly before two in the afternoon, and soon after leave again through the back gate. She had not seen him since. Not long after, the vicar had arrived. He had loitered for a few minutes, before trying first the front door and then the back. Mrs Dallimore was not sure if the vicar had entered Madame Farr's house or not, but half an hour later she'd heard "the most awful hue and cry", which she had first mistaken for one of Madame Farr's rare daytime séances. Mrs Dallimore claimed she saw or heard nothing more, until she was alerted by the sounds of the vicar's carriage leaving the vicinity—but of course, Holmes and I both knew that the vicar had not arrived in his fly. When she looked through the window, she saw the vicar and James Crain driving off. The only unusual detail she recalled was that Crain had been the driver.

"One more thing," Holmes asked, as we were about to take our leave. "How long have you lived next to Madame Farr?"

"Oh, about a year, maybe less. Since his nibs moved her in here. Used to be Frank Higginbotham's place, this, but he died. I s'pose it's been nice for Frank to have someone to talk to. He never did like living alone. 'Spect I'll be able to ask him meself, afore long."

"Now do you see, Watson?" Holmes asked as we gathered near the coach. He kept his voice low so that Benson might not overhear. "Let us piece together the sequence of events. Cole, whichever of the twins it was, arrived back at the house and deposited the bag of evidence. He exited soon after along the back lanes. His intention could only be either to escape, or to return to Crain Manor in the hope of receiving some instruction from his mistress."

"Or to free his brother," I said.

"A real possibility," Holmes nodded. "If he did so, he would have seen us confine his brother, and leave the house. Let us hope in that case Constable Aitkens has his wits about him. Still, with a house full of staff on the lookout, I don't fancy the man's chances of slipping through."

"So back there… The vicar?" I prompted.

"Yes. Our man Parkin had followed Cole all the way here. That he tried to sneak into the house would suggest he knew Cole had already left, for it would be folly to accost a known criminal directly. Parkin probably came down the back lane and saw Cole leaving, which gave him the opportunity to enact his plan. We know Parkin did not approach the house immediately. He watched from a safe distance until sure Cole would not return. He was seen approaching the front door. There are several narrow paths adjoining the two roads, as you can see here. Parkin must have doubled around in order to lend an air of innocence to his visit; a rural clergyman can rarely go anywhere in his parish without attracting some notice, after all. He would have found the front door locked, and realised he was being observed by Mrs Dallimore. And so he went around the back, out of sight of the neighbour, and loitered for a short time, before dislodging a window and entering the property.

"The vicar intended to leave the codicil somewhere obvious, to be found by the police. He must have deduced that we would come here eventually to make a search. While looking for a likely place to stow his forgery, however, he would have come across the bag of evidence. Now this was a good find indeed, for the red dress of the so-called Lady Sybille would certainly have looked like the proverbial smoking gun. Remember he was inside for half an hour at least before any commotion was heard—I expect curiosity may have got the better of him, and he made a search of the house, much as we did. Indeed, upon finding the ledgers, too, he may even have considered abandoning his plan entirely, for if the authorities were to find all that evidence, they might naturally assume that the spiritualists murdered Lady Esther.

"What happened next is less certain. Either your friend Crain has a key to Madame Farr's house, or else he ran into Parkin as the vicar was leaving. In any case, Crain arrived in the vicar's fly, and became aware that Parkin was already inside. He forced the vicar back into the house, and an argument took place. Crain must have seen the codicil, and guessed what had happened given our conversation with him earlier in Lord Berkeley's study. If the vicar was upstairs nosing through those ledgers, Crain would have had time to read the forged document, perhaps not even knowing that Parkin was still in the house. Parkin, meanwhile, might have been terrified at the sound of someone else entering, thinking perhaps the thuggish Cole had returned.

"In a rage, Crain tore the codicil in twain, crumpled it up and tossed it aside. To Crain, whose mind was already made up, this was all the evidence he needed. In his mind, the vicar was framing Madame Farr for a crime he had committed—Crain has spent a good deal of time in that woman's thrall, don't forget, and would want nothing more than to believe her innocent of all charges. At this point, Parkin must have tried to escape the house, or made some noise that caused the paths of himself and Lord Berkeley to cross.

"Imagine if Parkin had shown Crain the bag. Even though Crain himself saw Cole carrying the bag when he left Crain Manor, he would now have just cause to doubt Cole's guilt. He might think Parkin had brought the dresses along, and stashed them in the bag. Crain must surely have known that the other items belonged to Madame Farr, but better to believe her guilty of a few parlour tricks alone, than guilty of killing his sister.

"More angry words were exchanged, and Crain attacked Parkin. The next we know, Parkin is bundled into his own fly, and Crain drives them both off."

"And to what end? Do you think Crain would do something… terrible… to the vicar?"

"I barely know Lord Berkeley, save the haunted, grieving wreck I encountered today," Holmes said, flatly. "He is your friend, Watson. Do you think him capable of murder?"

"No," I said, although I doubted my own words. Crain had been quite unlike himself earlier; I had never seen him so troubled, even in the darkest days. I forced more confidence into my words: "Not murder. Never that."

"Then we must believe the vicar is alive, and that we have time to find them both," Holmes replied. "We have tarried here quite long enough. Judith, you think you know where he would go?"

"There is only one place I can think of. An abandoned cottage by the river, which was very dear to him when his mother was alive."

"And do you know a path by which our coach may reach it?"

"We can go most of the way, yes, but then we must take a path on foot, by the old mill."

"Aye," said Hardacre. "I think I know it."

With that, we loaded the evidence into the carriage, lest Cole return to the house, bundled ourselves inside, and went on our way once more.

CHAPTER FOURTEEN

AN EYE FOR AN EYE

The coach was eventually forced to stop. Ahead of us, blocking the way, was a small two-wheeler, its horse still limbered; it was the vicar's fly. The road beyond it was so overgrown that further passage was impossible. We disembarked, paying our reluctant driver an extra half-crown to turn both coaches about, and see to the vicar's horse. That done, Holmes lit a lantern, and Judith led the way up a muddy track, over a footbridge that spanned a narrow stretch of river, and on towards an old watermill, which stood dark and silent on the north bank.

"This mill is disused?" I asked.

"Yes," Judith replied. "A new mill was built some ten years ago, a mile upriver. My father used to work there before he... Anyway, this one should have been pulled down before now, but I expect the work was too expensive for Lord Berkeley's tastes. James's father, I mean."

I wondered perhaps if her father had passed away, resulting in her conversion to spiritualism. Then I recalled her earlier contempt for her family name, and suspected something deeper.

"Is the cottage much further?" Holmes asked.

"Not much. It is the old miller's cottage, just behind that pasture there. It is in a worse state than the mill itself, fit to fall down. But that is a different prospect—it is special to James, and I expect he would have protested most strongly had his father tried to demolish it."

"You and the new Lord Berkeley must be close," Holmes said. "I note that you call him by his Christian name; though not always whilst in his presence, I would think."

Judith looked back over her shoulder at Holmes, a bashful look on her youthful features. "Well perhaps he… is special to me. Though he does not know it."

"Crain's will is focused in a singular direction," said I. "When a man makes a particular study his obsession, there is none so blind." I glanced at Holmes; if he inferred anything pertinent to his own nature from my observation, he did not acknowledge it.

We climbed a rickety stile, and made across an overgrown pasture behind the mill. A barely trodden trail wended round its edge, terminating at another stile. Only upon reaching it did we glimpse the cottage through the dark trees, and see the flicker of a meagre light at one of the windows. A strange sound carried on the night air, distinct against the creaking trees and the call of night-birds. We listened intently, and it came again; the muffled cry of a man.

Holmes cocked his head like a hound, then hissed, "Come on!"

He bounded over the stile and raced to the cottage, his long limbs so suddenly and swiftly springing to action it was as though they were charged with electricity. I struggled to keep up with him, though I considered myself fleet of foot, and Judith soon dropped behind as we sprinted away.

I reached the back door seconds behind Holmes. He tried

the handle; the door opened, and Holmes vanished inside without waiting for me, just as another muffled cry rang out from the gloom.

"Holmes!" I hissed, but to no avail. He had decided to throw caution to the wind, and I had no choice but to follow.

I saw my friend take a set of stairs three at a time, lantern-light swinging across grimy plaster and exposed brick. I raced up after him, putting my foot through a rotten tread in the process, crying out in alarm despite myself. At once I felt a hand at my arm, and Judith was there, helping me as best she could to get free. There was no time to delay; I clambered to the top of the stairs, where raised voices already exchanged high words.

"You stay back, Mr Holmes!" Crain was shouting as I limped into the room.

I had expected some desperate scenario, but had not been prepared for it all the same. Crain stood by a cracked window at the far end of a dilapidated bedroom, its ceiling exposed to the rafters, from which water dripped perpetually. A mattress lay in the corner nearest the door, and I knew then that, for all Sir Thomas's proselytising as to the virtues of his African drug, Crain had spent some time living in squalor here. A man of eminent means, sleeping in conditions reserved for the worst opium addicts, all the while lying to his family regarding his whereabouts.

Crain himself was barely recognisable, standing hunched like some wild, cornered animal. Worst of all, he brandished a knife, which had caused Holmes to stop near the door. Beside Crain, in the corner of the room, was the vicar, tied to a chair, mouth stuffed with a kerchief. His face was bruised and bleeding; to my great relief he was alive, though groggy. And all around the vicar, by the light of several candles, I saw pictures pinned to the wall. A few photographs, but mostly amateurish sketches. I could not fully discern them, but I knew the images were of

Crain's mother, Lady Agnes. This meagre room, as derelict as it had first appeared, was a shrine.

"Crain, what are you doing, man?" I said.

"Watson, dear Watson. You of all people will understand," he replied, his voice urgent, almost shrill. He trembled, the knife in his hand shaking.

"Talk to him, Watson," Holmes hissed. "I wish to end this amicably, but…" He glanced to his coat pocket, and my heart lurched; my friend was indicating that he was armed.

I knew that Holmes of all men would not flinch from shooting Crain if he thought the vicar to be in immediate danger of his life. I swallowed hard, and took a step forward.

"Stay where you are, Watson," Crain snapped. "As I told Mr Holmes, the vicar and I have much to resolve, and your presence is not required."

"But it is, Crain. If you ever considered me a friend, at least hear me out."

"You are a friend, Watson—but do you have any idea what this man has done?"

"I do! I know all that he is guilty of, and what you believe him to have done. They are not one and the same."

"You defend him? I caught him in the act! This… 'man of the cloth'… was attempting to defraud my family. After all my mother and father did for him, for the sake of money he tried to put the blame for everything on Madame Farr. I saw it, Watson—the costume of Lady Sybille, a white dress doubtless used to fool you into thinking Mary's ghost was abroad in the manor. And a forged codicil, which he hoped would send Madame Farr to prison.

"I see it all so clearly now. It was Parkin who somehow made those things happen at the séance—I mean, where was he all that time? He must have an accomplice—some servant girl who dresses up as a ghost at his behest. Maybe Simon is in his employ. All those things that Mr Holmes found earlier, don't you see? It was the vicar. And that means… Oh, Watson, can't you see what evil he has wrought? In order to discredit Madame Farr, in order to swindle a fortune from my family, he murdered my sister!"

At this, Crain pressed the knife to the vicar's throat, prompting a stifled yelp of fear.

Holmes reached into his pocket. I took two steps forward, placing myself in the line of fire.

"You're wrong, Crain!" I cried, desperately. "Whatever else this man has done, he is not guilty of murder."

"How can you say that? You were the ones who found that his fly had been taken out last night, before dinner. I can guess where he went, and why."

"You believe," said Holmes, "that he went to Sir Thomas's house, and stole some *Boophone disticha*."

Crain looked to Holmes, surprise in his haggard eyes.

"You believe this because you know only too well of the many exotic drugs in Sir Thomas's collection. Those drugs are the reason why even now your hand shakes, your vision blurs, and you cannot concentrate. Am I not correct, Lord Berkeley?"

"Lord Berkeley…" Crain repeated. "My father. Dead, at this man's hand."

"No!" Holmes shouted. "He did not kill your father, nor did he kill your sister. He did not know about Sir Thomas Golspie's poisons, and even if he had, he would not have known where they were kept. The killer lies rather closer to home."

Crain squeezed his eyes shut, and then opened them wide, looking at me with confusion writ large on his features. "What's he saying, Watson? Tell him to be quiet! I can't think."

I held a hand out behind me, signalling Holmes to stop. "The vicar did something very foolish," I said, softly. "He forged a codicil, hoping to exacerbate Madame Farr's predicament. But that is all he did."

"The fly…"

"If you had stayed with us just a few minutes more," I said, "you would have heard the whole story. The vicar's fly was taken out, yes, but not by him. Indeed, the note we discovered in his room at the manor is evidence that he was called away as a distraction while someone else took the carriage. The same person who went to Sir Thomas's house and stole the drug that killed your dear sister. Believe me, Crain, I would see justice done as well as you, but this is not the man."

"Then who?"

"Holmes has a theory, and if you come back to the manor with us, we'll have this all cleared up in no time."

"No!" Crain shouted, and now he pressed the point of the knife more firmly to the vicar's throat, causing a bead of blood to ooze onto Parkin's dog-collar. The vicar let out a muffled cry. His eyes widened. "Oh, he's a clever one," Crain went on. "He has covered his tracks well enough to fool even the great Sherlock Holmes, but he won't fool me! Madame Farr is not a fraud, Watson! I know her. She has helped me so much… I know Parkin is guilty, because I know that she is innocent!"

"No, James, she is not." Judith's voice came like a clear bell, at once throwing Crain into uncertainty. She must have been listening from the doorway, and now she entered the room, treading carefully past Holmes, past me, and towards Crain, arms held out. "Madame Farr is not innocent, and nor am I."

"Judith. What are you saying?" Crain asked, easing the knife away just an inch.

"I am saying that Madame Farr staged the séance… or, certainly all the more sensational tricks. I know because I helped her."

"No! Has he put you up to this?" Crain waved the knife at Holmes.

"James, please. Mr Holmes has helped me see the light, if anything. I believe in spiritualism, I really do. Ever since I was a little girl I have had a gift, to sense things that others cannot. But this gift never manifested itself in spectacular ways, or allowed me to predict the future, or transported me to the spirit world. It was just a sort of… sense. A feeling.

"When I met Madame Farr, she told me that I had a true gift, but that most people would not join our cause without more tangible results. She persuaded me to help in her illusions—stage magic, I suppose—in order for us to spread our message more widely, and to provide genuine help to those who needed it. I believed in her, James. I believed in her so completely I turned my back on my family, and embraced Madame Farr and Simon, and Arthur—as a new family. It's not easy to confess that you might be on the wrong path when you've taken such a step, and cut yourself off from all that you've ever known. I found myself turning a blind eye to things I should have run from. Part of me still believes in Madame Farr, but part of me knows now that what I did was wrong. I dressed up as Dr Watson's dear late wife, to try and bring him to our cause, not for his spiritual wellbeing, but to prove Madame Farr's power."

"How?" I interjected. "I was never a believer, and never would be."

"But you almost were, Doctor! Madame Farr was certain she could convince you of the truth of spiritualism, and James had already let slip that you were going through some upheavals in your life. The thought of selling your practice and moving from the marital home you had shared with Mary had dragged up old memories, and it was these memories that Madame Farr sought to exploit. If the famous Dr Watson could be convinced, even for a short time, then who could truly doubt her? Of course, she was very keen to stop you from moving back to your rooms with Sherlock Holmes, the famous detective, for surely he would investigate as soon as he heard the story. She did not truly believe Mr Holmes to be the genius you painted him, and nor did I, until now. But by the time her plan was complete, she hoped it would be too late to stop her." Judith looked again to Crain. "I did not play my part in that deception just to line Madame Farr's pockets, I swear. I did it because I knew you would be galvanised by the doctor's story, and would seek to persuade him to join with us. And then we could buy our new church—a grand building that would attract believers from miles around. It was a dream! And in the pursuit of that dream I thought I could bend a few rules, tell a few lies, and maybe all would be well, because in the end it's all about the greater good, isn't it? But now… I think we have given you false hope, when really, you needed help of a less esoteric kind."

"False hope? What… what do you mean, Judith? Tell me that you weren't lying about Mama!"

"For my part, no. At least, not always. I do sense her presence. I feel her here, most strongly. But Madame Farr… she insisted on giving you messages from the other side, and at first I was astounded by her powers. As time went on, I realised she was lying. She was inventing the messages, and putting words in the mouth of your mother's spirit. Only… I was too deep in the mire by then. I could not tell you the truth, for fear that you would hate me."

Crain staggered back against the wall, shaking uncontrollably. "Hate you…" His voice was very quiet now. "Is that not the least you deserve? Do you know what you have done to me?"

"I think I do," Judith said, and in the candlelight I saw tears glisten upon her cheeks. "But fear of your rejection is the one thing that stopped me from confessing. Because you see, James…

Lord Berkeley… I love you. I have loved you from the first day we met here at this cottage. And I don't believe you ever knew it."

"Oh Lord…" Crain said, in a broken whisper. And then, loudly, he cried, "What have I done? Oh God!"

Crain raised the knife, and my heart fair stuck in my throat. Time slowed to a crawl. Crain took a step forward, and I knew not if he was about to bring the dagger down upon the vicar, or whether he meant to attack Judith. The girl stood there regardless, as though she would accept whatever fate her love deigned to deal.

"Watson!" Holmes shouted. I was dimly aware of the revolver in his hand. Did he urge me to get out of the way, or to stop Crain from doing something irredeemable?

I would not lose my friend, either to a blade, a bullet, or incarceration. I sprang forward, mustering all my speed and strength, reaching Crain even as the knife plunged towards his own stomach. I barrelled into him, flattening him against the wall, taking the wind from him. The blade flashed to the floor. I sank to my knees, Crain sobbing uncontrollably in my arms.

Once the surge of energy pursuant upon his rash crime had subsided, Crain fell into exhaustion, and a malleable, child-like state. I feared the worst for his health: the drugs he had taken had allowed no time for natural grieving, and the succession of shocks were too much for him to bear. Not least of these shocks was his loss of faith; Madame Farr had been his greatest comfort in dark times, even though we now knew that "comfort" to have been the worst of all worlds. Crain's eagerness to embrace spiritualism had given him false hope, forcing him now to confront the most awful truth—that he must grieve for his mother, father and sister all at once.

We bundled Crain into the vicar's fly, and Holmes instructed me to drive him back to the manor, while Benson would take the rest of us, including the wounded vicar. I had argued at first for Parkin to be returned home to his own bed, but Holmes convinced me otherwise. My bag was at Crain Manor, and I might need it to treat the man's wounds, which were thankfully superficial. And besides, Holmes had said, everything must be straightened out satisfactorily, so that all parties over whom a cloud of suspicion hovered might receive justice or absolution accordingly.

We arrived back at the manor cold, tired and hungry. It gave me only a modicum of cheer to see a few lights burning within, and a small sense of relief when we were greeted by Eglinton, who told us that he had received a new guest in our absence. How great a surprise and a comfort it was when we were greeted on the front steps by a familiar face.

"Lestrade!" Holmes said. "Better late than never."

"Late?" Lestrade said with a frown. "Scotland Yard does not grind to a halt whenever a civilian snaps his fingers—even one such as you, Mr Holmes. I'll have you know I have worked a double shift to be here."

"I am certain the Yard will remunerate you, Lestrade," Holmes smiled, "just as soon as you return to them successful in resolving a diabolical scheme of fraud and poisoning. Not to mention the favour you are about to do for one of the great old families of England."

Lestrade considered this as if for the first time, and seemed to rather puff up at the prospect of the Crain family being in his debt.

"When did you get here, Lestrade?" I asked, instigating pleasantries, for it was clear Holmes was not about to.

"About an hour ago. I would have got here sooner, were it not for some fallen tree on the tracks near… What-ho, who's this?" Lestrade nodded to the bedraggled forms of the vicar and Crain, the former helped to the manor by the driver we'd hired at the village, and the latter being half-carried by Benson. Judith loitered behind, for Crain had not so much as glanced in her direction, if he was even lucid.

"Allow me to introduce the Reverend Parkin," Holmes said with absurd cheerfulness, "and Lord Berkeley, the former Lord Beving. They are in urgent need of refreshment after a… minor mishap, shall we say? Come along, let's all get inside."

We had taken but two steps into the hall when we were spotted by the party, and met first with annoyance at their continued detention, and then with great curiosity and concern for Crain and the vicar. Servants were sent for, hot water, tonic and blankets fetched, and soon Crain and Parkin were attended to, though kept separate, lest any ill will resurface. It took no small time to quell the house-guests, during which Holmes brought Lestrade into our confidence.

"You have been made aware by now of the circumstances?" Holmes asked the inspector.

"I have heard a good many tall tales since I arrived at this house, Holmes," Lestrade said. "Those constables have appraised me of what I hope are the facts, whilst everyone else seemed content to tell me ghost stories over supper."

"Supper!" I groaned.

"There will be time to fill your belly when our work is done," Holmes chided. "Lestrade, I shall give you the full facts of the matter in private, later. For now, know this: the spiritualists are wanted felons in Newcastle, for the crimes of fraud and poisoning—that latter charge was never proven, but has been repeated here, the victim being none other than poor Watson. The appearance of the mysterious Red Woman that I'm sure you've heard all about, and the death of Lady Esther Crain, have nothing to do with the spiritualists, save that they provided an excellent cover for the true culprit." Holmes leaned in conspiratorially, and lowered his voice. “I am about to upset several members of this party, Lestrade, by making accusations I cannot yet prove. I assure you, I shall provide all the evidence you could want by the time this night is done, but only with your help.”

Lestrade looked to me. “My, my! Did Sherlock Holmes just ask for my help?” He smirked.

“Concentrate, Lestrade, for time is short. I need you to back me to the hilt, in the most officious manner you can muster, if you can bring yourself to offend your new hosts.”

“Well… it had better be worth it, is all I’ll say.”

“It will be. Especially as the man most likely to have his feathers ruffled is the esteemed barrister over there, Geoffrey Melville. You’ve crossed his path a time or two, if I recall correctly.”

Lestrade glanced over Holmes’s shoulder at Melville, who was standing aloof from the clucking and fussing of the others. “Oh yes,” he said. “You remember Jack Bloomfield, the Bond Street jewel thief? It was Melville that got him off, and I tell you that man was guilty as sin. Procedural errors, he said. On the part of my men! Procedural errors, my eye! And tonight, he didn’t even remember me, or pretended not to.”

“Then you may yet live to see him squirm,” Holmes winked, “though no more than is strictly necessary.”

“And, erm… Holmes… the vicar and his lordship. What’s the real story? Gentlemen’s disagreement?”

“Something like that,” Holmes said. “I hope that it will not require your intervention, though that will depend on how magnanimous Mr Parkin is feeling when our business is concluded. Now, are you ready? Good!” Holmes turned and cleared his throat. “Ladies and gentlemen,” he called loudly, bringing the chatter at last to an end. “May I have your attention. It has been a long and trying day, and the time has come finally to bring these distressing matters to a close.”

CHAPTER FIFTEEN

SECRETS REVEALED

"When I arrived at Crain Manor this afternoon," Holmes said, pacing the hall, "it was with every confidence that the mystery would be solved by dinner time. Perhaps this was due to my own hubris. In truth, I broke one of my own rules: I was prejudiced regarding the facts."

This was a fine thing for Holmes to admit, and I could scarce believe my ears.

"Knowing that Watson would be attending a weekend party with a group of spiritualists," Holmes continued, "and knowing that their leader, Madame Farr, had exerted some strong influence over Lord Berkeley—then Lord Beving—I took the liberty, as I said earlier, of investigating Madame Farr. When I received Watson's telegram informing me of the death of Lady Esther in mysterious circumstances, I immediately assumed Madame Farr to be somehow involved. The initial facts of the case—the haunted tower, the Red Woman, the warnings issued to Lady Esther over her disbelief in spiritualism—all these things pointed to the same conclusion. But the more time I spent in this house, the more I realised some far more intricate plot was in action.

"By dinner time, far from seeing the case resolved, I was further from the truth than ever. And yet my digressions had brought me to a deeper understanding of the puzzle that lay before me. Indeed, now we have several crimes to consider. First, the poisoning of Watson. Second, the attempt to defraud James Crain through confidence trickery. Third, the forging of a codicil to the late Theobald Crain's will, in order to make Madame Farr appear a murderess. This point may be news to you all, and I shall come to it in good time. For now, I shall give this codicil to Mr Cavendish." Holmes removed the now tattered paper and handed it to the rather overawed solicitor. "For safekeeping, and an expert opinion," he explained. "I maintain that the death of Lord Theobald Crain was a natural one, but it was precipitated by the sudden and tragic passing of his beloved daughter, Lady Esther, and her death was anything but natural. That is not to say she was murdered by a vengeful spirit, but rather by mortal hands.

"I have met with obfuscation at every turn during this investigation, and the time has come to interview the one person who has so far eluded me: Lady Esther herself."

"What is the meaning of this?" Melville cried. "Would even you, the great Sherlock Holmes, deign to resort to table-rapping to solve a case?"

"Not at all, Mr Melville. I merely suggest that the evidence left behind by the victim will, in this instance, be more telling than any amount of testimony from the living. And to that end, I must be somewhat indelicate in my search. Inspector Lestrade, you will come and bear witness; we shall make a search of Lady Esther's room."

"You will do no such thing!" snarled Melville.

"We do not need your permission, Mr Melville, if Lord

Berkeley gives us his. Lady Esther was not yet your lawful wife. Lord Berkeley?"

"Do whatever you need to do, Mr Holmes," Crain said wearily, huddled beneath his blanket.

"What is your purpose?" Melville asked.

"My purpose is to put an end to this sorry charade once and for all," said Holmes. "To reveal the truth of Lady Esther's death and, I might add, to save you from the gallows."

"Me? Of all the ridiculous—"

"Hardly ridiculous!" Holmes interrupted. "For all appearances, it looks as though you murdered your fiancée. Do not look so outraged, Mr Melville, for I know it is nothing more than an act. I suggest you save such theatrics for your closing statements in court in future."

"No one has ever dared speak to me this way," Melville said, drawing himself up to his full height, and staring at us down his nose.

"Which is precisely why you have managed to get away with it so far," Holmes snapped. "The evidence, incomplete though it is, suggests that you, with the aid of your fiancée's lady's maid, stole a potent African drug—*Boophone disticha*, to be precise—from the home of Sir Thomas Golspie yesterday evening. Whilst feigning a headache that supposedly kept you in your room, you actually crept from the house and took the Reverend Parkin's fly, making sure first to distract the vicar with a faked note. This was to ensure that, should a servant see the fly leaving or returning, she would attest that the vicar was indeed out and about, and everyone would assume that he had gone out in his own conveyance, which was why he was late for dinner. The note was a mistake on your part, Mr Melville, for the letters were carefully trimmed from several newspapers, most of which were particular to London, and at least one of which was from

Thursday's *Financial News*. Besides Watson here, I believe you were the only guest to travel in from the City.

"In truth, it was you who took the fly. Under instruction from Sally Griggs, and carrying a key to the back door which she doubtless provided, you entered Sir Thomas's home. You knew that Sally's mother was hard of hearing, and would be unlikely to notice you as long as you were careful. You knew also that Sir Thomas's dog is old and lethargic, and would be unlikely to raise a fuss. And so you crept upstairs, found the key exactly where Sally had told you it was kept, and took the drug from its strongbox in the library. The entire enterprise would have taken no more than ten minutes, allowing you to be back for dinner, albeit a few minutes late and wet from the rain.

"At this point, it had not been agreed upon to hold a séance, but Lady Esther must have surely guessed that this was her brother's reason for holding the party."

"She knew my intent," Crain interjected, glumly.

"Thank you, Lord Berkeley," Holmes said. "Then it stands to reason that she would have discussed this matter with her fiancé, and expressed her strong opposition to it.

"You could not have known, Mr Melville, that Lady Esther would later volunteer to spend the night in the Red Tower, unless, of course, it was you who first suggested it. After all, procuring the poison bulb powder at no small risk shows premeditation on your part. Perhaps you intended to administer the poison regardless, but I rather think not.

"You see, as a local girl, Sally Griggs would have heard about the supposed secret passage in Crain Manor, and could easily have shared that knowledge with you. It would have been a simple matter for a servant to spy discreetly upon Madame Farr and her entourage, which is precisely what she was doing on Friday night, when she saw one of the Cole twins help Judith out of the passage, and let her into Watson's room. Whilst they were distracted, Sally must have slipped into the passage and investigated its extent, discovering the secret way into the tower. While there, she found that the spiritualists had been excavating the abandoned cellar for some time, looking for the fabled buried treasure, but coming up empty handed. However, the discovery of the passage, and the connection to a rather gruesome episode in the family history, doubtless gave Mr Melville and Miss Griggs an idea. Now, the plan fell into place.

"Together, you plotted to interrupt the séance by having Sally dress as Lady Sybille, the fabled 'Red Woman', using the passage to disappear into thin air. This was an act of genius, I must confess; Madame Farr must have known then that the game was up, but could say nothing.

"The preparations were made for Lady Esther's vigil in the tower room. At some point, the poison was administered, perhaps using the same trick that the spiritualists used on Watson, dissolving it in her water—water that Sally would have brought for her. Slowly, the poison would have gone to work, causing first fitful dreams, then nightmares, then rousing Lady Esther to wakefulness, probably in a painful manner. She might have tried to reach the nightstand to drink more water, an act which would only have hastened her demise. She would have suffered hallucinations. I wonder, would Sally have been required to make one final appearance as the Red Woman? Whispers were heard in the walls not long before the household was awakened. Was it you and Sally, meeting in the secret passage, preparing once more the Lady Sybille costume? In Lady Esther's state, it would perhaps have been unnecessary, but it would have added certainty to the plot: the sudden appearance of a murderous ancestor in the room would have caused Lady Esther's heart to race beyond human endurance. She screamed in terror, and literally died of fright."

Crain sobbed as Holmes spoke these words, and Holmes paused, a look of regret on his angular features. I think perhaps he knew he had been beyond indelicate in his summation; his thrill at clinical deduction so often got the better of him.

Presently, Holmes continued, though his manner was more subdued. "As to your motives, who can truly say? Watson here saw a strange scene between yourself, Sally and Lady Esther on Saturday, which looked like the aftermath of some argument. Had Lady Esther uncovered some uncomfortable fact about your relationship with Sally Griggs? Watson's observation the previous night, of you and Miss Griggs in an embrace in the morning room, would support this theory. Ah, I see this is the first you've heard of that! A man of your standing could not allow such a scandal. Alternatively, James Crain's threats to disavow his sister might have been a worry to you. Perhaps she had expressed her intention to leave Crain Manor with nothing, for she certainly seemed to be a woman of principle. That would have made her a less attractive match to an ambitious London barrister, I dare say."

"I thought you were saving me from the gallows, Mr Holmes," Melville growled. "It rather sounds as if you are making a case to send me there."

"I concur," said Lestrade. "I may as well arrest him now, because such a testimony would surely be enough to convict any man."

"Ah, but I said this is how the case against Mr Melville *appears*. This is what I meant when earlier I said I had come to an incorrect conclusion. The facts, such as I could find, supported my hypothesis. But facts are a curious thing: when they are incomplete, they can lead even the best of us astray. There are several elements that do not ring true from that first theory. Add to that several other complications, and we have the makings of a far more ingenious plot.

"First, as Watson will swear, the whisperers he heard in the passage that night were both female."

"That's true," I said.

"One might wonder, therefore," Holmes went on, "whether Madame Farr and Judith had entered the secret passage to ensure their own plot had not been uncovered. Madame Farr was, after all, fully attired when she made an appearance in the early hours.

"And yet, if the spiritualists had been in the passage, surely they would have moved the sack full of evidence. Or, at the very least, they would have examined it and noticed the presence of the red dress. I do not think Madame Farr, so meticulous in her confidence tricks, would have overlooked this detail.

"Then we have the more complex matter of administering the poison. How would Mr Melville, or Miss Griggs, have known the correct amount of poison bulb to give to Lady Esther? Their goal was to achieve a slow descent into an hallucinogenic state. If they had laced her water, they could not have known how much she would drink. Perhaps she was taking some medication for her recent chill, which was replaced with the poison bulb, but again they would have required a remarkable knowledge of prescribed dosages worthy of the Wasimbu tribe of Western Africa. Far simpler to do it once Lady Esther locked the door—perhaps by creeping into the room via the secret passage and administering a lethal dose. But why then were there no signs of a struggle? Why was no alarm raised other than that single scream?

"There was one thing—Inspector, would you be so kind as to open the wardrobe and search for a dress of blue silk?"

Lestrade frowned, but complied. He searched through the rails, finding a blue dress, but not one made of silk. "There is no such dress, Holmes," he said at last.

"Can anyone here present confirm that Lady Esther owned a blue silk dress?" Holmes asked.

I confirmed it, as did Langton.

"Miss Griggs?" Holmes asked. "Where is the dress?"

"Sent away, sir. To… to be mended."

"Mended indeed. Because of a tear just above the right hip, where it was caught on a nail. At roughly the height of the tear on your jacket there, Watson, wouldn't you agree?"

"Good heavens, Holmes. Yes, of course."

"I wonder if perhaps Eglinton would conduct a search downstairs and find the dress? It is no pressing matter, but I have a fragment of silk found on a nail in the secret passage that I am certain will match the fabric of the dress."

"Nonsense!" Melville snapped. "Lady Esther was in no condition to traipse around that musty old passage."

"Really? And how would you know how musty the passage is, Mr Melville? The fact remains, however, that the silk was found in the passage, and the location of the aforementioned nail corresponds rather neatly with a cut on Lady Esther's body.

"And on the subject of the body, Watson's examination throws up some other rather interesting findings. The redness around the eyes, the swelling at the throat and the blue fingernails are not entirely congruent with the post-mortem effects of boophone poisoning. There is also the matter of the small red spots around the throat. She was poisoned—do not doubt that for a moment—but there was something else at work. Something relating, I believe, to the needle marks found on Lady Esther's arm."

"Needle marks?" Crain groaned.

"These were not what you might think, Lord Berkeley," Holmes said, "and very soon I shall prove it. What say you, Lestrade? Shall we make our search and bring these suppositions to an end?"

"I jolly well wish we would," Lestrade said.

There was little more to be said. Melville made some meagre protest, but there was nothing he could do, and so we allowed Crain to lead the way, gingerly, to the room of his late sister.

Once inside, Holmes paced the room, casting his eye scrupulously over every surface. It was immaculately tidy; everything in its place. He stopped at a pretty French cabinet, and tried the handles. It was locked.

"The key to this cabinet?" Holmes asked.

Crain shook his head.

Holmes looked to the doorway, where Melville and Sally stood, glaring daggers our way. "Miss Griggs," he said. "The key, if you please."

"No," she said, defiantly.

Holmes nodded to Lestrade, who stepped towards the maid. "Come on now, miss, or I'll have your room searched for the key."

She looked in desperation to Melville, who sighed heavily.

"It's all right, Sally," he said, very quietly and gravely. "Give him the key."

To my small surprise, Sally reached to her collar, and pulled out her necklace—actually a thin chain—upon which was a silver key. This she unclipped and handed to Holmes, her dark eyes full of sadness and resentment in equal measure.

Holmes unlocked the cabinet, and carefully went through the myriad tiny bottles, tins and jars within. It was an awkward business, and I could tell that even my friend, famous for his detached reason, was uncomfortable going through Lady Esther's most private things, especially with an audience present.

At last, Holmes began to remove certain items from the cabinet, arranging them neatly on the nightstand beside it as he went.

"An amount of concealing powder and rouge," he said first. "Not altogether suspicious, but there is an unusually large quantity. Now this is interesting. One bottle of laudanum, part used. An unlabelled bottle of pills—Watson, would you take a look please?"

He passed me the bottle, and I emptied a few pills into my hand.

"What we call 'pink pills,'" I said. "I think I have some in my bag. Otherwise known as Blaud's Pills."

"For the promotion of healthy blood cells," Holmes said.

"Yes," I confirmed.

Holmes nodded, and returned to the cabinet. Finally, he withdrew another bottle, and this time stood up straight, holding the bottle up for us all to see. "And this," he said, "can surely lead us to only one conclusion."

I looked at the bottle in Holmes's hand, and a terrible truth dawned upon me. "Fowler's solution," I said.

"Your medical opinion, Watson?"

I knew Holmes was already several steps ahead of me, for his encyclopaedic knowledge of medicines would rival that of most apothecaries. But I humoured him all the same. "One might at first think a patient taking such medication to be suffering from anaemia, for they promote the production of red blood cells over white. Laudanum alone is not suspicious—many ladies take small amounts for headaches and feverishness, and Lady Esther said she had suffered recently from a severe chill. But the presence of Fowler's solution suggests something more grave. It is not commonly prescribed, for the arsenic it contains is dangerous in its own right. And so it is often given to patients whose conditions are terminal, to relieve their symptoms and improve their quality of life, at least temporarily."

"And your examination of Lady Esther's body, Watson? Does the discovery of these items now change your initial verdict?"

"It does, Holmes." I turned to Lestrade and Crain. Behind them, by the bedroom door, stood Melville and Sally, and beyond

I saw other expectant faces crowding in, waiting for my answer. I took a deep breath, and said, "As Holmes described earlier, Lady Esther's body displayed a redness around the eyes, a swelling at the throat—which I would now consider symptomatic of a lymphatic irregularity—and a faint rash, or *petechiae*, about the throat. We know also that she bruised easily and was prone to breathlessness, and that she had complained of occasional nosebleeds. Her brother remarked recently on the amount of weight she had lost. There are many medical reasons for all these symptoms, but the discovery of these drugs can point to only one possibility. Lady Esther had leukaemia. A cancer… She was dying."

There were gasps from the corridor. Sally Griggs fell to her knees and wept.

"This… this can't be," said Crain. "I would have known. She would have told me."

"No," Holmes said. "She kept it a secret. She used the Fowler's solution to disguise the worst symptoms. She used laudanum to mask the pain, and make-up to hide the toll the illness was taking on her face. The marks on her arm that Watson saw…"

"A transfusion," I said. "A risky business, but sometimes effective in terminal cases. So, Mr Melville—I thought it strange that you would take Lady Esther to a physician in London. Her family could surely afford the finest care right here. You took her to a cancer hospital, didn't you?"

All eyes turned now to Melville. He staggered back, leaning on the door-frame, looking exhausted. He pinched at his eyes, and said, "Yes. You are correct, Dr Watson. The transfusion was a desperate gamble. Such treatment provides relief in only a small number of cases, but I insisted that we explore every avenue. It helped, for a short time, but then the symptoms returned, and we had to plan how we would spend what remained of the short time we had left together. I even suggested we simply elope and have done with it all, but Esther's loyalty to her family name was fierce, God love her. She would not abandon the family to these vultures."

"So why not tell the family?" Holmes said. "Why the secrecy?"

"Because of Madame Farr. That terrible, terrible woman… Esther was afraid that Farr would use her condition to dig her claws even deeper into James. Imagine if Madame Farr had known Esther was at death's door! She would have become a ghost in her own lifetime, with all preparations made for her passing, so that James might have her company in death. She would not be used so. She would not have her brother's grief used so! We decided to keep it all a secret. At best, we might be able to draw some nonsense prediction out of Farr, as Esther did at the séance. You remember don't you, Watson? That message about Esther and I having a long and happy marriage, and children… No chance of that. But better still, we hoped we could find some way of exposing Madame Farr before the end came, to reveal her as a trickster before the whole community."

"And finally you saw an opportunity, when a certain Dr Watson was invited to Crain Manor," Holmes ventured.

"I see no reason to continue the charade, Mr Holmes," Melville said. "I went along with Esther's wishes, and among those wishes was for you to come here and solve the case, for she had a great deal of admiration for you, fostered by a love of Dr Watson's accounts of your adventures. She made sure to mention you to Dr Watson at every opportunity, saying how she wished you could be here, and she bade me say the same. Do you remember, Doctor? Her theory was that if Madame Farr could use the power of suggestion to manipulate others, then so could she. After her plan unfolded, you would be sure to send for Holmes.

"She was a woman of incredible strength and fortitude. If you only knew the pain she suffered, and yet she hid it even from her family, allowing herself to lapse only in my presence. She would show no sign of weakness to the spiritualists, whom she saw as invaders into her realm. But more than that, Esther was the cleverest woman I ever knew, and I loved that about her more than anything. She knew you would focus your ire on Madame Farr, and expose her for what she really was. Esther had tried and failed, yet remained convinced of Madame Farr's trickery. She has accomplished in death all that she could not accomplish in life—she has freed her brother from the clutches of that vile woman, and I know she will be at peace now that her family is rid of Madame Farr's malign influence.

"There is really no need to compound Lord Berkeley's distress further." Melville turned now to Crain, who sat on Esther's bed, shivering. "Lord Berkeley—James. Forgive me. I only did as Esther asked, out of love for her. But neither of us could predict the terrible consequence of our plan. Your father… he…" Melville paused, and cleared his throat. "That is my only true regret. The late Lord Berkeley always appeared so strong. I had no idea the loss of Esther would take such a toll, and I very nearly lost my nerve when he passed away. If you never forgive me for that, I will understand."

He turned back to Holmes, reached into his pocket, and took out a folded letter, bearing a waxen seal imprinted with the Crain family crest. "Here, Mr Holmes. Esther recorded her final testimony for you, to be handed to you on successful completion of the investigation. She wrote it yesterday, when we had finally agreed on our plan. She gave it to Sally for safekeeping, knowing that, even should her maid fall under suspicion, no one would be so indelicate as to search her person."

Holmes took it, broke the seal, and leafed through the numerous pages. "This explains one minor detail," Holmes said. "Watson observed that Lady Esther's middle finger was indented slightly, as though she had written a letter moments before her death. But she had not—rather, she had written a very long letter earlier that evening, and her fingertip remained depressed due to deficiencies in her blood. I am sure she could not have foreseen that detail, but it proved to be a more complicating factor than she could have known."

"You really are clever, Mr Holmes," Melville said, with a curt bow. "I wish you and Esther could have met; she desired it more than anything. But in this small way, she has added to the casebook of Sherlock Holmes, and that is a fitting memorial, don't you think?"

Holmes smiled, and I believe he was more touched by this last remark than he could admit.

"Thank you for your candour, Mr Melville," he said. "For the record then, let us hear the truth of it, in Lady Esther's own words."

CHAPTER SIXTEEN

THE TESTIMONY OF LADY ESTHER

To whom it may concern,

If you are reading this, then I am dead.

There, it's said. I knew those first words would be the hardest to write. No matter how long I have taken to get used to the idea of my own mortality, it still feels too soon now that the hour is nigh. And it is nigh, because I intend to die this night. April 15, 1894. I suppose I should write it out formally: My name is Esther Agnes Crain, born December 1, 1870. I am of sound mind, but not, sadly, of body. For my body has betrayed me most cruelly.

I hardly know where to start, so I shall begin with the illness, because it changed everything, and led to this point. Shortly after Christmas, I began to feel increasingly lethargic. I was never free of cold. No matter how much I ate, I felt weak and thin, my skin pale and spotted. Dear Geoffrey feared I had anaemia, and while I visited him in London, he insisted I go right away to see his doctor. I endured all manner of tests, and eventually discovered the awful truth. I had leukaemia, and it was terminal. The doctor told me I had six months to live, at most. That was January.

I wanted nothing more than to return to my family, and to fall into my father's arms and feel sorry for myself. But my return to Crain Manor made all that impossible. First of all, Father had taken a nasty turn, and our family physician prescribed for him so many different drugs that I'm astonished Father managed to remember which was which. As soon as he was fit to walk the grounds, he at once threw himself into his work, such was his way; but there was something different about his manner. He was working so hard, against his doctor's advice, that I knew he was trying to put his house in order, in case he should die. When I saw Mr Cavendish visit the house the following week, I knew I was right. And Father should, of course, have been able to rely on James at such a difficult time, but he could not, for James was otherwise indisposed. With this scenario before me, how could I tell them my own news? I knew I would have to bear it alone, at least for the time being.

It was not my brother's fault. Please do not think for a moment that I blame him. He had never been the strongest willed of our family, and he had never recovered from the loss of our mother. He had become rather reliant on the curious pills provided him by Sir Thomas out of some misguided sense of loyalty. They had much the same effect on James's faculties as any opiate, though supposedly with fewer physical impediments. But it was not the physical he should have been concerned with, but the metaphysical.

While I was in London, the spiritualist group James had been visiting for some time had seemingly tightened their hold over him. My brother was changed, mesmerised by Madame Farr. Her spy, Judith, had inveigled her way into my home. Her servant, Simon, was everywhere, all the time. It was obvious what Madame Farr wanted—James's money, and influence, and patronage. Madame Farr had ambitions to elevate her station from rural table-rapper to court magician, like some latter-day John Dee. If I were to reveal my condition to the family with Madame Farr about, then I might as well be dead already. And when I was gone, what then? Would I be supposedly summoned up, with that woman putting words in my mouth at the séance table for the amusement of her clientele? Would she tell everyone, as if with my own words, that I was so dreadfully sorry for ever having doubted her? Would my demise help ensure that James would be forever in her thrall—a noble lord of a noble old family, reduced to a sycophant? You may think ill of me for saying this, but I would not let that happen to our family.

I attended one of Madame Farr's séances. I had read as much as I could find about the practices of spirit-mediums and their tricks. I had read every story of Sherlock Holmes penned to date by James's old friend, Watson, that I might learn the art of deduction, and unmask Madame Farr as a charlatan. I wanted to heal the family, so that I could at last reveal my own secret without causing further harm. I failed. She was too clever for me. When I saw her using a spirit cabinet, I thought I could expose her at once. But the cabinet, just moments after emitting strange lights and smoke, was found empty. As I was about to search the room more thoroughly, Simon—the very man whom I had loudly proclaimed to be the real cause of the psychical phenomena—appeared at the back of the room, with a nasty smile on his face. Simon, it seemed, could be in two places at once. With that, I lost all support from the other sitters, and Madame Farr dismissed me as a non-believer, and a disruptive influence. To this day, I don't know how she performed her tricks, but I am still convinced that tricks they were.

And so, disheartened, and with James pushed even further from me, I returned home. I helped my father run the estate as best I could, taking a dangerous mix of drugs to keep up appearances. I played the role of dutiful daughter, as James was manipulated by that woman like a puppet on a string. I could entrust the truth only to my loyal maid and confidante, Sally. And it was Sally, inadvertently, who planted the seed of a plan in my mind—a seed that would eventually germinate.

Sally one night overheard James and Judith talking about the Red Tower, and the legend of Lady Sybille. Madame Farr had apparently made some comment about a secret treasure hidden somewhere in the manor, and thought perhaps its discovery might lead to the laying of the famous ghost—the 'Red Woman'. I knew this secret treasure was whispered of in the village. Father had always refused to speak of the passages, perhaps because of his own father's superstitions. And so I set Sally the task of spying on Judith—the cuckoo in our nest would herself come under secret scrutiny! We found no secret passage, or buried treasure—but we did observe Judith twice in the act of searching for a passage: tapping panels, turning wall-sconces, and the like. And so I closeted myself away in the library as often as I could, and began to research the legend of Lady Sybille, in the hope that I could find something with which to beat Madame Farr at her own game.

Much time passed. I became so ill at times that I

could not travel, and so Geoffrey spent more and more time with me here. Madame Farr attempted to ensnare him with messages from his poor first wife, who died most tragically some years ago. It was vindictiveness that drove her: she knew I was wise to her games, and sought to drive a wedge between Geoffrey and me. It only drove us closer together. Geoffrey had first thought I was paranoid, but now saw Madame Farr for what she really was, and vowed to help me mend my family before my time was up. We increased my dose of Fowler's solution, provided in strict confidentiality by Geoffrey's doctor, so that I might travel to a London clinic for a blood transfusion. This gave me weeks of comparatively good health; an illusion, perhaps, but a godsend nonetheless. Upon our return, Sally told us that the spiritualists must have found the secret passage, for the servants had been hearing strange whispers around the back stair, as of ghosts. It had got some of the maids into an awful panic. Doughty old Eglinton had dismissed the noises as rats in the abandoned tower cellar, but I knew that in our absence a passage must have been found.

Everything else happened rather quickly. James arranged for a weekend party, and invited none other than Dr Watson, the very writer I had so long admired. He wanted a rational man to proclaim the veracity of Madame Farr's psychical power from the rooftops, but instead he gave me a means to summon the one man in all of Christendom who could undo her: Sherlock Holmes. The man who had himself "returned from the dead"—who better to defeat a spiritist? This is where I myself engaged in the most unforgiveable deception. I knew that Dr Watson was a chivalrous man, who has more than once gone to great lengths to defend the honour of a lady in need. And so I have rather shamelessly played upon this most noble of traits, in the hopes that Dr Watson will doggedly pursue my murderer to the very end. I hope that he can forgive me.

Our plan was put together hastily, and I rather fear that it has driven an irreconcilable divide between Geoffrey and me. But in the end, both he and Sally agreed to help me in this desperate gamble. I must hope that this, my final testimony, is sufficient to clear them of blame in any wrongdoing, for they acted in accordance with my dying wishes, against their own better judgement, entirely out of love for me.

I know you have all worked it out by now. I was not murdered; not by a ghost, nor by Madame Farr.

I have taken my own life.

Or, rather, I have hurried along my inexorable demise, to a time and manner of my own choosing.

And there you have the start of the plan. Last night, Sally caught Judith and Simon in the act of duping poor Dr Watson. I wanted so much to tell him what I knew, for it was clear he was much affected by their prank. But I needed to guard what I had learned: the location of the secret passage. My own researches into my family's history had revealed that the supposed treasure was a fanciful myth, but that the secret passage was likely real, constructed out of necessity during the Civil War, and used by Lady Sybille in opposition to its original purpose when she betrayed her husband.

After seeing how Judith had played the part of the ghost, we have arranged for Sally to do the same as Lady Sybille, in order to interrupt the séance at a suitably dramatic moment. She will materialise suddenly, before seemingly disappearing into the sealed tower. I shall have to put on a performance worthy of the stage to persuade everyone that I should spend the night in the tower. Once the tower room is prepared, I shall make a great show of locking myself inside with the only key. Sally will then meet me by entering through the secret passage, and give me a very strange and powerful drug.

This is where another innocent party may well be hurt, and I cannot apologise enough for it. Sir Thomas Golspie is the dearest man, but he has in his possession a powerful poison, which earlier tonight Geoffrey stole from him. He calls it the 'poison bulb', and has many times talked to us of its dark effects. I choose this method for several reasons. First, it cannot easily be detected, except by a true specialist in exotic poisons. Were I simply to take laudanum, Dr Watson would be on hand to record a verdict of suicide, and the plan would all be for nought. I know my chosen method will cause the most terrifying, nightmarish hallucinations; but from what Sir Thomas has described in the past, it will also drive me insensible, and is that not a better way to meet one's end than a slow wasting sickness? Does that make me a coward? Perhaps it does. I doubt very much I shall be in my own mind when the end comes, no matter how agonising it may sound. And I want the mystery to be worthy of the most gruesome penny dreadful. I shall die with a look of horror on my face, and not a mark on my body, within a locked room. I rather imagine our party guests will think the ghost has killed me, while Mr Sherlock Holmes surely will not be able to resist such a tantalising and abstruse puzzle!

The original intent was for me to imbibe the drug before retiring, allowing its slow effect to overwhelm me as I settled down to sleep. But we realised very quickly that none of us have the skilled hand of the herbalist, like Sir

Thomas. Then I had thought that I could steal through the secret passage and collect the drug myself before returning to the tower and taking it. Alas, the air in the passage is so thick that I could not go more than a few yards before being overcome, and I caught myself on a protruding nail that tore through my dress and caused me to bleed more than it should have. After that, I knew I had to ask poor Sally to be the bearer of the poison.

As for the rest, I have instructed Geoffrey to tell everything to the authorities when questioned. He knows the risks, but has deemed them worth the cost. Everything that I know of Sherlock Holmes, from the accounts that I have read, depict him as a fair man. I can only hope that he will judge Geoffrey kindly, and heed my plea for leniency.

I have been writing now for too long already, and the hour of this preposterous séance draws near. I shall spend what little time I have left on this earth with Geoffrey.

Adieu, adieu,
E

CHAPTER SEVENTEEN

A RETROSPECTION

In the immediate aftermath of Holmes's revelations, there was a great deal to do, and very few members of the household in a fit state to do it.

We were lucky to have on hand Inspector Lestrade, to rally the two exhausted local constables. I shared their weary reluctance to carry out any further tasks; not that we had any choice in the matter. If Holmes was tired, he did not show it, so buoyed was he by the successful resolution of another investigation.

And yet, had we truly achieved success? Crain was a broken man, barely able to string together a sentence. No sooner had the letter been read than he collapsed, and had to be carried to his room. The vicar, so long in the bosom of the family, was now embittered and frightened, and not without cause. Yet his own duplicity would surely cast a shadow on his future relationship with the Crains. And then there was Judith—so long the quiet confidante of Crain, now heartbroken that her part in his deception had surely caused him to reject her. Indeed, Crain Manor was not a happy house.

On the matter of Judith, it was her with whom we dealt first. Lestrade and Holmes found themselves in rare agreement, and after some lengthy ruminations the inspector assured the girl that no charges would be brought against her so long as she swore to testify against Madame Farr and the Cole twins. For Crain's sake, she wholeheartedly agreed.

The Reverend Parkin was a tougher prospect. His forging of the codicil had been a cynical plot to throw blame upon Madame Farr for murder. If his intentions had been pure, there would have been some recourse to let him off lightly, but this was not the case.

"All that you truly cared about," Holmes had said, "was increasing the financial provision for your church, at the expense of Madame Farr's continued liberty. I can think of no less Christian a way to settle one's score. However, although he was misguided in his actions against you, Lord Berkeley has already provided a rather unorthodox and violent punishment, which you might call retribution, but which I am disposed to think of as your penance. Any man, in such circumstances, would have been forgiven for thinking you had killed Theobald Crain, and with such a belief, who could blame his lordship's son for his anger? Knowing his delicate state of mind, it is that most Christian of virtues, forgiveness, that I would ask of you. If you agree to keep Lord Berkeley's name out of the police files, and the newspapers for that matter, then I shall not have to ask the inspector here to arrest you. Does that sound fair?"

The vicar expressed an opinion that none of it sounded fair, but in the end he agreed regardless.

"Very well," Holmes said. "In that case, know this: the late Lord Berkeley made a substantial provision to St Mary's in his will, and you shall still receive it. He had planned to increase the amount, though you presumed to think he was set to write the church out of his will altogether. It is therefore in your best interests to mend this rift between yourself and the new Lord Berkeley. Perhaps he will honour his father's wishes. Besides, you cared for Theobald Crain too, did you not?"

This last point changed the vicar's attitude considerably, and not just the promise of more money. I genuinely think he did care for Theobald Crain—his anger at the old man's deathbed had been genuine.

The hour had been late indeed when we visited Melville, and we had summoned Sally Griggs, too, that they might share in the knowledge of their fates. Holmes reminded the two of them of the toll their actions had taken on the Crain family, but the deep remorse shown by both was evidence enough that no reminder was required.

"So what is to be done with you?" Holmes said.

"I doubt very much any charges will stick," Melville said, albeit gloomily. "My fiancée committed suicide, and that's all there is to it. I must be the one to live with that."

"Indeed you must," said Holmes. "But that is not all there is to it! You assisted Lady Esther in her suicide—both of you—and regardless of your reasons, that is a crime. In order to go about this plan, you, Mr Melville—a respectable High Court barrister no less—took a private vehicle without permission, broke into a man's house, and stole a deadly poison with the sole intent to kill."

"You make it sound like murder!" Melville's eyes moistened now with tears, and I felt a pang of guilt at Holmes's rough treatment of him.

"Not murder, no; although the end result is much the same. But the most serious crime, Mr Melville, is perverting the course of justice. The two of you, and Lady Esther, conspired to pin the blame for nothing less than murder on an innocent party."

"They were not innocent!" Sally cried, now in floods of tears.

"Quite," said Holmes. "And that is your only saving grace. Your actions did, in a strange way, bring justice upon a cabal of criminals. You say that the truth was always intended to come out, but when? If I had not discerned Lady Esther's plan, how long would you have waited to reveal the plot? Would you have let Madame Farr swing for conspiracy to murder?"

"No. Never," Melville said. "I still respect the law. You have my word as a gentleman."

"What say you, Inspector Lestrade? Is Mr Melville's word as a gentleman sufficient to stay the hand of Scotland Yard?"

"In this instance, Holmes, I am not so sure. A gentleman who would stoop to common burglary is not a man to be trusted. And don't forget, this is the same man who successfully argued for the release of the Bond Street jewel thief, and he was guilty all day long."

I saw Holmes roll his eyes, and knew Lestrade had said entirely the wrong thing.

"Jack Bloomfield?" Melville asked. "Ah, now I recognise you! Is this all some petty attempt at revenge? If I remember correctly, your sergeant was caught red-handed paying a witness, which threw the rest of your eyewitness testimonies into severe doubt."

Lestrade went red in the face. "My sergeant was—"

"I warn you, Inspector," Melville said, "I have friends in high places. You would be hard-pressed to find a judge to convict me; and think of the repercussions to your own station as a result."

Holmes intervened. "Mr Melville, might I remind you that the deceased woman, your fiancée, had connections at court? I would be wary of invoking friends in high places, when you had a hand in the death of a friend of royalty. That said, I am personally inclined to be lenient. That leniency has limits; threats against my friends in Scotland Yard being chief amongst them."

A sudden change came over Melville. Here was a man unused to being challenged, but either as a result of his recent tragedy, or of Holmes's stern disposition, he became cowed, casting his eyes downwards, nodding apologetically.

"I... I apologise, Inspector Lestrade," he said. "This has been a very trying time. Arrest me, if you must. After all, what have I left, without Esther? I only ask that you show mercy to Sally, whose only crime was loyalty to her mistress, whom she loved. Whom we all loved."

Lestrade now appeared less sure of himself, and looked to Holmes. "This surely all depends upon whether charges will be pressed. What about this Sir Thomas fellow? Is he not upset about the theft from his house? What about Lord Berkeley?"

"I doubt you will find any man or woman in this house willing to report a crime, Lestrade. Mr Melville, at your earliest convenience you should return to London," Holmes said.

"Holmes..." Lestrade interrupted, but Holmes ignored him.

"I do not think a man so prominent as you, and so steeped in the rule of law, would attempt to abscond, am I right?"

"I shall take what is coming to me, whatever the consequences," said Melville.

"Good. I shall write to Sir Thomas Golspie, informing him of all the details of this matter. He might decide to press charges, but I shall advise him to wait until Lord Berkeley is better, that they might discuss the best course of action. It is not for me or Lestrade to decide, for we are not the injured parties.

"As for you, Miss Griggs; until Lord Berkeley has recovered sufficiently to manage his household, it is up to you whether to petition Eglinton for a place on his staff, for no lady's maid is presently required in this house of mourning. I doubt Mr Eglinton is the type of man to throw a grieving woman out on her ear, and I shall speak with him to that effect. If you wish to remain in service, we might hope that a good reference can be written. Otherwise, the same warning applies to you as I gave Mr

Melville: should Lord Berkeley decide to take the matter further, then my opinion matters not one jot."

Sally Griggs nodded. Melville stood, and shook Holmes firmly by the hand.

"You are not only a clever man, Mr Holmes, but a fair one. I shall not forget this."

"Don't thank me yet, Mr Melville," Holmes said. "Now, Watson, you were grumbling about being hungry. Let us see what we can find for you. Come along, Lestrade—our work here is done, I believe."

The next morning, for all Holmes's eagerness to depart, we were not the first to leave the manor. We learned from Eglinton that the vicar had taken his leave almost at first light. And now Langton was smoking his pipe near the front door, as a footman loaded up the coach with his cases. Mrs Langton had already alighted, looking rather stern.

"Ah, Watson, Holmes," Langton said, looking not entirely as cheerful as he sounded. "Sorry to beat you to the punch, but I really must be getting back."

"Is everything all right?" I asked.

"It will be, I think. Look, I came clean about the gambling. Constance isn't in the best mood over it, but I'm sure she'll come round when she sees things are different now. The thing is… all this… it sort of puts everything in perspective, don't you think? I paid my last respects to Uncle Theobald just now. They say money is the root of all evil, and it certainly brought ill upon the family. I have resolved to turn around my own fortunes through hard work and fair trade. No more horses. And no more billiards with the likes of Watson!"

"This change of heart seems awfully courageous," Holmes

ventured. "It has nothing to do with Theobald Crain's will, I take it?"

Langton gave us the most devilish grin. "Mr Holmes, the reading of the will is not for another week. Any provision left for me and Constance would surely be a mystery until then. It's not as though a certain solicitor is on hand to let slip some details over a strong nightcap—that would be a terrible breach of professional conduct." He gave us the most conspiratorial wink, and tapped out the ash of his pipe on the wall. "As I said, Constance isn't happy about the gambling, but I'm sure she'll come round. Sooner than you might think. Goodbye, gentlemen, it was a rare honour!"

With that, Langton turned and walked briskly to the carriage, taking his place in uncomfortable silence beside his wife.

"Well I never," I said, as the carriage trundled off. "I take it Langton has fallen on his feet."

"He seems the sort who always does," said Holmes. "Do not judge him harshly, Watson. He is one of life's chancers, certainly, but his grief at the death of his uncle and cousin seemed genuine to me. If some good has come of all this, it is that Langton has earned another chance. What he does with it, however, is up to him."

We went back inside, where Cavendish and his wife were arriving for breakfast, with Lestrade beside them. All three had dark rings about their eyes through lack of sleep.

"Good morning," Cavendish said. "Mr Holmes, I have that codicil for you. I can attest that it is a forgery, should you need anyone to testify in court."

"I doubt that will be necessary," Holmes said. He took the paper, and handed it immediately to Lestrade. "The inspector should keep it as evidence, just in case. Mr Cavendish, I trust you have Lord Berkeley's real will?"

"Of course," Cavendish said. "There will be a reading next week, after the funeral."

"And until then, the will's contents are a closely guarded secret?"

Cavendish reddened a little. "My lips are sealed, naturally."

"Excellent," Holmes said. "Shall we breakfast then? And perhaps afterwards you would care to share a carriage when Benson returns? I'm sure you are eager to return to the office, Mr Cavendish, and we should all like to make the 10.30 train."

It was agreed, and the remainder of our time passed without incident. I, however, excused myself from the breakfast table early, so that I might go in search of Crain to say my goodbyes. I was surprised indeed to find him lucid, sitting at his father's desk of all places.

"Ho, Watson," he said. "I know what you're going to say. I should be resting. But I tell you something, old fellow, I've had more than enough rest of late. I feel as if I've been sleep-walking the past months; so much so that I have missed out on the love of my family. Father and Esther… all this happened so that I might wake up finally, and take charge of my life. And by God, to honour their memory I shall do exactly that, starting today if I can find the strength."

"Well this is a turnabout," I said, "and a welcome one if it sees you in brighter spirits."

"Don't talk about spirits!" Crain said, laughing, until it turned into a wheezing cough. He frowned, and I saw that the strain upon him was still a heavy one, for all the brave face he presented.

"I wish I could stay longer, but I must return to my own patients."

"I am sorry your professional services have been overused this weekend," Crain said, solemnly. "It wasn't quite the holiday either of us expected."

"No, it wasn't," I said. There passed an awkward silence. We both had much to think on, though I knew it was worse for

Crain. I would be able to return to London, and set aside all thoughts of ghostly visitations and diabolical plots. Crain would have to endure it all, become lord of the manor, and do his duty. "Well," I said eventually, "I must go. I shall visit again, hopefully to see you better."

"I should very much like that, Watson," he said. "You are a true friend."

I nodded to Crain, and took my leave.

I trod the gloomy corridors for the last time, past the death-room of Theobald Crain, and past my own room, with the stern portraits of generations of Crains looking down at me. Amongst them, I saw for the first time, were the dark eyes of Lady Sybille, in her blood-red dress. It was a small portrait, almost hidden away amongst the many faces, but my eye was drawn to it now. I paused beneath the picture for a moment, and then hurried on my way.

At the landing, I stopped again. A dark cloud had passed over the manor, turning day almost to night. And as I trod the boards at the top of the stairs, a slow, ominous creak came from the north-west corner. The door to the Red Tower groaned slowly open, revealing utter darkness behind.

I tarried no longer. It was all in my mind, I knew it must be, and yet I had no desire to stay longer at Crain Manor. Holmes was bemused when I met him in the hall and fair bundled him out the door. Although I felt foolish then as afterwards, when we eventually got under way in the carriage, I did not so much as glance back at the house. For I had the queerest sensation that the Red Tower would be staring back at me.

It was on the journey home that I made up my mind to sell my practice to Dr Verner. Indeed, as soon as I returned to work I arranged to meet him, and also began proceedings to sell my house. I had learned several valuable lessons at Crain Manor. First, that life is to be embraced, and lived. Second, that for all his aloofness and cerebral coldness, Sherlock Holmes was ever my friend—his anger when he learned what the spiritualists had done to me would forever warm my heart in dark times. And finally, I had come to realise that the excitement of investigation still thrilled me. Since Holmes's supposed fall at Reichenbach, I had allowed myself to settle into a comfortable routine; but the mystery of the Red Tower instilled within me a desire to cast off security like a pair of worn-out slippers, and embrace adventure once more.

Of course, when I later learned that Dr Verner was a distant relative of Holmes's, and that my friend had engineered the generous offer that had procured my practice, my faith in Holmes's magnanimity was a trifle dented. Despite that, I have rarely had cause to regret the decision, so perhaps Holmes does have some knowledge of matters of the heart after all.

That would be the end of the tale, but for a few loose ends that were tied up in our absence.

After an investigation by Scotland Yard, Madame Farr was proven to be Mrs Gertrude Mellinchip, just as Holmes had deduced. She was sent back to Newcastle for trial, accused of embezzling almost a hundred pounds from grieving customers. However, doubtless aided by the criminal fraternity with whom she was well acquainted, Mrs Mellinchip managed to abscond before her case was heard, saving me a trip to the north to give evidence. She remains at large, and Holmes regularly scans newspapers the length and breadth of Great Britain for any rumour of her malign enterprise starting afresh. We always wondered, however, whether she had found some other means to secure her passage to America.

The other Cole twin, whom we learned was indeed Arthur,

was picked up by chance some weeks later, almost passed over as a vagrant, trudging the road to Newbury. He revealed that he had returned to Crain Manor after stowing the evidence of the spiritualists' crimes at Madame Farr's house, presuming it to be safe for the time being. At the manor, he had learned that his brother, Simon, was locked up under the supervision of Constable Aitkens, and as he plotted to liberate Simon, he was spotted by the footmen, who chased him off. He returned first to the house, where he found the bag of incriminating evidence gone, and signs of a fierce struggle. He did not know what to make of it, but knew his game was up, and so he grabbed what few things he dared and headed out of the village with little more than the clothes on his back. In court, neither twin would give up the other for the crime of benzene poisoning, and even Judith's testimony could not identify a clear culprit between them; so he and his brother were sentenced to two years apiece at Her Majesty's pleasure.

Of Judith, there was at least some good to come from it all. Her love for Crain would go unrequited, for although he forgave her part in Madame Farr's schemes, I could barely imagine the painful memories she must have stirred in him whenever they saw each other. However, Crain helped reunite her with her estranged father, restoring and reopening the old mill so that her family—whose name we finally learned was Sugden—could secure a decent living for themselves.

It was some months before Crain was fully fit, his own doctor tactfully recording an official diagnosis of brain fever. Lestrade informed us that Crain had written to him, expressing a desire that no action should be taken against Melville, and vouching for the character of Sally Griggs, who had gone on to find a good position in a household in Windsor.

It was the following spring when I received a letter from

Crain announcing his impending marriage to a fine lady from an old Cambridgeshire family. I was happily surprised that the Reverend Parkin was to officiate at the wedding. Apparently Theobald Crain's provision for the church was sufficient to begin restoration of St Mary's, and after near a year, Parkin and Crain had agreed to settle their differences amicably. Both Holmes and I were invited to the wedding.

Sherlock Holmes, naturally, declined.

ACKNOWLEDGEMENTS

A novel of detection, especially one with such intricate medical and ghostly aspects as this, would hardly ring true without (far too) many hours of research, much of which never even makes it to print. In this case, however, special thanks must go to my crack science advisor, haematology specialist Dr Carolyn Voisey, for her insights into historical leukaemia treatments and symptoms, and the effects of various toxins on sufferers, as well as advice on the best ways to drug poor Watson. She has made Watson's life all the more difficult, but his victory all the sweeter.

On the spiritualist front, I was well served by a lifetime of compulsively collecting books from and about the nineteenth century, including a fair number of titles dealing with matters of the occult, and Victorian psychical phenomena. Some apology should probably be made to those advocates of the broader field of modern Spiritualism, as for the purposes of this novel I have delved only into the chequered history of proven fraud. For a glimpse at the other side of this particular coin, readers are humbly invited to peruse my other series for Titan Books, the Apollonian Casefiles. For readers wishing to look into the fascinating topic of Victorian spiritualism for themselves, I include a very short bibliography here of the material I found most useful, comprehensive and illuminating:

Doyle, Arthur Conan, *On the Unexplained*, Hesperus Press 2013

Lunt, Edward D, *Mysteries of the Séance: And Tricks and Traps of Bogus Mediums*, 1903; Kessinger Publishing 2010

Pearsall, Ronald, *The Table-Rappers: the Victorians and the Occult*, Sutton Publishing 2004

Price, Harry, *Revelations of a Spirit Medium*, Forgotten Books 2017

Souter, Dr Keith, *Medical Meddlers, Mediums and Magicians: The Victorian Age of Credulity*, The History Press 2012

ABOUT THE AUTHOR

Mark A. Latham is a writer, editor, history nerd, frustrated grunge singer and amateur baker from Staffordshire, UK. A recent immigrant to rural Nottinghamshire, he lives in a very old house (sadly not haunted), and is still regarded in the village as a foreigner.

Formerly the editor of Games Workshop's *White Dwarf* magazine, Mark dabbled in tabletop games design before becoming a full-time author of strange, fantastical and macabre tales, mostly set in the nineteenth century, a period for which his obsession knows no bounds. He is the author of the Apollonian Casefiles series, published by Titan Books.

Follow Mark on Twitter:

@aLostVictorian

SHERLOCK HOLMES
THE PATCHWORK DEVIL

Cavan Scott

It is 1919, and while the world celebrates the signing of the Treaty of Versailles, Holmes and Watson are called to a grisly discovery.

A severed hand has been found on the bank of the Thames, a hand belonging to a soldier who supposedly died in the trenches two years ago. But the hand is fresh, and shows signs that it was recently amputated. So how has it ended up back in London two years after its owner was killed in France? Warned by Sherlock's brother Mycroft to cease their investigation, and only barely surviving an attack by a superhuman creature, Holmes and Watson begin to suspect a conspiracy at the very heart of the British government…

"Scott poses an intriguing puzzle for an older Holmes and Watson to tackle."
Publishers Weekly

"Interesting and exciting in ways that few Holmes stories are these days."
San Francisco Book Review

"A thrilling tale for Scott's debut in the Sherlock Holmes world."
Sci-Fi Bulletin

SHERLOCK HOLMES
LABYRINTH OF DEATH

James Lovegrove

It is 1895, and Sherlock Holmes's new client is a high court judge, whose free-spirited daughter has disappeared without a trace.

Holmes and Watson discover that the missing woman—Hannah Woolfson—was herself on the trail of a missing person, her close friend Sophia. Sophia was recruited to a group known as the Elysians, a quasi-religious sect obsessed with Ancient Greek myths and rituals, run by the charismatic Sir Philip Buchanan. Hannah has joined the Elysians under an assumed name, convinced that her friend has been murdered. Holmes agrees that she should continue as his agent within the secretive yet seemingly harmless cult, yet Watson is convinced Hannah is in terrible danger. For Sir Philip has dreams of improving humanity through classical ideals, and at any cost…

"A writer of real authority and one worthy of taking the reader back to the dangerous streets of Victorian London in the company of the Great Detective."
Crime Time

"Lovegrove does a convincing job of capturing Watson's voice."
Publishers Weekly

SHERLOCK HOLMES
THE THINKING ENGINE

James Lovegrove

It is 1895, and Sherlock Holmes is settling back into life as a consulting detective at 221B Baker Street, when he and Watson learn of strange goings-on amidst the dreaming spires of Oxford.

A Professor Quantock has built a wondrous computational device, which he claims is capable of analytical thought to rival the cleverest men alive. Naturally Sherlock Holmes cannot ignore this challenge. He and Watson travel to Oxford, where a battle of wits ensues between the great detective and his mechanical counterpart as they compete to see which of them can be first to solve a series of crimes, from a bloody murder to a missing athlete. But as man and machine vie for supremacy, it becomes clear that the Thinking Engine has its own agenda…

"The plot, like the device, is ingenious, with a chilling twist…"
The Sherlock Holmes Journal

"Lovegrove knows his Holmes trivia and delivers a great mystery that fans will enjoy, with plenty of winks and nods to the canon."
Geek Dad

"James Lovegrove has become to the 21st century what JG Ballard was to the 20th..."
The Bookseller

TITANBOOKS.COM

SHERLOCK HOLMES
GODS OF WAR

James Lovegrove

It is 1913, and Dr Watson is visiting Sherlock Holmes at his retirement cottage near Eastbourne when tragedy strikes: the body of a young man, Patrick Mallinson, is found under the cliffs of Beachy Head.

The dead man's father, a wealthy businessman, engages Holmes to prove that his son committed suicide, the result of a failed love affair with an older woman. Yet the woman in question insists that there is more to Patrick's death. She has seen mysterious symbols drawn on his body, and fears that he was under the influence of a malevolent cult. When an attempt is made on Watson's life, it seems that she may be proved right. The threat of war hangs over England, and there is no telling what sinister forces are at work…

"Lovegrove has once again packed his novel with incident and suspense."
Fantasy Book Review

"An atmospheric mystery which shows just why Lovegrove has become a force to be reckoned with in genre fiction. More, please."
Starburst

"A very entertaining read with a fast-moving, intriguing plot."
The Consulting Detective

SHERLOCK HOLMES
THE STUFF OF NIGHTMARES

James Lovegrove

A spate of bombings has hit London, causing untold damage and loss of life. Meanwhile a strangely garbed figure has been spied haunting the rooftops and grimy back alleys of the capital.

Sherlock Holmes believes this strange masked man may hold the key to the attacks. He moves with the extraordinary agility of a latter-day Spring-Heeled Jack. He possesses weaponry and armour of unprecedented sophistication. He is known only by the name Baron Cauchemar, and he appears to be a scourge of crime and villainy. But is he all that he seems? Holmes and his faithful companion Dr Watson are about to embark on one of their strangest and most exhilarating adventures yet.

"[A] tremendously accomplished thriller which leaves the reader in no doubt that they are in the hands of a confident and skilful craftsman."

Starburst

"Dramatic, gripping, exciting and respectful to its source material, I thoroughly enjoyed every surprise and twist as the story unfolded."

Fantasy Book Review

"This is delicious stuff, marrying the standard notions of Holmesiana with the kind of imagination we expect from Lovegrove."

Crimetime

SHERLOCK HOLMES
THE SPIRIT BOX

George Mann

German zeppelins rain down death and destruction on London, and Dr Watson is grieving for his nephew, killed on the fields of France.

A cryptic summons from Mycroft Holmes reunites Watson with his one-time companion, as Sherlock comes out of retirement, tasked with solving three unexplained deaths. A politician has drowned in the Thames after giving a pro-German speech; a soldier suggests surrender before feeding himself to a tiger; and a suffragette renounces women's liberation and throws herself under a train. Are these apparent suicides something more sinister, something to do with the mysterious Spirit Box? Their investigation leads them to Ravensthorpe House, and the curious Seaton Underwood, a man whose spectrographs are said to capture men's souls…

"Arthur Conan Doyle was a master storyteller, and it takes comparable talent to give Holmes a second life… Mann is one of the few to get close to the target."

Daily Mail

"I would highly recommend this… a fun read."

Fantasy Book Review

"Our only complaint is that it is over too soon."

Starburst